D1432994

FOUR PUDDINGS AND A FUNERAL

OXFORD TEAROOM MYSTERIES
BOOK SIX

H.Y. HANNA

CONTENTS

CHAPTER ONE

Nobody likes going to a funeral—especially when the person being buried isn't the only dead body.

Of course, I didn't have an inkling of what was in store as I headed towards the church that Saturday morning. In fact, I was looking forward to the event. Oh, not in some kind of ghoulish way. No, it was simply because I—or rather, my business, the Little Stables Tearoom—had been asked to cater for the funeral reception. This was the largest catering job we had received so far and I was excited.

People were already coming from far and wide to the quaint Cotswolds village of Meadowford-on-Smythe to sample my famous English scones and traditional afternoon tea, and my tearoom business had been going from strength to strength since my starting it eight months ago. But I knew that getting a foot on the catering ladder would be the next big step. Especially as—with Oxford University on my doorstep—there would be all the associated colleges, departmental faculties, and university societies, with their luncheons, receptions, and parties all offering a wealth of catering opportunities.

And today's job at the funeral would help too— even though it was taking place in Meadowford rather than Oxford. Rex Clifford had been a prominent local businessman with many ties to the historic university city. I knew there would be a lot of "important" guests at the post-funeral reception who could help spread the word about my tearoom's delicious baking.

As long as I impress them, I thought, looking worriedly at the trays of food lining the rear compartment of the car. Carefully arranged on trays and platters were an assortment of traditional afternoon tea treats, from dainty finger sandwiches filled with cucumber and mint, and honey-glazed ham with English mustard, to a moist, fluffy Victoria sponge cake bursting with juicy strawberries. And of course—perhaps the most important item on the menu—a large platter filled with freshly baked scones, alongside mini pots of home-made jam and clotted cream.

"Do you think the scones look okay?" I asked anxiously. "You know, they are our signature dish."

My best friend, Cassie, straightened from the

back of the car and gave me a playful punch on the arm.

"Relax, Gemma. Dora's really outdone herself today—I think these are some of the best scones she's ever baked. Mmm... perfect buttery goodness with a rich golden crust... and those mini lemon meringue pies look so delicious too. I'm dying to pinch one. Oh, and the sticky toffee pudding! Now, I did sneak a taste of *that* before we loaded up in the kitchen. Oh my God... *divine.* If you're not careful, one of the big London hotels will be pinching your baking chef to go and work for them," Cassie chuckled. She tilted her head to one side and considered the trays in front of us. "Hmm... the only thing I was wondering is: do you think there are too many puddings? I mean, do we really need a treacle tart, lemon meringue pies, a sticky toffee pudding, *and* the Victoria sponge?"

"You know how much people love desserts," I said. "And this order came in so last-minute, we had to make do with what Dora could rustle up at short notice. I didn't have the chance to plan a menu properly. Anyway, the widow—Adele Clifford—specifically told me that her husband had always had a sweet tooth, so she wanted to have as many cakes and sweet treats as possible, in his honour."

"Well, she's certainly getting the best puddings in Oxfordshire," said Cassie with a smile. Then she put a hand on her hip and regarded me curiously.

"Speaking of the best, how was your dinner last night with the handsome detective?"

I avoided her gaze. "Oh, the food was fabulous. You can see why the Cherwell Boathouse is often voted one of the top restaurants in Oxford. Their butternut squash soup was—"

"Oh, stuff the butternut squash soup!" said Cassie. "I want to hear about the romantic date with Devlin."

"It... it was great."

Cassie raised her eyebrows at my flat tone. "And...?"

"And what?"

"Aww, come on! Give us the sordid details, Gemma! I know you guys were going through a bit of a rough patch—so did you kiss and make up?" She winked and leered at me.

I blushed slightly. "I told you... it was a lovely time. The food was great, the setting was really romantic, and Devlin didn't even talk about work once. We just spent a lot of time reminiscing about our college days together and laughing at the old jokes—"

"And what about that mysterious blonde he was seen with? Did you ask Devlin about that?"

"Oh. That."

Cassie rolled her eyes, "Yes, *that*. You said you were finally going to ask him about it and get a proper answer." As I hesitated, she grinned. "Don't tell me—I was right, yeah? It was nothing and

4

you're feeling embarrassed now for being so paranoid."

I shifted uncomfortably. "Actually... I... er... sort of forgot to ask Devlin about that."

Cassie stared at me. "What do you mean? How can you *forget* to ask about something like that? It's been bothering you day and night for the past week!"

"Well, I..." I twisted my hands together. "Okay, I didn't forget, but I just decided... well, I decided it wasn't really the right time to bring it up."

Cassie gave me a severe look. "*Gemma.*"

"I couldn't do it, okay?" I burst out. "It was all so beautiful and romantic, and Devlin had sent me roses, and the food was delicious and we were laughing and I just... I couldn't bring myself to spoil the mood."

"I bet it was spoiled for you anyway because that question was burning in your head the whole time."

I dropped my eyes. Cassie was right.

"I can't believe you sat through the whole of dinner without asking, just because you were afraid... What were you afraid of?" she demanded. "For goodness' sake, you don't really think that Devlin is cheating on y—"

"No!" I said quickly. "No, I'm sure he's not. I mean, I'm sure he can't be. I know Devlin isn't that kind of man. I'm sure he's not having an affair and there's a good reason why he's been acting so weird and distant recently... But..." I paused, then looked at her miserably and said in a small voice, "What if... what if I'm wrong?"

"Well, avoiding the subject isn't going to help you get answers," said Cassie in exasperation. "Gemma, this is getting ridiculous."

I gave her a wan smile. "You know, Robert Louis Stevenson said: 'to travel hopefully is a better thing than to arrive'."

"Oh, that's pants!" said Cassie impatiently. "I just don't understand—what could be so terrible about asking? Don't you want to find out the truth?"

"I do... but I'm... I'm scared about what the truth might be." I sighed. "It's hard to explain, Cassie, but a part of me feels like... like it's better to live in fear than to know for certain."

Cassie's expression softened. "I suppose I can understand that." She gave my arm a squeeze and said gently, "But you can't keep brushing it under the carpet forever, Gemma. It won't go away, you know. It'll fester inside you and destroy the trust in your relationship. You've got to have it out with Devlin."

I knew she was right. I was being a coward. But still, I shrank from the thought of confrontation. I took a deep breath, then let it out.

"I... I *will* ask him about it," I said. "I promise. I just need to find the right time to do it."

Cassie threw her hands up in a gesture of surrender and turned back to the trays of food. "All right... I suppose we'd better move these things into the hall."

I helped her lift some trays out of the boot of the car, and together we walked into the small parish hall adjoining the village church. This was a later addition, but it had been designed to blend with the Saxon architecture of the church. In fact, with its traditional oak-wood flower boxes and air of country charm, the parish hall was as frequently photographed by the tourists visiting Meadowford as the church itself.

The interior was a large space with high, vaulted ceilings, often used for village community events and weddings. Today, it had been solemnly decorated for a funeral reception, with large white candles and arrangements of white lilies, carnations, and ivory roses scattered about the room. A long buffet table with a linen tablecloth had been erected at one end of the hall, and Cassie and I set our heavy trays down on this gratefully.

"We should probably put some of this in the fridge," said Cassie, eyeing the food on the trays. "Do you know how long the service is going to take?"

I shook my head. "No, but you're right—even if it's only a short one, it's going to be a while before people are eating and it's quite warm today." I glanced at the window next to us, which showed blue skies and bright sunshine, then looked across the hall. "I remember Adele telling me there's a fridge in the kitchen that we can use. I'm not sure how big it is, though."

"Okay, well, let's put these in," said Cassie, grouping some items together on two trays. "The scones and teacakes should be okay to stay outside—we'll just need to cover them. You go and put these in the fridge. I'll bring the rest of the stuff."

Carefully, I balanced the two trays on top of each other and carried them across the hall, making my way to a door at the far end. I found myself in a short hallway with various doors leading off from it. They were all shut and none were clearly marked as the kitchen. I was about to open the door nearest to me to check when I heard the sound of raised voices coming from behind the last door in the corridor.

Ah. That must be the kitchen. Most likely place for people to congregate, I decided. *Perhaps some of the family are here already...*

I walked to the last door, then paused as I realised that it was slightly ajar. I caught a glimpse of the interior of the room. Yes, it was the kitchen, including a dining area on one side with a large round table encircled by chairs. Several people were huddled around the table, all dressed in mourning black: a dark-haired young woman with a pinched, angry face, another young woman of similar age with short blonde hair and an even deeper scowl on her face, an older, distinguished-looking man with grey hair and a trim beard, and—my eyes widened—a formidable-looking old lady with a helmet of woolly white hair and sharp, shrewd eyes.

Mabel Cooke. What was she *doing here?*

Mabel was the leader of a group of senior ladies, known affectionately as the "Old Biddies", who ruled the village of Meadowford-on-Smythe with a meddling fist and prying nose. Like many retired pensioners, Mabel and her three friends—Glenda, Florence, and Ethel—had time on their hands and energy to spare. The problem was, instead of directing it towards knitting, gardening, and grandchildren, the Old Biddies seemed to have developed an unhealthy interest in crime. When they weren't reading Agatha Christie novels, they were busy trying to re-enact one, and their meddling in recent murder cases had already given local police a big headache.

"...but there must be some mistake!" Mabel was saying, her usually booming voice becoming even louder with incredulity. "I have known your father for years and he was always a great supporter of the Happy Hedgehog Friends Society. He had always pledged to leave a large sum to the charity in his will. Rex Clifford would never go back on his word. There must be some misunderstanding. You should insist that your solicitor check things again."

"There's no mistake," said the dark-haired young woman bitterly. "We saw the solicitor yesterday and it seems that Dad *has* left his entire estate to *that woman.*" She nearly spat out the last two words.

"But we're going to contest the will, aren't we, darling?" said the other young woman, reaching out to rub her back.

"Yes," said the first young woman, sitting up straighter. "Yes, we're not going to just sit back and accept it! We're going to appeal."

"I'm not sure that would be wise, Rachel," murmured the older man.

She turned towards him angrily. "You can't expect me to just sit here and do nothing! The money is mine by right!" She gave him a contemptuous look. "I should have known that you'd take Adele's side. I suppose she's got her claws into you too, Uncle Miles? Batted her false eyelashes at you and had you falling for her helpless little woman act?"

The older man didn't react to her taunting. "I merely meant that it might be very difficult to contest the will and you could find yourself with an expensive fight on your hands," he said.

"But I'm sure there would be grounds for an appeal!" cried Rachel. "After all, you have to be of sound mind when you sign a will, don't you? Well, I can't believe that Dad was of sound mind. He would never have cut his only daughter out of his will and left everything to that... that floozy! I mean, for heaven's sake, they'd only known each other three months before they got married, and she was nearly twenty years younger than him."

"There's no fool like an old fool," said Mabel,

pursing her lips.

"This wasn't just foolish—it was crazy! I'm sure Dad can't have really approved that will," declared Rachel.

"I think you're going to find that very hard to prove, my dear," said her uncle Miles Clifford gently. "For one thing, there must have been a witness who also signed the will and who can testify that my brother acted under his own volition. I'm sure the lawyers would have made sure that everything was legal and above board."

Rachel's bottom lip jutted out. "I don't care. Witnesses can be bribed, can't they? Besides..." She glanced at her friend. "Kate says it just doesn't make sense why Dad would suddenly change his mind like that. Did something happen? If he was angry at me for something I'd done—enough to cut me out of his will—why didn't he say anything to me about it?"

"I'm sure it's not anything you've done, Rachel," said Miles Clifford quickly. "It might have nothing to do with you at all—"

"You mean it was just Adele somehow getting her sticky fingers into the whole thing and convincing Dad to change the will in her favour? That's called 'undue influence', isn't it?"

Her friend nodded. "That's more than enough for an appeal!"

Miles Clifford shot the other girl a look of dislike, but addressed his niece. "Rachel, I know the situation seems unfair but I don't see how anything can be done. Sometimes—"

"I'm not giving in!" she insisted. "I'm not! I've got to do something—I can't just let that woman win. I don't care what it takes—I'm not letting Adele get the money!"

At that moment, the door in the hallway behind me swung open and I jumped, guilty at being caught skulking and eavesdropping outside the kitchen. I whirled around to see Adele Clifford coming towards me. The widow was an undeniably attractive woman, somewhere in her mid-fifties, with a carefully preserved face and figure, and dark hair that had been expertly tinted and styled. She was wearing a black silk dress and matching stilettos, which clearly had designer labels attached to them.

However, as she came towards me, saying: "Ah, there you are. I saw your friend settin' up outside..."—her voice gave her away. As any Brit will tell you, class is defined as much by your accent as the clothes you wear and the car you drive, and Adele Clifford's sugary voice betrayed her East London Cockney origins. And the fact that she was trying very hard to alter her pronunciation and speak with an exaggerated "posh" intonation showed that she was self-conscious about it.

"I was just about to put these in the fridge," I said quickly, nodding to the trays in my hands. I shouldered my way through the kitchen door and walked in to find the room's occupants already on their feet, their expressions wary as Adele followed me in.

"Oh, you're all 'ere!" said Adele with a tinkling laugh. "What a cosy little family gatherin'. I 'ope I was invited too...?"

Rachel maintained a stony silence but her uncle hastily stepped into the breach.

"It was just an impromptu affair," he said. "We were having a private moment to remember Rex before the official service."

"Darlin' Rex..." Adele made a great show of wiping an imaginary tear from one eye. Then her gaze narrowed on Mabel. "What are *you* doin' 'ere, Mrs Cooke?" she asked, her voice changing.

Mabel bristled at her tone. "I beg your pardon?"

"Well, you're not family," said Adele pointedly.

"I have been a friend of dear Rex for years," said Mabel indignantly.

Adele gave a sneering laugh. "Friend? Don't kid yourself. Just 'cause Rex took pity on your pathetic little charities and tossed a few quid to your latest Save-the-Fuzzy-Dormouse or wha'ever campaign doesn't mean that 'e saw you as a friend. 'E wouldn't—"

"I saw Mrs Cooke outside and invited her to join us," Rachel cut in, her voice tight and angry. She added with false sweetness, "I realise that you're the mistress of Clifford House now, but I assume—the parish hall being public village property—that I don't need your permission to invite people in here?"

Adele flushed, then quickly recovered her aplomb. "Oh, sure... I suppose you 'ave to make allowances for these sad old pensioners who wouldn't otherwise 'ave anythin' else to do. Poor dears. I can just imagine 'ow *desperate* they are to fill their days and find events to go to. I suppose they bore their own families and now 'ave to look for someone else to latch on to." She gave a theatrical sigh. "And your father was always such a kind, generous man—no matter 'ow tedious 'e found these old biddies, 'e always made time for them. I suppose today, of all days, we should 'umour them one last time."

Mabel went red and began spluttering in anger. Hastily, I stepped forwards and held up the trays of food. "Um... is it all right if I put these in the fridge?"

"Cor, those look delicious!" said Adele, stepping closer and reaching a hand out, her fingers flickering over the tray. "I'm just itchin' to taste one! But I can't. I've just put on my lippie so I'll 'ave to resist!" She gave me a coy smile and dabbed at the corners of her bright red lips.

"You can enjoy them at the reception later," I said, reflecting that Adele was hardly behaving like a grieving widow. And from the disapproving looks the other occupants in the room were giving her, they shared my thoughts.

I hurried across to the fridge and carefully stowed the trays inside, then escaped the tense atmosphere in that room with some relief. Outside, I found that Cassie had brought the rest of the food from the car and I helped her arrange the platters attractively across the buffet table. Then my best friend gave me a cheerful wave and left to return to the tearoom.

I watched her go slightly anxiously. Weekends were usually our busiest times as not only the tourists but many of the locals also arrived at the Little Stables Tearoom for their fix of delicious baking. I hoped Cassie would be all right coping on her own. The Old Biddies usually helped out—they loved the chance to gossip with everyone, and tourists seemed to enjoy their nosy, chatty style—so we'd worked out an arrangement where they lent a hand during busy times, in return for treating the tearoom as their personal HQ and helping themselves from the menu. But with all of them attending the funeral this morning, Cassie would be completely on her own. Still, a lot of the village residents would probably be at the funeral too, I remembered, so the tearoom shouldn't be as busy as normal.

Glancing at my watch, I realised that the funeral service was about to begin. I left the parish hall and made my way out to the adjoining cemetery, where a substantial crowd was gathering around a freshly dug plot. I found a position at a discreet distance from the group and watched as the vicar greeted Rachel Clifford and her friend, and made space for them next to the gleaming mahogany coffin. The rest of the mourners shuffled to form a semi-circle around the grave and I saw Mabel with the other Old Biddies—Glenda Bailey, Florence Doyle, and Ethel Webb—jostling for a position at the front of the crowd.

Minutes passed. The mourners began fidgeting, whispering, peering around the cemetery. The vicar glanced back towards the church, an expression of puzzlement and slight annoyance on his face. The service couldn't start without Adele Clifford, the deceased's widow—but where was she?

Then a couple in black stepped out of the parish hall and began walking towards the crowd. It was Adele, escorted by her brother-in-law, Miles. She was hastily re-applying lipstick and making a great show of dabbing her eyes with a tissue. I wondered cynically if the whole thing was an act. From the coy glances she kept darting at the crowd, it seemed like she enjoyed the attention. In fact, I wouldn't have been surprised if Adele had purposefully delayed her arrival until everyone had gathered by the graveside, so that she could make a grand entrance.

All eyes were on her as she sashayed around the coffin to stand next to Rachel, sniffing loudly as she did so. Miles Clifford took a position behind her, his tall distinguished figure dwarfing those around him.

He clasped his hands behind his back and lowered his head, his expression unreadable. Whatever he might have thought of his sister-in-law's theatrics, he was too courteous to comment on them. His niece, however, was not so tolerant. Rachel Clifford flushed angrily as she watched her stepmother continue the exaggerated show of grief; she opened her mouth as if to say something, then her friend put a protective arm around her shoulders and the two girls pointedly turned their backs on the widow.

Looking slightly uncomfortable, the vicar cleared his throat and raised his arms to begin the service. It was a fairly short one—it seemed that Rex Clifford was a man who didn't like pomp and ceremony, and he had asked for a simple graveside service in his will. As the vicar's solemn voice rose and filled the quiet of the cemetery, I was touched to notice that many of the mourners were in tears, their genuine grief easy to see. Rex Clifford's widow might have been more show than substance, but it was obvious that many residents of the village and the wider Oxford community would really miss him.

Then, as the vicar began the familiar prayer of: *"The Lord is my shepherd; I shall not want..."*—I noticed something beyond the crowd.

I squinted into the distance. It was a tall figure— a man—lurking behind the row of yew trees on the far side of the cemetery. His face was in the shadows and I couldn't see his expression properly, although I could see his dark gaze trained on the coffin. Like the rest of the mourners, he was dressed all in black, but his outfit had something of the feel of a "costume" about it. In fact, with his long black trench coat and sleek black hair, he reminded me of Keanu Reeves in *The Matrix*. I half expected him to pull out a sinister black machine gun or similar weapon from behind his back! Then I gave a self-deprecating laugh and chided myself for my overactive imagination.

Still, as the vicar continued the prayer—"...*Yea, though I walk through the valley of the shadow of death, I will fear no evil*..."—I found my gaze returning to the mysterious stranger and, for some reason, I shivered.

CHAPTER TWO

The service was over faster than I expected and I hurried to get back into the hall ahead of the crowd, and in particular to retrieve the rest of the food from the fridge and arrange it on the buffet table. Stepping back to survey my efforts, I smiled in satisfaction. The platters of cakes, finger sandwiches, scones, and pies looked elegant and professional, while still retaining a home-made appeal, and the lovely buttery smell of fresh baking was mouth-watering.

I walked around the table to check it from every angle, pausing to adjust the tray of lemon meringue pies which showed a gap in their midst. I smiled to myself and shook my head. Cassie must have pinched one after all. Then I smiled again as I saw that she had thoughtfully left a stack of the tearoom's business cards in the centre of the table. *Good ol' Cass*! I was so grateful to my best friend for taking over the marketing of the tearoom. Not only had she set up the website, but she'd also personally designed the business cards, providing one of her own beautiful illustrations as the tearoom's logo.

The hubbub of voices behind me told me that the mourners were arriving. I turned around and saw them entering via the open double doors at the other end of the hall, many of them making a beeline for the food. I moved back from the buffet table, hovering at a discreet distance to watch people's reactions, then relaxing slightly as I saw many begin to eat enthusiastically.

"These are absolutely delicious!" declared one lady, biting into half a scone which had been generously slathered with jam and clotted cream. She swallowed, then licked her fingers. "I don't think I've tasted such wonderful scones in years!"

"They *are* fabulous, aren't they?" agreed the man next to her. "I wonder where they're from?"

"Oh look, here's a card..." said the woman, leaning across to lift one of the tearoom's business cards from the stack at the centre of the table. "The Little Stables Tearoom, Meadowford-on-Smythe... Hmm, we should check it out the next time we come to Meadowford—what do you think, Harry?"

"Certainly, certainly," said her companion, talking with his mouth full.

I retreated farther from the buffet table, a smile on my face and a warm feeling in my heart. My happy thoughts were interrupted, however, by the sound of Mabel's familiar voice saying loudly:

"...well, of course she could be easily murdered!"

I turned in surprise and saw a group of senior village residents, all spectacles, white hair, and woolly cardigans, gathered eagerly around Mabel Cooke and the other Old Biddies. Curious, I drifted closer and joined the back of the group.

"It's not a question of whether it could be done—it's whether anyone would do it," one of the old ladies closest to me was saying.

"Oh, I'm sure there are many who would love to murder her," said another lady, shooting an acerbic look across the hall at the glamorous widow, who was chatting with a group of men. "I have never met a more unpleasant woman in my life. Did you hear what she did at bingo last week? Denise Palmer had just settled down in her usual chair when Adele arrived and insisted that was her seat! And she wouldn't stop harassing poor Denise. We tried to intervene—we explained that Denise is going deaf and needs to sit closer to the caller to hear—but Adele wouldn't listen. She even tried to shove Denise out of the chair. Poor Denise left in tears."

"She tried to do something similar the week before, but Mabel stopped her," said Florence Doyle, folding her plump arms and nodding with satisfaction.

"Yes," said Mabel grimly. "And if I had been there last week, she wouldn't have got away with such disgraceful behaviour towards Denise!"

I looked at Mabel with interest. So that was why Adele had seemed so hostile to her when they met in the kitchen earlier! The two women were obviously enemies, and, from the sound of things, had clashed several times already.

"I just don't understand how Rex Clifford could have ever married her," said one of the other pensioners, tutting and shaking her head. "I mean, his first wife, Susan, was such a lovely lady. And so different from Adele."

"Perhaps she drugged him," someone suggested.

"Or practised witchcraft on him!" said someone else with a laugh.

A soft voice spoke up. "People do get lonely as they get older, you know." Ethel Webb, the gentlest of the Old Biddies, looked around the group. "When I used to work at the library, I saw that happen very often. People who were left alone after their spouses died would often come to the library just for some human contact. They weren't really interested in the books—they just wanted someone to chat to. I spent hours recommending books to people before I realised that. There was one gentleman who had lost his wife and he came in almost every day, often staying by my desk for hours!"

"Perhaps it was a particular type of chat that he wanted, Ethel," suggested Glenda Bailey with a giggle.

Ethel looked at her blankly. "What do you mean?"

"He wanted an up-chat," said Glenda.

"An 'up-chat'?" Ethel looked even more puzzled. As the only one of the Old Biddies who had never married, she was almost the cliché of the twittering spinster, with her fluffy white hair, gentle manners, and modest smile.

"Yes, that's what the young people say these days. When somebody up-chats you," Glenda simpered. The very opposite of Ethel, Glenda was eighty-going-on-eighteen, with a perpetual soft spot for handsome men and romance.

I cleared my throat and spoke up, "Er... Glenda, I think you mean, 'chat you up'." Turning to Ethel, I added, "That means they're romantically interested in you."

Ethel blushed a pretty pink and twisted the tissue in her hands. "Oh... I'm sure not..."

"Well, I certainly can sympathise with Rex Clifford if he was lonely, but I still say it was a terrible day for this village when he married Adele," one of the pensioners said and several others nodded in agreement.

"I cross the street if I see her coming," a woman said emphatically.

"Really, if somebody *did* murder her, it would be a community service!" another woman declared.

"But how would you do it?" asked the first senior

eagerly. "I mean, it's not so easy to kill someone by stabbing, is it? You have to stick the knife in at just the right place."

"You could strangle them," suggested another pensioner. "Though you'd want a pair of non-arthritic hands to get a good grip."

I looked at them all in slight alarm. I might have been away from England for eight years, but since when had little old ladies become so bloodthirsty?

"Wait, wait... you ladies aren't serious, are you?" I said, laughing weakly.

Several pairs of beady old eyes turned towards me. Nobody laughed. I gave them a nervous smile. "I mean, come on... it's fun to talk about murdering someone you dislike but it's not realistic—"

"Nonsense!" Mabel's voice boomed. "As I said, it's extremely easy to murder someone, if you know what you're doing. And especially if you use poison. Then you would not even have to worry about providing an alibi—you could be at a safe distance away from the victim when they expire."

Mabel's voice carried across the hall and several of the other mourners at the reception turned around to stare.

"Er... ha-ha... they're just joking," I assured the other guests, waving a hand at the Old Biddies and trying to put on a jovial face. People gave me odd looks, but, to my relief, politely turned away after a moment.

I looked at Mabel and hissed, "Mabel, you can't

say things like that! People won't realise that you're joking."

"But I'm not joking," protested Mabel. "Poison *is* the perfect murder weapon. Agatha Christie once said: 'Give me a decent bottle of poison and I'll construct the perfect crime.' You know, she used poisons in most of her mystery novels."

Glenda piped up, "Ooh, yes, my favourite one is *Sparkling Cyanide*—I always think Colonel Race sounds very dashing, don't you? I do so like a military man." She giggled. "Of course, he's only a bit over sixty, it says in the book, and that's a bit young for me—although I suppose he could be my 'toy boy'. I haven't ever had one of those! Marjorie Smith has one and she says he's done wonders for her skin—"

"I didn't like that book," said Ethel with a shudder. "The deaths sounded horrible. Going blue in the face and fingers twitching from convulsions..."

"Well, *I* wouldn't use cyanide," said Mabel. "Arsenic is what I would choose."

All eyes turned back on her. "Arsenic?"

Mabel nodded authoritatively. "It's the ideal poison. Odourless, tasteless, and its symptoms are so similar to many common stomach ailments, no one would suspect."

"But how would you get her to take the arsenic?"

"That's easy. You simply add powdered arsenic to her food when she's not looking. For example, any of those cakes there—" Mabel waved a hand towards the buffet table, "—could easily hide powdered arsenic in all that icing sugar and whipped cream."

"Uh... not my cakes!" I said hastily. The last thing I needed was for the wrong rumours about my tearoom to start spreading!

"What a shame we can't really poison Adele," said a pensioner wistfully.

I glanced quickly across the room to where the widow was, wondering if Adele herself might have overheard, but thankfully she was engrossed in conversation with a middle-aged businessman. She was laughing and fluttering her eyelashes, one hand holding a wine glass and the other on his lapel. I felt slightly repulsed by her behaviour. Even if she didn't really mourn her husband, it seemed in extremely bad taste for her to flirt at his funeral reception!

As if in response to my thoughts, I saw Rachel Clifford stride across the hall towards her stepmother, her face set in a scowl. She stopped beside Adele, yanked her aside and snapped:

"Can't you show a bit of respect? This is my father's funeral, for God's sake!"

Adele gave her an insolent smile. "Your father wouldn't want me to brood."

"He wouldn't want you trying to shag every man at his funeral either!" said Rachel.

Adele tossed her head. "I know you're bitter

about the terms of the will, Rachel, but there's no need to take it out on me. I can't 'elp it if your father decided I was more worthy, can I? Maybe if you'd been a better daughter, 'e wouldn't 'ave cut you out of 'is will."

Rachel drew back as if she had been slapped and I felt a rush of sympathy for her. Okay, so she didn't seem like the most pleasant person from what I'd seen of her so far, but that had been an unnecessarily cruel comment, especially at her father's funeral.

"I... I *was* a good daughter to him," said Rachel, tears smarting in her eyes. "I'm sure my father didn't intentionally cut me out of his will. It was you! *You* did something—you lied to him or conned him or something—and you made him change the will in your favour. That's what I'm going to tell the courts!"

"Oh, you better think twice about doin' anything," said Adele with a superior smile. "You'll lose the case. Just ask Gavin 'ere..." She reached out to a man standing nearby, grabbed his arm and hauled him close. "You've met Mr Sexton, right? 'E'll tell you that the will is completely watertight and you'd end up makin' a very expensive mistake."

She looked at the lawyer, who shifted uncomfortably. "Er... I don't feel it's really appropriate to discuss such matters here today, Mrs Clifford."

Adele laughed and turned back to Rachel.

"'Course, if you're very nice to me, I might consider lendin' you some money. I know you're desperate for some capital to expand your business... Well, I can be generous too. But you need to show me some proper respect. Don't forget, I 'old the purse strings now!"

Rachel looked as if she might explode. She bit her lip, spun on her heels, and marched away with Adele's jeering laughter following her.

CHAPTER THREE

There was an awkward silence, then Adele looked at me and said brightly, "Well! Now that's out of the way... I'm lookin' forward to tastin' some of your nosh." She rubbed her abdomen. "I'm so hungry, I'm gettin' stomach cramps. Come and tell me what you recommend!"

She dragged me and Sexton over to the buffet table, and gestured to the spread in front of us. "So which one should I 'ave?"

"The treacle tart would be my choice," came a booming voice opposite.

I looked up to see Mabel Cooke facing us on the other side of the table. She was holding a cake knife and server, and had just cut a large wedge from a round pie with a golden pastry lattice covering.

"Treacle tarts were my favourite puddings as a

boy," Sexton spoke up, his serious face breaking into a smile. "They don't seem to taste as good as they used to, though. I had some at a café recently and I was very disappointed."

"That's because they didn't make it properly, young man," said Mabel. "When they are made the traditional way, as we do at Gemma's tearoom—with golden syrup, breadcrumbs, and a dash of lemon juice to cut through the sweetness—and served with a dollop of clotted cream or ice cream, there is nothing to beat it. Here..." She placed the wedge on a plate and thrust it across the table.

"Not for me, thanks—but you have some, Mrs Clifford," said Sexton, handing the plate to her.

Adele hesitated, obviously reluctant to take something that Mabel had recommended, then she accepted the plate with bad grace. She picked up a fork from the table and was about to leave when another voice called her name.

"Adele... you must have some of this sticky toffee pudding. It's absolutely delicious."

I turned in surprise to see Rachel standing next to us, holding a plate out to Adele. But a very different Rachel from the girl who had stormed off a few moments ago. Instead of her habitual scowl, she had a bright smile pinned on her face and was looking at Adele invitingly.

"I've already got some treacle tart, thanks," said Adele, indicating the plate in her hands.

"Oh, but you must try some of this too!"

exclaimed Rachel, leaning forwards and using her fork to slide the piece of sticky toffee pudding from her plate onto Adele's. "It's the perfect mix of gooey moist sponge and lovely chopped dates... mmm, and the toffee sauce on top..."

Adele started to protest, then caught a whiff of the rich toffee smell and capitulated. "All right. It does look really good."

"Would you like a napkin?" asked Rachel as Adele took a generous bite with her fork.

"No, I'm all right. I'm goin' to look for a place to sit down for a while," said Adele. She massaged her temples and frowned. "This funeral is givin' me a splittin' 'eadache."

I winced slightly at the disrespect to her dead husband and glanced at Rachel, but the girl's face remained bland.

"There are some chairs by the wall there," I said, pointing to a spot nearby.

Adele nodded and walked off. Rachel helped herself to another piece of sticky toffee pudding, then grabbed a glass of wine and went to join her friend, Kate, on the other side of the hall. I was left alone with the lawyer. He was a solemn-looking man in his mid-forties, with a weak chin and pale blue eyes behind thin, wire-rimmed glasses. He cleared his throat now, obviously unsure how to continue the conversation.

"So... you're the one responsible for providing the food today?" he asked politely.

I smiled. "Yes, I'm catering the event. I own the Little Stables Tearoom in the village. And you... are you with Sexton, Lovell & Billingsley, by any chance?"

He held his hand out. "Yes, I'm Gavin Sexton."

I shook his hand. "My parents are with your firm, although I thought it was '*Richard* Sexton'? That's who my mother usually mentions seeing."

"He's my uncle," said Sexton. "He's due to retire this year and hasn't been in good health, so I've been taking over many of the responsibilities and dealing with most of his clients."

"Like Rex Clifford," I said.

He inclined his head. "Yes, Mr Clifford was one of my uncle's oldest clients. I've been looking after his estate this past year."

"Was his death unexpected?" I asked.

"Well, everyone knew that he had a weak heart, although, after the last operation, they were hopeful that he would recover and live for many years longer. I think his heart attack took everyone by surprise."

"And... er... I understand that the way he left his affairs took everyone by surprise as well?"

He gave me a dry look. "You're referring to the will, aren't you?"

"Yes," I admitted with a sheepish smile. "I couldn't help overhearing some of the family members discussing it earlier. Actually, I was a bit surprised that they knew the details of the will already. I always thought the will wasn't read out until after the funeral—"

Sexton chuckled. "You've been watching too many old movies. It might have been done that way in the past, but nowadays wills are usually read as soon as the death is confirmed. There's no need to wait until after the funeral for everyone to 'gather together in the library'. In fact, the beneficiaries are often not even present—it's up to the executors to inform them about the bequests, by letter or phone afterwards."

"And... do you think there would be grounds for contesting the will?"

The smile left Gavin Sexton's face. "I wouldn't advise it. That's what I've told Miss Clifford, although whether she will heed my advice is another matter. She is understandably very angry about the situation—but unfortunately, if Rex Clifford wished to leave all his money to his widow, there's nothing anyone can do about it, however unjust it might seem."

"Rachel—Miss Clifford—seemed to feel that she could cite 'undue influence' in this case—"

"She could try but I doubt the case would stand up in court. There was a witness to the signing of the new will, who could verify that Rex Clifford was of sound mind." Sexton shrugged. "Really, the only way Miss Clifford could get her hands on the money now would be if Adele were to die. The terms of the will state that the estate would fall to the next of kin and—as Rex Clifford's only child—Miss Clifford would inherit the whole lot. In fact..."

He trailed off suddenly as his attention was distracted by something over my shoulder. I saw an expression of dismay mingled with anger cross his face. I turned around to see what he was looking at and my own eyes widened as I caught sight of a figure moving through the crowd.

It was the young man in the black trench coat, who I had observed in the cemetery earlier. He was sauntering along, making his way towards the front of the room, and as he came closer I was struck by how handsome he was. Almost too handsome—like a male model in a magazine, with high cheekbones and slanting dark eyes, a tall, slim physique, and jet black hair, styled long and slicked back from his face. There was something faintly Oriental about his looks and I wondered if he was of Eurasian descent—the child of a mixed marriage, perhaps. He certainly moved with the smooth confidence of a model and, combined with his almost theatrical clothing and his air of mystery, he was drawing a lot of attention from the other guests.

"Excuse me," said Gavin Sexton suddenly, turning and walking away.

I barely heard him, all my attention riveted on the handsome stranger. I wondered what he was doing at the funeral and I could see my thoughts reflected on several of the faces around me, especially those of the local residents. Meadowford was a small village and all newcomers were greeted with interest, even if they were just tourists. The sight of such a mysterious and dramatic-looking stranger at a resident's funeral was enough to send the local gossips into overdrive.

The stranger walked past where Adele was sitting and seemed to trip just as he passed her chair. He stumbled, put out a hand to catch himself, then fell heavily against her, knocking her plate off her lap.

"Oh!" Adele cried as the plate smashed on the floor, spilling flaky pastry and toffee sauce everywhere. I winced to see my food squashed on the floor and wasted.

"Ah! Sorry!" the young man cried. He bent to pick up the pieces of broken china, then said earnestly, "I'll get you a new one!" He hurried past me to the buffet table and returned to Adele a moment later with a large slice of Victoria sponge cake.

"Uh... I'm not sure I want any more pudding," she said, looking slightly queasy as she accepted the fork and plate. Then she glanced down at the moist sponge cake, bursting with fresh whipped cream and juicy strawberries, and licked her lips. "Mm... this does look good, though. I 'aven't tasted the Victoria sponge yet and I 'ad my eye on it earlier..."

"Yeah, go on—why don't you try some?" said the stranger. "Anyway, sorry again."

He made her a sort of bow, then drifted to the

other side of the room. I watched him curiously as he paused beside a table where a framed photograph of Rex Clifford was on display next to candles and a large flower arrangement. A minute later, Gavin Sexton walked up to him. I couldn't see the lawyer's face—he had his back to me—but from the tension in his shoulders, it was not a friendly conversation. I wondered if he was checking whether the stranger was gate-crashing the funeral. The handsome Eurasian's face darkened and he seemed to be arguing with Sexton, but before I could ponder further, a clinking sound rang out across the hall.

As the hubbub faded and guests turned expectantly towards the sound, I saw Rachel Clifford standing by the table with the photograph, a raised glass in her hand. She was holding a fork in her other hand and tapping it against the rim of her glass. The crowd fell silent.

Rachel raised her voice. "Thank you so much, everyone, for coming today. I'm sure my father would have been touched to see how many people had come to remember him."

There was a rumble of agreement from the crowd and several people raised their glasses, as if in a toast. I darted a look at Adele, wondering how she was taking this. By assuming the role of hostess and addressing the guests, Rachel was usurping her stepmother's position as the new mistress of Clifford House. The widow didn't look happy about it. She was flushed, her expression slightly nauseated, as she leaned against the opposite wall.

"... and now I'd like to propose a toast to my father," Rachel said, raising her glass to the framed photo on the table next to her. "To Rex Clifford, who—"

"Hey... can I say a few words?" a new voice spoke up.

Rachel stopped and everyone turned towards the speaker. It was the handsome stranger. He was standing on the other side of the table, a hand placed lovingly on the framed photo.

"I beg your pardon... Who are you?" asked Rachel, looking at him askance.

He gave her a tentative smile. "My name's Tyler. Tyler Lee... I'm your brother. Well, your half-brother, actually."

There were gasps around the room and I saw several eyebrows waggling wildly.

"My *brother?*" said Rachel. She stared at him, then gave an incredulous laugh. "You've got to be joking. I'm an only child—"

"Yeah, well, you wouldn't know about me," said the handsome stranger with a sad smile. "Even our dad didn't know. My mother was a proud woman and she knew that he had a family back here in England. I mean, it was tough for us—we didn't have much and she had to work really hard—but she didn't want to beg." He took a step forwards and raised a clenched fist. "But I know he really loved her! They didn't have much time together but you don't see passion like that every day and... and I'm sure he would have looked after me—after us—if he'd known."

People's eyes were practically popping out of theirs sockets now. Everyone was holding their breath—it was so still, you could almost hear a pin drop in the room. Rachel Clifford had her mouth hanging open and she looked as if she didn't know how to respond.

"My mother told me all about my dad, from the time I was a baby," Tyler Lee continued, unperturbed by the reaction around him. "She said he was a good man—really kind and generous... and I always wanted to find him one day." He sighed dramatically. "Who knew that when I finally found him, it would be too late?"

There came a sound like a choking sob nearby. I glanced over to see Adele staring at the young man, her face convulsed and her hand clutching her middle.

Blimey. I didn't think that she would be the type to be moved by a sob story. I guess I was wrong.

Tyler Lee reached a hand out to Rachel across the table. She recoiled from him.

"It's wonderful to know I have a sister," he said, his voice quavering with emotion. "Especially now that my mother is gone too. At least I know I'm not alone anymore!"

It was a moving speech but I couldn't help feeling

that it had been carefully rehearsed. Tyler Lee obviously had a flair for drama and, although his words were directed at Rachel, I noticed that he faced the crowd, projecting his voice so that it carried to the farthest reaches of the hall. This was a man used to "working" an audience and who enjoyed the attention. I wondered again whether he might be an actor or a model...

He leaned across the table and caught Rachel's limp hand. "I can't wait to get to know my new family. We can share memories of the wonderful man who was my fa—"

His speech was suddenly interrupted by a strangled cry.

I turned to see Adele stagger forwards, then slump over the buffet table, face down in the sticky toffee pudding. Someone next to her screamed as her body began to jerk spasmodically.

"She's having a seizure!" someone shouted.

Adele rolled off the table and fell to the floor, dragging the tablecloth with her and pulling half the food off the table. There were more screams, mingled with the sound of shattering china, as scones, cakes, and sandwiches fell to the floor, and fresh cream splattered everywhere. I rushed towards Adele just as several other people ran forwards as well. She was retching and moaning, clutching her abdomen and twisting in agony.

"Call an ambulance!" I yelled as I bent down next to Adele and helped others roll her over.

"Is there a doctor here?" cried a woman next to me.

"Yes, I'm a doctor!" said a short, balding man, elbowing his way through the crowd. He crouched down beside me and examined Adele, who seemed to have stopped vomiting and was moving less and less now, her moaning fading away. But her stillness and silence were not reassuring.

"Is she all right?" someone asked in a hushed voice.

The doctor looked up, his face grim. "I hope the ambulance gets here quickly. It doesn't look good."

CHAPTER FOUR

I looked up from my bowl of breakfast cereal as the sound of persistent meowing came from the other side of the living room. My little tabby cat, Muesli, was sitting by the glass door which led out to the garden at the back of the cottage. She stretched up towards the doorknob and looked back at me, saying, "*Meeeeeeorrw!*"

"All right, Muesli..." I said absently, rising from the dining table and crossing the room towards her.

At least my way wasn't barred by stacks of cardboard boxes any more. I had moved into my new cottage several weeks ago, but long days at the tearoom meant that I was usually too exhausted to unpack in the evenings. Things had been chaotic until last weekend when I had finally set aside the time to empty all the boxes and try to get everything in the right place. There were still a few items piled here and there, but overall, my cottage was beginning to look quite neat and cosy, I thought, glancing around and smiling with satisfaction.

Then my gaze fell on the assortment of weird-looking plants that filled one corner of the sitting room and I sighed. Courtesy of my mother—who seemed to have gone on a rampage at the local garden centre—I was now the proud owner of a Taiwanese rubber tree, a Jurassic sago palm, a spiky bromeliad, a weeping fig, and several sprouting spider plants. Still, I was relieved that my mother's botanical fervour seemed to be waning at last. I hadn't received a new plant from her in three days—which was significant progress.

Muesli meowed again, her tone becoming impatient now.

"All right, all right..." I said as I reached the garden door and opened it for her. The little cat poked her nose out of the gap and sniffed the air, whiskers quivering.

I looked down at her. "Well? You wanted to go out. Go on then!"

Muesli looked up at me, then turned and strolled back into the living room.

Arrrghh! Cats! Why did I ever adopt one?

I shut the garden door and stalked back to the dining table. But I had barely sat down to start eating again when Muesli was beside the garden door once more, meowing insistently.

I gave her an irritable look. "I just opened the door for you and you decided that you *didn't* want to go out."

"*Meorrw!*" said Muesli petulantly.

"No," I said. "I'm not opening the door for you again."

"*Meorrw?*"

"No."

"*Meeeorrw?*"

"No!"

"*MEEORRW! MEEORRW! MEEEEEOOORRWW!*"

"Oh... all right! *All right*!" I stomped back to the door and flung it open. Muesli took a step, then another... then she sat down on the threshold and began washing her face.

I stared at her disbelievingly. The little minx! What was she doing?

"Muesli! Are you going out or not?" I demanded.

She ignored me and continued washing her left ear until she was satisfied. Then, finally, she got up and strolled out into the courtyard. I shut the door, grumbling to myself, and returned to my now soggy breakfast. *If she returns to the door in a minute, asking to come back in, I'll wring her little neck!* I thought balefully.

Thankfully, Muesli decided to stay in the garden long enough to let me finish my breakfast in peace, wash up the dishes, and check my emails before getting ready to leave for work. I let her back in, checked that she had fresh water and a clean litter tray, then—throwing a quick look around to make sure that I hadn't forgotten anything—I grabbed my tote bag and went into the foyer, where my bicycle was parked.

A little furry grey head popped out of the wicker basket in front of the handlebars. It was Muesli.

"*Meorrw?*" she said, her big green eyes looking at me hopefully.

In spite of my recent irritation with her, I felt my heart soften. Poor thing. I knew Muesli hated being left alone in the cottage all day. She was an inquisitive, sociable cat who loved company and delighted in meeting strangers. Before I had adopted her, she used to live in Meadowford, with access to the woods at the back of the village and the chance to come to the tearoom every day. Her life with me must have been very boring in comparison and I felt a twinge of guilt.

"I'm sorry, sweetie," I said as I lifted her out of the basket and set her down on the floor. "You can't come with me. You know animals aren't allowed at the tearoom."

"*Meorrw...*" said Muesli, her little face forlorn. She watched me place my tote bag in the basket where she had been. I felt my heart contract again but ignored it as I wheeled the bicycle towards the front door.

"I'll try to get back a bit earlier today," I promised her.

Then, on an impulse, I popped back into my

kitchenette and grabbed a packet of cat treats. Extracting a few chicken-liver-flavoured biscuits, I gave them to Muesli. "Here you go."

Feeling slightly guilty that I was bribing her with food, I took advantage of Muesli's distraction with the treats to quickly wheel my bicycle out of the cottage and shut the door behind me. As I set off along the towpath beside the river, I was pleased to remember that it was Sunday and that there would be no early morning rush hour traffic to worry about. Not that the roads wouldn't still be busy. Oxford wasn't a big city—it was really more like a large town—but with its world-famous university, not to mention all the museums, theatres, and historical attractions, it was a major tourist destination every day of the week. And the old cobbled lanes and one-way streets that weaved their way through the historic city didn't cope very well with heavy traffic. Still, there were many back alleys and hidden lanes that a bicycle could access, and most of the students and local residents got around on two wheels instead of four.

I'd grown up in Oxford and then spent time as a student in the university, so I knew the city like the back of my hand. I cycled almost on auto-pilot as I made my way up from the south end of the city, where my cottage was situated, and headed north-west into the Cotswolds countryside and the little village of Meadowford-on-Smythe. Once I was free of the city boundaries, I let the bicycle freewheel as I leaned back and breathed deeply, feeling the warm breeze on my face. With June just around the corner, summer was finally coming to England and it was a wonderful feeling!

I laughed suddenly at my thoughts. You would think that after living for eight years in Australia—where sunny days were the norm—I would have got blasé about sunshine and warm weather. But there was still something glorious about an English summer (when it finally arrived!). Somehow, nowhere else seemed to compare to the sight of the British countryside in full bloom, with bluebells and daisies everywhere, cow parsley lining the roads, and hedgerows alive with butterfly wings...

I slowed the bicycle as I entered Meadowford-on-Smythe and cruised down the High Street until I reached the front of my tearoom. Housed in a lovingly restored Tudor inn—complete with the half-timber framing and white-washed walls, and an inglenook fireplace taking pride of place in the main room—the Little Stables Tearoom was the quintessential image of "Olde England". I was surprised to see a substantial crowd outside it already, obviously waiting for it to open. Not a group of eager tourists either, but a crowd of village residents chattering excitedly to each other. I saw the Old Biddies amongst them, busily speaking to several other pensioners.

"Morning!" said Cassie as I walked into the tearoom kitchen via the back door.

She was standing by the big table in the centre of the room, next to my baking chef, Dora Kempton, who—as usual—was up to her elbows in flour as she expertly kneaded a piece of dough. They had obviously been discussing something important because Cassie's cheeks were flushed with excitement.

"...I do hope he comes back today, Cassie. I'll keep my fingers crossed for you!" Dora said.

"Who comes back?" I asked.

"You missed all the excitement here yesterday while you were at the funeral," said Dora with a smile. "There was a Canadian tourist who took a liking to one of Cassie's paintings on the wall. He even asked her how much it would cost to ship it back to Montreal."

"Oh, Cass, that's fantastic!" I said, beaming at my friend.

Cassie's eyes sparkled. "When your mother suggested that I hang my paintings up in the tearoom, I never really expected that anyone would be interested in them... Oh, Gemma—this will be my very first sale!" she said, clutching her hands together with a dreamy sigh. Then she added hastily, "Not that he's definitely buying it yet. He said he'd think about it. He's staying at the Cotswolds Manor Hotel and said he might pop back in today, after doing some sightseeing in Oxford."

"What's his name? Just in case you're not around—I don't want to miss him."

"Scott Leblanc. He's a really big guy, wears a lot of denim."

I nodded and reached for an apron to put on as well, whilst Cassie went out first to open up the tearoom.

"Don't forget to check the cupboards in the pantry, and the back of the fridge today," Dora reminded me as I prepared to follow Cassie. "The Food & Safety inspector is supposed to be coming sometime this week."

I made a face. "Oh, heavens, I almost forgot! I hope we don't get the same chap as last time—he was awful."

I'd had one inspection shortly after the tearoom first opened and I could still remember the finickity little man who had come in his cap and white coat, peering into every jar and running a finger over every surface. It had been a relief to gain the five-star rating on the Food & Safety certificate, which was proudly displayed in the tearoom's window, and I didn't want to do anything to jeopardise that.

"I'd better go around and check all the corners for cobwebs too. I don't want to give him any excuse to write a bad report on us." I paused, then added, "By the way, what's going on outside? Why are all those people there?"

Dora looked up and said in surprise, "Haven't you heard?"

"Heard what?"

"I thought you'd know, given that you were at the

funeral."

"Oh, you mean what happened to Adele Clifford?" I asked. "Yeah, that was a bit horrible. She had some kind of seizure or something. Is that why half the village is here? To gossip with the Old Biddies over morning tea?" I knew that Mabel and her friends loved holding court in the tearoom, and the big table by the window was usually reserved for them and their cronies.

"Oh, everyone's been talking about it in the village," said Dora. "I mean, you just don't expect a second death at a funeral, do you?"

"Wait—what are you talking about?"

"Didn't you know? Adele Clifford is dead."

CHAPTER FIVE

I stared at her. "Dead?"

Dora nodded. "She died in hospital last night."

I sat down in one of the chairs by the table. "Bloody hell... really? I can't believe it! I mean, she did seem to be in a bad way... but the ambulance arrived pretty quickly and I thought she'd be fine once she got to the hospital..."

I hadn't liked Adele Clifford and I couldn't really pretend that I was upset about the news—but still, it was always a shock to hear about a sudden death. Then my head jerked up in horror as something occurred to me.

"It wasn't an allergic reaction, was it?" I asked anxiously. "Oh God, I hope it wasn't something she ate! She was really stuffing her face with several of the puddings we provided for the reception. I did ask her about allergies, of course, when she put in the order, and she told me she didn't have any… but you know how these rumours always get around and it will give the tearoom a bad reputation."

Dora frowned. "I don't think anyone knows the cause of death yet. Even Mabel didn't seem to know more when I talked to her at church this morning."

I sighed. Well, if Mabel and the other Old Biddies didn't know, then no one else in the village would. I'd have to content myself with waiting for the post-mortem results. *Perhaps I can ask Devlin*, I thought suddenly. As a leading detective in the Oxfordshire CID, he would be in charge of the investigation anyway if there was any hint that the death could be suspicious. *Yes, I'll call him later—as soon as I have a moment free. It'll be nice to speak to Devlin anyway and hear his voice*, I thought, smiling in anticipation.

A horde of pensioners swarmed into the tearoom as soon as the doors were opened, led by the Old Biddies who marched straight to their "usual" table and settled down, surrounded by their friends. They were followed by a few tourists who were keen for some refreshment before lunch.

Cassie went to look after the Old Biddies and their posse, whilst I served the tourists. One American couple, in particular, was very friendly and I lingered by their table to chat as they told me about their travel itinerary.

"We started in London and we're heading north," said the husband, who had a drawling accent that reminded me of the cowboy movies my father liked watching. He had the leathery, weather-beaten skin of a cowboy too, and eyes that crinkled at the corners, although he was dressed like a respectable businessman on holiday in an expensive sports jacket, polo shirt, and chinos.

"Y'all got some mighty fine architecture in this country," he added with a smile.

"Yes, we just love all the history and culture," his wife chimed in, a pretty woman with curly brown hair and a fondness for floral patterns, if her outfit was anything to go by. Even her shoes were made of floral-patterned canvas fabric. "We thought the buildings we saw in London were amazing—and then we got to Oxford! Oh my! Are all the towns in England like this?"

I laughed. "No, not at all. I mean, some are, but places like Oxford and Cambridge aren't a very realistic representation of modern England. There are a lot of big industrial cities—like Manchester and Liverpool—which are probably much more the norm. But hey, if 'Olde England' is what you want, then you've come to the right place for it. The Cotswolds area is full of medieval market towns and quaint little villages that haven't changed for hundreds of years."

"We're so looking forward to seeing them!" said the wife. "Tomorrow we're going to Bourton-on-the-

Water, and Upper Slaughter and Lower Slaughter... don't you just love the names of these places? And we'll also be visiting Stow-on-the-Wold, Cheltenham Spa, Burford, and Chipping Campden later in the week..."

"They're all gorgeous villages and market towns," I said. "Will you be heading up north to Stratford-upon-Avon as well? You can't miss William Shakespeare's birthplace!"

"We were actually thinking of heading west, towards Bath," said the husband.

"Oh, that's gorgeous too. Very elegant Regency city," I said enthusiastically.

The wife beamed. "Yes, I can't wait! I'm a huge Jane Austen fan and it's always been my dream to visit Bath. We're from Texas, you see, and you just don't get that kind of architecture back home." She looked around the interior of the tearoom and added warmly, "And can I just tell you, honey, how much I love this place? I adore traditional English teashops and we've visited quite a few on this trip but yours is the best by far!"

"Oh... ah, thanks," I said, slightly embarrassed by her effusive praise. "Maybe you should wait until you've tasted the food before you say that," I added jokingly.

"Oh, I'm sure I'm gonna love it!" said the wife, looking down at the menu with relish. Then she furrowed her brow in confusion. "Wait... this section called 'Puddings'... it's got things like apple pie and

Victoria sponge cake... but those aren't puddings, are they?"

"'Pudding' has two meanings in England," I explained. "It can mean any kind of 'dessert' in general or it can mean an actual pudding. So if someone asks you what you want for pudding, they're asking what kind of dessert you would like." I gave her a crooked smile. "British language is often like that. There are a lot of words that have completely different meanings, depending on the context. 'Tea' is another one. It can mean the hot beverage... or it can mean an afternoon snack of cakes and scones, accompanied by the hot beverage... or it can mean that time of day when you'd have this snack... or it can even mean an early evening meal for people who live in the North of England. They don't call it dinner or supper— they call it tea." I chuckled at the bewilderment on her face. "Don't worry, you'll get used to it!"

After taking their order, I left the couple still pondering the "puddings" on the menu and returned to the counter, where Cassie was already busy stacking the first tray with scones, teacups, and a pot of tea. The rest of the morning flew by. Several tourist coaches stopped in Meadowford and the tearoom was soon filled with the sound of voices talking in all kinds of accents: Japanese, French, American, Brazilian, German, Singaporean, Italian, Chinese... but no Canadian. I could see Cassie's gaze dart hopefully to the door every time someone entered, then her face fall in disappointment each time her Canadian admirer didn't appear.

"He's not going to come, is he?" she said despondently when we finally paused for a breath during a lull. "He probably decided that my painting wasn't that good. Maybe I'm asking too much for it? I mean, I'm a nobody, right? I probably shouldn't charge anything for my paintings. They're all crap, really, and—"

"Stop it, Cassie," I said fiercely. "You're a great artist and you know it!"

I looked at her in exasperation. I could never understand how Cassie could be so confident in all other areas of life and yet be a completely different person when it came to her art: anxious, insecure, and second-guessing herself at every turn. I knew her paintings were fantastic and that she was incredibly talented—I was sure it was only a matter of time before she was "discovered".

"Your painting is priced exactly as it should be," I said firmly. "In fact, I think it's worth much more. If it was in some posh gallery in London, they'd probably be selling it for double the price!" I reached out and squeezed her hand. "Don't sell yourself short, Cass. You're very talented and I'm sure once you make a few sales, word-of-mouth will spread and people will be coming to commission paintings from you. You'll see!"

She gave me a wan smile. "Thanks, Gemma."

The door of the tearoom swung open and we

both looked over eagerly. But it wasn't a big, denim-clad Canadian—it was a uniformed police constable, followed by a short young man in a bright blue blazer, a tight T-shirt which did not flatter his skinny chest, and maroon drainpipe jeans which hung so low that they looked as if they would drop to his ankles at any moment. His hair was gelled to within an inch of its life and he wore trendy loafers with no socks. He had "Trying Too Hard" written all over him.

He swaggered over to the counter and said, "I'm looking for the owner, Gemma Rose."

"That's me," I said. "Can I help you?"

He flashed a badge at me. "Detective Inspector Dylan Pratt of Oxfordshire CID."

Cassie snorted with laughter, then clamped a hand over her mouth.

I blinked at the young man. *Surely he must be joking?* "I'm sorry? I must have heard wrong... I thought you said your name was—"

"Dylan Pratt—Inspector Pratt," he said curtly. He glanced at Cassie, then took my elbow and pulled me aside. "I need to ask you some questions."

"Um... sure. What about?" I looked at him uncertainly.

"I understand you provided the catering for Rex Clifford's funeral reception yesterday morning?"

I nodded. "Yes, I provided the food. Not the drinks."

"Did you make all the food yourself?"

"Well, not myself—my chef, Dora, baked most of the items. But yes, it's all home-made and was made in this tearoom."

"Can you vouch for the safety of all the ingredients?"

"I... I think so. It's the same ingredients that go into the normal tearoom menu and as you can see—" I waved a hand, indicating the busy tables around us, "—there are lots of people coming in every day, eating the same baking. We haven't had any complaints."

"Hmm..." He wrote something down in a notebook. "I'd like to speak to your chef afterwards and check the contents of your kitchen. Now at the reception, was the food under your supervision the entire time?"

"Well, no... that's impossible," I said. "It was displayed on the buffet table and, although I was hovering close by, I can't guarantee that I was watching it all the time. People were coming and helping themselves and there was quite a crowd around the table."

"So it's possible that someone could have tampered with the food without your knowledge?"

"Um... yeah, I suppose so. But who—"

"And am I right in saying that you went up to the buffet table with Adele Clifford to help her choose something to eat?"

"Well, actually, she dragged me with her. She—"

"What did she have?"

"She... she had a slice of treacle tart, I think."

He gave me a hard look. "Who served it to her?"

"Um... it was Mabel Cooke. One of the village residents."

A satisfied smile crossed his face. "Yes, good—I wanted to see if you would confirm my suspicions.

"What suspicions?" I asked.

He ignored me and said, "And did you observe Adele Clifford after that? Did she seem all right to you? Show any signs of illness?"

"I think she had a headache—I remember her rubbing her temples and complaining about it as she went to sit down with her plate. Oh, and she mentioned having stomach cramps a bit earlier— but she said it was just because she was hungry."

"That's all?"

I frowned in an effort to remember. "Well, actually, now that you mention it, she did look quite queasy. Her face was a bit funny and she was clutching her middle... but that was when the... um... when that guy called Tyler Lee was speaking. I thought she was just getting emotional listening to him. It wasn't until she slumped over that I realised something was wrong." I looked at him sharply. "But wait—are you saying that Adele Clifford's death is suspicious?"

He crossed his arms and smiled smugly. "She was poisoned."

I took a sharp breath. "*Poisoned?* Are you sure?"

He gave me an irritable look. "Of course I'm sure.

The doctor who was looking after her in Intensive Care had a brain wave and tested her urine—came up positive for arsenic. The autopsy is being done today but I'm sure the post-mortem results will confirm that."

I stared at him. "*Arsenic?* But... but I thought nobody got poisoned by arsenic any more."

"Oh, you can still get poisoned by arsenic, all right," he said darkly. "It's just a lot harder to get hold of the stuff nowadays. Right. I need you to provide a statement. The constable here will sort that out with you. Now, I need to speak to Mabel Cooke..." He scanned the room, his gaze zooming in on the table by the window where the Old Biddies were still sitting with some of their friends. "I was told that I would find her here in the tearoom. Which one is she?"

"She's the old lady in the purple cardigan, right by the window," I said reluctantly. "But I don't understand... why do you need to speak to her?"

He gave me a look, like I was very stupid. "Because I'm investigating Adele Clifford's murder and Mabel Cooke is the top suspect."

CHAPTER SIX

I started to laugh. "What? You're joking, right? You're not seriously suspecting an eighty-year-old granny of being a murderer?" Then my laughter died away as I realised that his face was deadly serious.

"This is no laughing matter, Miss Rose," he said, scowling. "Age makes no difference. There are several cases of pensioners murdering people. There was an old woman of a hundred-and-two who strangled her roommate in a Massachusetts nursing home only a few years ago... and another ninety-six-year-old woman in Florida who shot and killed her nephew."

"Yes, but..." I trailed off helplessly, looking over to Mabel, then back at him again. "If you knew Mabel Cooke, you'd know it's ridiculous to think that she could murder anybody!"

"Is it?" he retorted. He flipped back a few pages in his notebook and said, "I have witness reports from the funeral reception saying they overheard Mabel Cooke describing how easy it is to murder someone, especially using poison. And she specifically mentions favouring the use of arsenic."

I groaned inwardly. "Yes, but she was just joking!"

"You seem to think that people joke about murder a lot, Miss Rose," he said coldly. "In my line of work, that would be called a death threat."

"Aww, come on!" I said, starting to lose patience. "Don't tell me you've never done it yourself? Talked about wanting to kill someone that you find really annoying? You might even fantasize—for fun—how you'd do it, but you'd never really do it."

"I don't fantasize about killing people," he said. "And anyone who does is a criminal in my book." He turned away.

"Wait!" I grabbed his arm. "Okay, if you're going to go down that route, then... Mabel isn't the only person who served Adele Clifford."

"What do you mean?"

"Well, Rachel Clifford also came up to Adele while we were at the buffet table and she insisted that Adele have some sticky toffee pudding. In fact, she transferred some from her plate to Adele's." I hesitated, feeling slightly guilty for "snitching" on the young woman. "Rachel Clifford stands to inherit the whole estate if Adele dies. Don't you think that would make her a stronger suspect? And she would have had ample opportunity to doctor the piece of sticky toffee pudding she gave Adele.

"Oh! *And—*" I added excitedly as I remembered. "There's also that stranger—Tyler Lee. I saw him bring Adele some cake as well. He could have added poison to the cake before he gave it to her. If he really is Rex Clifford's love child, then he'd have a good motive to kill her too, because—just like Rachel—he'd be eligible to inherit some of the estate!" I finished triumphantly. "So you see—Adele had three different puddings from three different people. How can you be so sure that the poison was in the slice of treacle tart that Mabel served her?"

Pratt looked taken aback. "I haven't heard about these other people giving food to Adele," he said, eyeing me suspiciously.

"You can check with Rachel Clifford and Tyler Lee if you don't believe me," I said.

"I don't need you to tell me how to do my job." Pratt scowled. "And in any case, neither of them was overheard plotting to murder Adele. Mabel Cooke is still our strongest suspect." He held up three fingers, ticking each one off. "She had the means, the motive, and the opportunity!"

I resisted the urge to roll my eyes. The guy sounded like he was reciting from a *Detective Work for Dummies* manual.

"But Mabel doesn't *have* a motive," I argued.

"She had no reason to kill Adele. She certainly didn't gain anything by the widow's death—she's not the next of kin and she's not a direct beneficiary of the estate in any way."

"Ah, but a charity she supports was named in the original will and may benefit again, if Adele is removed from the picture."

"Happy Hedgehog Friends?" I gave a sceptical laugh. "Give me a break! You're not seriously suggesting that Mabel murdered someone to get a few hundred quid for some homeless hedgehogs?"

"It was not a few hundred pounds—it was a sizable donation," said Pratt stiffly. "And that's not the sole reason. You see, I've done my homework—I've been speaking to some of the other village residents and I heard rumours that Mabel Cooke and Adele Clifford came to blows at bingo."

"I would hardly call it coming to blows," I said dryly. "I think the village gossips have been exaggerating. Mabel and Adele probably just had some heated arguments—from what I know, Mabel was trying to protect some of the other pensioners from being bullied by Adele."

"Ah, but you see—that ties in with my theory perfectly!" said Pratt with satisfaction. He flipped through the pages of his notebook. "I have witnesses from the funeral reception saying that when Mabel was discussing how to murder Adele, many of her friends agreed that killing the widow would be—I quote—'a community service'."

I rolled my eyes and heaved an exasperated sigh. "It was a *joke*, Inspector! You've got to stop taking it all so seriously! Trust me, I know Mabel and her friends very well—they love mystery novels and murder investigations and that sort of thing. They have an overactive imagination. They're always talking about how a murder could be done—it doesn't mean anything.

"Besides," I added, "don't you think that if Mabel really planned to murder Adele, she wouldn't be announcing it to everyone at the reception?"

"Criminals are known to like boasting about their cleverness. It's a well-known part of the criminal psyche. You haven't done criminal profiling—you wouldn't understand," he said loftily.

Before I could say anything else, Pratt spun on his heels and was marching across the room towards the Old Biddies' table. I started to follow but was waylaid by a Japanese tour group leaving the tearoom who wanted to thank me for the delicious food. I responded to their compliments absently, nodding and smiling, whilst my eyes followed Pratt anxiously. The Old Biddies might have been a bit exasperating at times but I was very fond of them and I didn't want them suffering from Pratt's bullying tactics. After all, Mabel—for all her bossy manner—was still an old lady...

However, when the tour group finally left and I was able to hurry across to the Old Biddies' table, I discovered that I had been worrying for nothing.

Inspector Pratt was leaning across the table and wagging a finger at Mabel:

"...and I believe you served cake to Adele Clifford at the post-funeral reception—just after you talked of murdering her with poison. What do you say to that?" he demanded in the best aggressive TV-detective manner.

But Mabel looked unimpressed. Instead, she eyed him up and down and said, "Is there something wrong with your trousers, young man? They're falling down."

The other Old Biddies and the rest of the pensioners giggled.

Pratt reddened and I saw him tug surreptitiously at the waistband of his jeans. "These are called hipster. It's a style," he informed her stiffly.

"Are you sure you haven't forgotten your belt?" said Mabel, still assessing him.

"No, madam, I have *not* forgotten my belt! These... these are meant to be worn low on the hips," snapped Pratt. "Look... never mind my jeans. You didn't answer my question."

"Oh... no, I didn't serve Adele cake," Mabel said.

"Aha! You are lying!" Pratt said with glee. "I have witnesses—including Miss Rose here—who can testify that they saw you serving Adele from the buffet table. Do you dare deny that fact?"

Mabel looked surprised. "I wasn't denying it."

"But you just said you didn't serve her," said Pratt, looking confused and angry. "Don't try to wriggle out of it! Everyone here heard you!"

"I'm not trying to wriggle out of anything," said Mabel with a disdainful sniff.

"Then why did you say you didn't serve Adele cake?"

Mabel pursed her lips. "Well, it wasn't cake. It was a treacle tart. A cake is usually made of sponge with a cream filling and frosting on top. A tart, on the other hand, is made with a pastry crust on the bottom and sides, though this particular one had a shortcrust pastry lattice on top, so I suppose one should really call it a pie—"

"*Aaarrgh!*" Pratt made a strangled sound in his throat. "Mrs Cooke, I do not care whether it was a pie or cake or double chocolate sundae that you served!" he said through gritted teeth. "I want to know whether you admit to serving Adele Clifford a piece of dessert!"

Mabel blinked. "But you just said you have witnesses who can verify that. Why do you need to ask me?"

There were sniggers from around the room. By now, the whole tearoom had stopped eating and were avidly watching the scene unfold. Pratt glanced around and flushed angrily, then turned his attention back to Mabel.

"And do you also admit to boasting about how easily you could murder Adele Clifford by poisoning her?"

Mabel looked at him indignantly. "I certainly

wasn't boasting, Inspector—that's very poor manners. I was simply stating a fact. It *is* very easy to poison someone if you know how."

I groaned inwardly again. "Mabel," I said, leaning towards her, "maybe you shouldn't answer any more questions until you speak to a lawyer—"

"Nonsense! I have nothing to hide."

"Ah! Then you'll have no objection to coming down to the station with me," said Pratt, reaching over, putting a firm hand under Mabel's elbow, and hustling her to her feet.

"Hey! Wait—you're not *arresting* her?" I said, scandalised.

Several of the other pensioners stood up as well, turning to face Inspector Pratt, arms akimbo. He faltered slightly as he faced the row of white-haired old ladies glaring at him. Then, before he could answer, the door to the tearoom swung open again and a dark-haired man stepped in.

An audible sigh of relief swept through the tearoom. It was Devlin O'Connor, looking broodingly handsome as usual in an elegantly tailored charcoal-grey suit, his piercing blue eyes scanning the room quickly as he assessed the situation. Tall, lean and muscular, he dominated every other man around him. The difference between him and Pratt was striking, not just in their appearance but in the air of quiet authority that Devlin exuded compared to Pratt's arrogant belligerence.

Devlin strode over to the Old Biddies' table and

gave Pratt a nod. "Dylan—may I ask what's going on here?"

Pratt stiffened. "Nothing that concerns you, O'Connor."

"I think I'll be the judge of that," said Devlin pleasantly.

Pratt went red. "Are you telling me how to do my job, O'Connor?" He leaned towards Devlin and jabbed a finger in his chest. "I've spoken to the DCC, all right? You're off the case! It's mine!"

Everyone looked taken aback at the man's unprofessional manner but Devlin kept his cool.

"I think we should discuss this back at the station," he said, his voice calm. He glanced around the tearoom. "I'm sure the Detective Chief Constable would not appreciate CID internal affairs being deliberated in public."

Pratt followed Devlin's gaze around the room and flushed an even darker red. Then he snarled, "Fine. But I'm taking Mrs Cooke here in for questioning, whether you like it or not!"

Devlin looked as if he would argue, then he said in a neutral voice, "I'm sure we can ask Mrs Cooke if she would be willing to come down to the station with us, to help with enquiries."

"I'm not asking—I'm telling her!" growled Pratt. "And if she won't come, I won't hesitate to arre—"

"But of course I will go!" Mabel boomed.

"You... you what—?" Pratt looked nonplussed.

Mabel rubbed her hands together. "I have always

wanted to see the inside of an interrogation room! Will you speak into one of those recorders on the tables first before we start, just like they do on telly?"

Pratt spluttered furiously, "How dare you! This is a serious matter!"

Mabel looked at him in surprise. "And so it should be! I'm glad the police are finally recognising my talents in this area. I have been offering to help with enquiries for months now and the Oxfordshire CID have never taken me up on the offer. I must say, you're a much more enterprising young man, Inspector Pratt." She picked up her handbag, tucked it under her arm, and gave him a brisk nod. "When do we leave?"

Devlin turned away to hide a smile. Pratt looked slightly dazed and, for the first time, I felt a wave of compassion for him. The poor man didn't realise what a can of worms he'd opened when he decided to tangle with Mabel Cooke!

CHAPTER SEVEN

After Mabel, Devlin, and Pratt had left, the tearoom buzzed with excited conversation. Mabel's pensioner friends got up quickly and came to the counter to pay, obviously keen to hurry out and spread the story through the village. The other three Old Biddies, however, drew me aside instead of leaving.

"Gemma, we have no time to lose!" said Glenda.

"What do you mean?"

"We have to find out who murdered Adele Clifford!" Florence declared.

"The police are investigating that," I said.

"They don't sound like they know what they're doing," said Ethel. "That Inspector Pratt can't even get his trousers to stay up properly."

"Well, Devlin's good," I said. "You know he's a

great detective. He'll make sure the investigation is handled—"

"Yes, but what if he isn't allowed to work on the case?" asked Glenda. "You heard what Inspector Pratt said! They might decide that since he knows Mabel personally, there would be a... a conflict of interest, I think it's called."

Florence nodded. "We can't rely on your young man, Gemma—we have to take care of it ourselves. That's what Mabel would say if she were here."

"But... what do you want to do?" I asked in exasperation.

"First, we need to make a list of all the suspects," said Ethel, her eyes sparkling with excitement. "That's how it's done in all the mystery novels."

"That's easy—Rachel Clifford is the most likely suspect," I said, getting caught up in their enthusiasm in spite of myself. "She has the most to gain in the event of Adele's death. And she had a clear opportunity to poison the sticky toffee pudding she gave Adele. In fact..." I paused, remembering. "In fact, I remember being surprised when she suddenly showed up and started offering Adele the pudding."

"Why were you surprised?"

"Well, she had been so hostile up till then! Always scowling and snapping at Adele... and then all of a sudden, she turns up full of smiles and goodwill, insisting that Adele try some of her pudding... That looks suspicious to me."

"What about that young Asian chap who came to the funeral?" asked Florence.

Glenda tittered, "Ooh, he was so very handsome, wasn't he? Perhaps he is a 'lady killer'... in every sense of the word!"

"If he really is Rex Clifford's son, then he would be entitled to an equal share of the estate," Ethel pointed out.

"That would give him a strong motive, yes..." I agreed. "But that's assuming, of course, that he knew the particulars of the will. If he didn't know that the entire estate had been left to Adele, he wouldn't have had any reason to want to kill her."

"Oh," said Ethel, slightly deflated.

"We have to find out when Tyler Lee arrived in the U.K. and if he made contact with the lawyers before he came to the funeral," I said, thinking out loud. "He's definitely a strong suspect because he gave Adele some food too." I told them about the way Tyler Lee had tripped while walking past Adele and fallen against her, knocking her plate out of her hands.

"He insisted on bringing her a replacement," I finished. "I saw him go to the buffet table and return with a slice of Victoria sponge."

Glenda gasped. "Do you think he did that on purpose?"

I shrugged. "Who knows? But it *would* be a good way to get Adele to eat some poisoned cake, don't you think?"

"We have to find out more about him!" Florence said.

"What about the brother, Miles Clifford?" I asked. "Isn't he 'next of kin' as well?"

"He's a respected professor at Oxford University—he's one of the senior tutors at St Frideswide's College," said Florence doubtfully. "He's probably quite wealthy in his own right."

"And his claim would come behind Rachel and Tyler Lee," said Glenda. "I know because Mabel told me. The 'next of kin' in the will specified children first, then siblings. So unless Rachel and Tyler Lee both die, Miles Clifford wouldn't get anything."

"Yes... hmm... in any case, he seemed to be the only family member sympathetic to Adele," I said, thinking back to the funeral. "And he definitely didn't give her any pudding. Okay... so who else? Any other enemies?"

"*Everyone* was her enemy," said Florence, giving me a dry look. "There are dozens of people in the village who could have happily poisoned Adele at the funeral."

I sighed. "Well, that doesn't really help us."

Ethel patted my hand. "Don't you worry, dear— we've made a good start."

"Yes, and once we do a bit of behind-the-scenes sleuthing, we'll have more clues to work from." Florence nodded.

"We'll make a start today, as soon as Mabel returns from the police station!" said Glenda.

I wasn't sure I liked the sound of that. "What do you mean, 'behind-the-scenes' sleuthing? You're not planning to snoop around again, are you? Don't do anything crazy, okay?" I pleaded.

They promised and toddled off, but I was uneasy. I'd seen the kind of escapades the Old Biddies got embroiled in, and I shuddered to think of what they were planning this time. Still, they had got me thinking about Adele's murder, and as I went about my work for the rest of the day, I couldn't help mulling over the case.

My thoughts kept returning to Rachel Clifford and the way she had looked that morning in the kitchen at the parish hall, just before the funeral. I had seen the hatred in her eyes and heard the fury in her voice as she spoke of her stepmother. Her words rang in my head: *"I've got to do something—I can't just let that woman win. I don't care what it takes—I'm not letting Adele get the money!"*

The Old Biddies might have been excited about Tyler Lee—after all, it was always more tempting to think of the murderer as a mysterious stranger from the Orient or something like that—but I knew that, more often than not, the killer was someone who was known to the victim, someone a lot closer to home.

That thought crossed my mind again late that afternoon when I was behind the counter, sorting through some paperwork, and came across a survey that Cassie had designed. It was a new idea she'd had—a questionnaire to be sent to all catering orders after the event, to see which areas we could improve on.

I smiled as I suddenly thought of the perfect first person to test the survey on. I glanced around the tearoom: the "Afternoon Tea" rush was almost over and several of the tables were empty.

"Hey, Cass—do you think you could hold the fort for a bit? I think I might pop around to Clifford House with our new survey. We just did a big catering order for them and it would be the perfect chance to test this questionnaire."

Cassie raised a sardonic eyebrow. "And maybe ask a few questions about Adele Clifford's murder while you're at it?"

I gave a sheepish smile. My best friend knew me too well. "The thought had crossed my mind," I admitted.

"Gemma, you'd better be careful. Devlin isn't working the case this time and that inspector really seemed to live up to his name."

"Yeah, he *was* a total prat, wasn't he?" I grinned.

"He's also likely to do his nut if he finds you meddling in a police investigation. He could get you in serious trouble."

"I'm only going to ask a few questions," I said defensively. "There's no harm in that. And it's only natural that I would be curious—everyone else is. Don't worry, I'll be fine."

"Famous last words..." said Cassie dryly.

CHAPTER EIGHT

When I rang the doorbell at Clifford House a short while later and Rachel's scowling friend, Kate, flung open the door, I felt my confidence slip a bit.

"Hi! Is Rachel around?" I asked, giving her bright smile.

"What d'you want?" snarled Kate.

"I'd like to speak to Rachel," I said, ignoring the girl's belligerent manner.

"She's busy. She's just had a death in the family, you know."

"Two, actually," I said quickly. "And yes, I know—I was there. I catered the funeral reception."

She paused, obviously recognising me, then muttered, "Yeah, well, then you'd know that everything's been a nasty shock for Rachel. She can't deal with anything at the moment, unless it's really urgent."

I hesitated. Even by a great stretch of the imagination, I couldn't really present a survey about my catering services as urgent. I was about to admit defeat and retreat, when I heard Rachel's voice from deeper in the house.

"Kate? Who is it?"

A moment later, Rachel Clifford came to the door. She was dressed in pair of faded yoga pants and an old T-shirt, and she looked at me without much enthusiasm, but I didn't waste the opportunity.

I gave her a dazzling smile. "Hi, Rachel—could I have a quick chat with you? I was hoping to get a bit of feedback on the catering I provided at the funeral reception. I'm just starting out, you see, and it would be *so* helpful to me...?" I trailed off hopefully.

Kate opened her mouth to protest, but Rachel's face softened and she said, "Is it your own business, then?"

I gave a proud smile. "Yes, I opened the tearoom in the village about ten months ago. I'd never run a business before so it's been a pretty steep learning curve," I said with a laugh.

Rachel thawed even further. "I've got my own business too, and I know what you mean." She pulled the front door open wider, ignoring her friend's disapproving look, and said, "Would you like a cup of tea?"

A few minutes later, I was installed in the Cliffords' large, comfortable sitting room with Kate perched on the arm of the sofa next to me, eyeing me like a suspicious guard dog.

Rachel set my mug of tea down on the coffee table and offered me a bowl of what looked like little squares of cardboard. I took one and nibbled it cautiously. It tasted a lot better than it looked— salty and crispy, with a slightly nutty flavour.

"These are very good," I said in surprise.

"They're home-made tofu chips," Rachel said. "I'm following the Blood Type Diet, you see, and I have to be careful about eating too much chicken or red meat, because I have low stomach acid and can't metabolise meat efficiently. Tofu is a great alternative source of protein. I also mustn't eat any shellfish or corn or oranges—especially oranges. They're an irritant to people of my blood type and interfere with the absorption of important minerals. What blood type are you?"

"Uh... I'm not sure. A, I think," I said, trying to remember.

"Oh, then you should have a primarily vegetarian diet," said Rachel earnestly. "And avoid dairy products—you just can't digest them properly. Definitely don't have any anchovies, mangoes, venison, sweet potatoes... oh, and kidney beans— they can cause a decrease in insulin production for Type As."

"Er... okay, I'll try to remember that," I said.

"Have you been on the diet long? You seem to know a lot about it."

"Well, I'm very interested in alternative therapies and diets," said Rachel with a smile.

"Is it part of your work?"

"In a way. I'm a yoga teacher. I believe in a holistic approach to health."

"Ah—is this the 'own business' you were talking about?"

"Yes." She smiled. "I started about a year ago, just making home visits and teaching classes at some of the local gyms, but what I'd really like to do is open my own studio. I need capital for that, though..." She trailed off. There was a loaded silence for a moment, then Rachel picked up the survey from the coffee table and glanced at the questions. "I'm not sure how much I can help with this. Adele did all the organising for the reception."

Delighted that she had brought up the subject of the murdered widow, I leaned forwards and said quickly, "Oh, I heard about what happened to Adele. I'm so sorry—I mean, it was terrible when she collapsed at the reception and everything turned into total chaos, but then for her to die! That must have been a shock."

"Oh, my God—I'll say!" Rachel gave a disbelieving laugh. "Here I was, wondering what to do with Adele, and then she ups and dies! Talk about the gods dropping things straight into your lap."

I drew back, slightly repulsed by her callous

reaction. Whatever sympathy I'd felt for Rachel at the funeral faded. In her own way, she was just as selfish and unpleasant as Adele had been!

"Rachel..." said Kate in a warning tone, darting a glance at me.

Rachel collected herself and gave me a guilty look. "Oh, yeah... I mean, of course I'm sorry she was murdered... but I can't pretend that it wasn't a blessing in a way."

I cleared my throat. "Yes... um... I heard about your... 'situation'. And I sympathise with you totally," I added smoothly. "I mean, anyone would be angry to discover that she was deprived of her inheritance by a relative stranger, who had only known her father for such a short time."

"Exactly!" cried Rachel. "I'm not going to be a hypocrite about it! I never liked Adele and I'm not going to start pretending now, just because she's dead."

"Did you hear that she was poisoned?" I asked in a gossipy tone. "It was all over my tearoom this morning. The police think it's murder."

Was it my imagination or did Rachel suddenly look slightly uneasy? Her friend, Kate, had definitely stiffened, and was now regarding me with a watchful intensity.

"Have the police come to question you?" I asked Rachel.

"Why should they? Rachel had nothing to do with the murder!" Kate snapped

"Oh, it's just that the police think the poison was in something Adele ate and they were questioning Mabel Cooke in the tearoom this morning, because she served Adele some treacle tart from the buffet table." I turned wide, innocent eyes on Rachel. "I remember that you gave Adele some pudding as well, didn't you? That's why I wondered if they'd come to speak to you."

Rachel flushed slightly. "Um… yes, you're right, I did. Your sticky toffee pudding was so delicious, I just had to share it…" Her eyes slid away from mine as she realised how lame that sounded.

"That was really nice of you," I commented, thinking that it was actually really weird behaviour for someone who claimed to hate Adele.

Rachel flushed even more as she guessed my thoughts. She gave a sheepish laugh. "All right—I'll come clean. I *was* really angry at Adele—but then I calmed down and thought about it. I realised that I had to swallow my pride: I need money to set up my studio, and if Adele was holding the purse strings… well, I decided it wouldn't kill me to butter her up a little."

It was a good story and it might even have been true. I couldn't help thinking, though, that it sounded very well rehearsed.

"If the police are looking for a murderer, they should investigate that half-Chinese bloke who turned up at the funeral!" growled Kate. "Mysterious guy in creepy clothes who conveniently turns up at the funeral, claiming to be the son of the deceased... if that's not dodgy, I don't know what is!"

"You mean Tyler Lee?" I said.

Rachel's face darkened. "If that's even his name," she muttered. "And that ridiculous story he told— all a pack of lies!"

I looked at her speculatively. "You don't believe him then?"

Rachel tossed her head. "I just can't see my father having a baby with some Chinese mistress. It's too ludicrous to even think about!"

"Didn't your father travel to China then?"

"He did," Rachel admitted grudgingly. "He had quite a few factories there and he used to go out often to inspect them... but I'm sure he didn't have some seedy lover there!"

I didn't say anything but, in spite of her vehement protests, I could see a flash of uncertainty in Rachel's eyes. After all, Rex Clifford had been a well-travelled businessman and no one could say for certain that he had never been tempted. China was a long way away and he could easily have indulged in a few affairs while he was overseas.

I thought back to the moving speech that Tyler Lee had made at the funeral reception. Could that all have been a lie?

"If he *is* your half-brother, does that mean that he would be entitled to half your father's estate?" I asked.

"I suppose so," said Rachel dourly. "But he would have to prove his identity first!"

"Did he try to speak to you again after the reception?"

Rachel shook her head. "He scarpered as soon as Adele collapsed and the ambulance arrived."

"Which makes him look extra guilty, doesn't it?" said Kate.

"But don't you think—"

"I think Rachel's tired now. And I don't think any of this is really helping you improve your catering service, is it?" said Kate pointedly.

I coloured slightly. I glanced at Rachel, hoping that she would protest, but she said nothing. I had to admit, though, that she did look quite pale and tired, and for the first time, I noticed dark circles under her eyes. The question was, were they put there by genuine fatigue—or by the strain of planning and concealing a murder?

CHAPTER NINE

I walked away from the front door of Clifford House, deep in thought. I had a feeling that Rachel might have been more talkative if she hadn't been under the watchful eye of her friend and I felt frustrated. If only I could have pushed her a bit more, she might have revealed more under pressure—but it looked like that was something that would have to be left to the police. Then I sighed as I remembered that it wasn't Devlin, with his keen intelligence and sharp wits, who was in charge of this investigation. It was Dylan Pratt—and from what I'd seen of the arrogant young detective so far, he didn't inspire much confidence. The fact that he hadn't even come to interview Rachel yet was a bad sign already.

My phone rang, distracting me from my

thoughts, and I answered it as I began walking down the garden path.

"Darling! Have you seen my iPad?"

It was my mother, sounding completely unlike her usual composed self.

"No, why?"

"I can't find it anywhere!" she said frantically. "I was wondering if I might have left it in the tearoom?"

"I'm not actually at the Little Stables at the moment, Mother—I'll have a look as soon as I get back. But I don't think so... I don't remember seeing your iPad anywhere and I had a good sort-out behind the counter this afternoon."

"Oh *sugar*! Where could it be?"

Wow. For my mother to be using that sort of language, she must have been *really* upset.

"When did you last see it?" I asked.

"That's just it, darling—I can't remember! I was sure I brought it home with me yesterday and I've been so busy today, what with tea at Helen's house and then going to the sale at Debenhams, that I never noticed it was missing until now!"

"Well, don't panic," I said. "It might be at my cottage. You popped over last night, remember? You probably left it in my sitting room somewhere. I tell you what, I'll check as soon as I get home and bring it over later."

"Oh, thank you, darling—that would be wonderful! In fact, why don't you have dinner here then with your father and me? I'm making a lamb roast with rosemary and garlic, and home-made mint jelly... oh, and apple crumble for dessert—your favourite!"

I hesitated. I loved my mother—but she was best experienced in small doses. An entire evening with her usually required mountains of patience and several pills for a throbbing headache. Still, I hadn't had dinner with my parents in a while and I felt slightly guilty.

"Okay, thanks—I'd love to come to dinner," I said. "Shall I come over around eight?"

"Super, darling! And while you're here, perhaps you can have a look at the internet. It's never been the same since you were here last and checked your emails," she said reproachfully. "I do think you might have broken it."

"What do you mean? How can I break the internet? Do you mean you can't get online? Is there a problem with your modem?"

"Oh, no, no, there's nothing wrong with the modem, darling. We had a lovely engineer from British Telecom come and check everything for us the other day. D'you know, he told me that house prices in Witney have soared and that his poor sister is having a *nightmare* trying to buy something. They've got a little girl and they wanted something with a garden but they were shocked at the asking prices, even for a semi. And it's not even in central Oxford! Of course, Dorothy Clarke says she thinks one is *much* better off investing in property overseas—I saw her in Debenhams this morning—did I tell you that her daughter is getting married? To this lovely doctor she met while on holiday in Malta. He fixes knees, I think. Or was it elbows? Anyway, Dorothy says he's bought the most enormous house in Malta and they're going on honeymoon to Hawaii—"

"*Mother!*" I said through gritted teeth. "What does all this have to do with me breaking your internet?"

"It's very rude to interrupt, Gemma," said my mother severely. "Haven't I taught you any manners?"

I sighed. "Sorry, Mother. It's just that—well, I can't really stop to chat right now and I wanted to know what was wrong with your internet."

"The Google just doesn't look the same anymore, darling. I don't like the way the letters look. I want you to put the original one back."

"Oh..." Understanding dawned. "You mean the logo? That's called the 'Google Doodle'—it changes all the time."

"Well, can't you stop it changing?"

"No, Mother," I said, laughing. "Anyway, it doesn't stop you searching for anything—it still works just the same. Anyway, I've got to go now. I'll see you later tonight!"

I hung up and started towards my bicycle, which was parked against a tree nearby. But I hadn't gone a few steps when I became aware of a movement on the other side of the hedge dividing the neighbouring property. It was a gnarled old hand, I realised with surprise, beckoning eagerly to me. I hesitated, then kept walking.

"*Psst! Psssst! Over here!*" came a loud whisper from over the hedge.

I hesitated again, then—curiosity getting the better of me—I cut across the lawn and went over to the hedge. I was surprised to find that the hand belonged to a white-haired old lady in gardening gloves and a floral smock. She was brandishing a pair of pruning shears but her interest was obviously not on the plants around her. Instead, she was eyeing the Cliffords' residence, and, as soon as I arrived at the hedge, she asked eagerly:

"Do they know who did it?"

I blinked. "Um... are you talking about Adele's—?"

"Of course! Who murdered her? Have the police made an arrest yet?"

"No, they've only just started the investigation."

"Taking their time, aren't they?" The old woman sniffed. "Haven't even been out to speak to me yet and you'd think they would want to know what the neighbour saw!"

"Er... did you see anything?" I asked.

"Oh yes... I could tell you something about the goings-on in that house..." she said, raising and lowering her eyebrows meaningfully.

I felt a surge of elation. I might not have got

much information out of Rachel Clifford but here was something even better: a nosy neighbour!

"What sort of goings-on?" I asked eagerly.

"Well, now..." She looked down with false modesty. "I'm never one to gossip..."

I smiled to myself and said in an indifferent voice, "Oh, that's a shame, but I do respect your feelings. Well, it was nice chatting to you..." I turned as if to go.

"Wait!" She reached across the hedge and clamped a hand on my arm. "Don't be so hasty, young lady... I wouldn't mind talking to *you*. I mean, you're the girl who runs the tearoom in the village, aren't you? I'm Mrs Wiseman," she added. "I haven't been to your tearoom yet but my friends say you have the best scones in Oxfordshire."

I blushed slightly. "Thank you. I hope you might have the chance to come and taste them yourself."

She beamed. "I'll make sure I do soon." She glanced at Clifford House again and added, "And after all, this isn't really gossip—not *really*—I mean, I'm just telling you what I saw. If the police came and questioned me, I'd be doing the same."

"Of course," I murmured.

Mrs Wiseman lowered her voice and leaned closer. "I'm sure the murder has something to do with the fight last Tuesday."

"What fight?"

"Oh, terrible it was—screaming and shouting so loud I could even hear it from my kitchen. So of course, I had to come out here to see what the fuss was all about..."

"Naturally," I agreed, grinning. "What did you see?"

"Nothing," she said mournfully. "I couldn't see into the house from here. I recognised the voices, though. It was Rex and his brother—you know, the one who's a professor at Oxford—they were having the most terrible row. I'd never heard Rex shouting like that before."

"What was the argument about?"

She frowned. "I couldn't really hear properly—even though they were shouting, the words were quite muffled. I did hear the name 'Rachel' several times, though, so I think the fight must have been about her." She gave me a dark look and added in a scandalised whisper: "Wouldn't be surprised if it was—the way she's taken up with that *girlfriend* of hers. Always going around together and never any young men in sight... Well! They say in the village that Rachel might be one of *those*..." she trailed off and waggled her eyebrows again.

"Er..." I tried to think of a diplomatic response. "They might just be close friends, you know. I mean, just because two women do a lot of things together doesn't mean... And anyway, even if they are... um... does it matter? As long as they're happy—"

"Oh, but it would have broken Rex's heart!" cried Mrs Wiseman. "All he wanted was for Rachel to settle down with a nice young man and have a baby in her arms. He would never have accepted all these newfangled ideas about two women... well, *being* together..." She shuddered. "It's no wonder that he changed his mind about his will."

I looked at her sharply. "Are you saying that Rex Clifford could have been so upset when he found out about Rachel's... er... lifestyle that he cut her out of his will?"

Mrs Wiseman shrugged. "Well, he was a very *traditionally* minded man. Unlike his brother. Now what was his name? Miles... yes, that's right. Miles. Professor Miles Clifford. He's a professor at Oxford University—did I say? And well, you know what academic types are like. They can be so... *liberal.*" She said it like it was some kind of disease.

"Do you think Miles was defending Rachel?" I asked.

"Oh, I wouldn't be surprised! He always seems to dote on the girl. But I'm sure in this instance, Rex wouldn't be mollified."

I thought back to Rachel's reaction the morning of the funeral. She had seemed genuinely shocked and puzzled that her father could cut her out of his will—but surely if she had told him about her gay lifestyle, she would have known that he was upset. So why had she still been surprised? Unless she *hadn't* told him? In which case, how had Rex Clifford known?

Adele.

Suddenly I had an idea of what might have happened. Rachel probably *had* been trying to hide the truth from her father—she probably knew that it was something he could never accept—but last Tuesday, Adele had spitefully told Rex Clifford everything. And the businessman had completely lost it. In spite of his brother Miles's best efforts to reconcile the two, he had turned against his own daughter and decided to change the will which had benefited her.

"Did you see Rachel? Was she there last Tuesday?" I asked Mrs Wiseman, keen to see if my conjectures were correct.

"Hmm... no, I didn't see her but she might have been out the back. Adele Clifford was there, though; I definitely saw her when Miles Clifford left—she saw him to the door. And then again a few hours later, when the solicitor arrived, she came to the door and let him in."

"The solicitor?"

"Yes, that nice young chap from Sexton, Lovell & Billingsley."

"Gavin Sexton?"

She nodded. "Yes, that's right. Old Sexton's nephew. He arrived with a briefcase and hurried into the house."

"I wonder if you're right and Rex Clifford called his solicitor to change his will," I mused.

"Oh, I'm sure," said Mrs Wiseman. "In fact, I think they asked their cleaning lady to be the witness. She normally comes on a Tuesday, you see, and she usually leaves by five thirty—but last week, she didn't leave until after seven. *After* that young lawyer chap arrived," she added.

I looked at her with admiration. I should have told Devlin to hire Mrs Wiseman for police stakeouts!

As if reading my thoughts, Mrs Wiseman gave me a coy look and said, "I heard that your young man is a detective in the Criminal Investigation Department."

"Yes, he's with the Oxfordshire CID," I said, wondering if there was anything the village gossips *didn't* know about my personal life.

"Well... maybe you could tell him that I have important information for the police," Mrs Wiseman suggested, looking unexpectedly shy. "Perhaps they would like to come and question me...?"

I smiled, realising suddenly that behind that gossipy exterior was a lonely old woman who wanted to feel important and needed.

"I'll definitely tell Devlin—er, I mean, Inspector O'Connor—that you have valuable information about the murder investigation," I promised. "He's not actually working this case, though, but I'm sure he will pass the information on and the detective in charge will be out to see you soon." I crossed my fingers behind my back and hoped that Inspector Pratt would live up to my promises.

Mrs Wiseman smiled in anticipation. "Oh, that

would be wonderful, dear. But make sure to tell them that I'm not around on Monday afternoons—that's my bingo day—and Wednesday mornings, I go to the Farmer's Market in Gloucester Green. Oh, and Friday I play bridge at my friend Marge's house, so I can't do that day. Saturdays, I sometimes go into Oxford to do some shopping, and Sunday there's church, of course, and then my book club meets in the evening."

I blinked rapidly. *Blimey.* Paris Hilton probably didn't have a social calendar as full as hers! "Er... okay, I'll make sure I pass that along."

Giving her a wave, I returned to the nearby tree to retrieve my bicycle and head back to the tearoom.

CHAPTER TEN

I couldn't stop thinking about the mystery of
Adele Clifford's murder the rest of the afternoon.
Cycling back into Oxford that evening, I was
pedalling slowly down towards Folly Bridge and the
development by the river where my cottage was
situated, when I glanced up and noted the imposing
facade of St Frideswide's College, which dominated
one side of the street. As one of the grandest of the
Oxford colleges, St Frideswide's was famous for its
wealth, its long list of powerful alumni, and its
Gothic tower, which was a key feature of the Oxford
city skyline. It was also, I recalled, where Miles
Clifford was affiliated as a tutor.

Impulsively, I slowed my bike and pulled over by
the front gate. Leaving my bicycle beside the college
bike shed, I hurried into the Porter's Lodge. A

middle-aged man in a black suit looked up from behind the counter. I glanced at my watch and wondered if Miles Clifford was likely to be in his college rooms at this time. Still, it wouldn't hurt to ask and I might strike lucky.

"Can you tell me where Professor Clifford's office is, please?" I asked, flashing my university alumni card.

He nodded. "Straight across the main quad, through the archway on the left, and into the Library quad. Staircase 5, Room 11. You might have a hard time seeing the staircase numbers—they are doing repairs to the stonework and there is scaffolding along the entire east side of the quad—but if you head for the staircase in the right corner, you can't miss it."

I followed his directions, cutting across the vast expanse of the huge main quadrangle, with its manicured green lawns and carved Gothic arches, and through a great archway to come out into another quadrangle, its eighteenth-century Palladian architecture in elegant and beautiful contrast to the previous buildings. Like many Oxford colleges, St Frideswide's was built and added to slowly over several centuries and its buildings displayed a variety of architectural styles, following the era they were constructed in. Somehow, though, everything always seemed to blend together into a harmonious whole (well, except for the ugly box-style buildings added in the

1960s... they always seemed to stick out like a sore thumb!).

I arrived, slightly breathless, at the foot of Staircase 5, and stepped into the stairwell. It was a typical Oxford college staircase, all winding wooden steps and multiple landings, and my heart sank slightly. I groaned, remembering my aching legs climbing these staircases from my student days. But I took a deep breath and gamely started up the steps.

Miles Clifford's office was on the third landing and a red-haired girl was backing out of the room just as I arrived. She turned and nearly bumped into me, then we did that funny dance where we each tried to step around each other and each kept blocking the other by mistake.

"Oops! Excuse me—"

"Sorry... I didn't mean..."

We caught each other's eyes and burst out laughing. She stepped to one side and gestured towards the door. "Here, I'll stand still."

"Thanks," I gave her another smile, then knocked on the door and entered.

It was a classic Oxford don's office, with dark wood-panelled walls and bookshelves overflowing with leather-bound volumes. A black scholar's gown and a tweed jacket hung from a coat rack beside the door, next to a raised stand on which stood a replica of a Neolithic stone circle. I realised suddenly that it was Stonehenge. And hanging on the wall above the model was a photograph of the real-life site, with the sun rising just behind the stone boulders. Next to it was another framed image—this time an illustration of a stepped pyramid, which looked like a Mayan temple. In fact, all around the room, there were photographs and illustrations of various giant structures built by ancient civilisations.

Miles Clifford looked up from behind the large mahogany desk by the window and his face brightened when he saw me. "Ah... it's Miss Rose, isn't it?"

I looked at him in pleasant surprise. "You remember me?"

He chuckled. "How could anyone forget the creator of those delicious scones?"

I laughed. "To be honest, I didn't bake the scones myself. But they *were* from my tearoom."

"Your tearoom?"

"The Little Stables Tearoom, in Meadowford."

"Ah... that's right. Yes, I've passed it several times and have been meaning to pop in. I must make the effort to do that next time I'm in the village. It'll be a nice treat after the torture."

"The torture?" I looked at him, puzzled.

He laughed. "A little joke of mine. There is an acupuncturist in Meadowford who I go to see from time to time. I get bad neck pain—probably from years of stooping over the textbooks!—and I find a session of acupuncture really does wonders. Still, one never quite gets used to seeing the needles..." He gave a slight shudder, then clasped his hands together and smiled at me. "Now, what can I do for you?"

"Er..." I froze, realising suddenly that I didn't have a pretext for coming to see him. I had acted impulsively when I popped into the college, recalling the way Miles Clifford had seemed so calm and reasonable during the morning of the funeral, and thinking that he would be a good person to pump for more information about the Clifford family dramas. But now faced with his well-bred, courteous manner, I didn't know how to bring up the subject of Adele's murder and Rex Clifford's sudden change of will. It seemed too rude, too personal, to just start asking him about his family and his niece's sexual orientation!

"Um... I just..." I groped for something to say as the professor waited patiently. Then I remembered that he was an academic and all academics loved talking about their subject. It might also soften him up for more questioning later. I pointed to the illustration of the Mayan temple and said, "I couldn't help noticing that when I came in. It looks fascinating. What's that place?"

Professor Clifford walked over to the framed picture and looked at it admiringly. "It's the Pyramid of Kukulkan—also known as *El Castillo*—at Chichén Itzá in Mexico. Stunning, isn't it? I have been there many times and yet each time it still takes my breath away."

"Oh, were you there for research...?"

"Yes, and also just to pay homage, really. It's one of the key sites of interest in my field and there's an endless fascination with it... the same way, say, all Egyptologists are fascinated by the Rosetta Stone."

I furrowed my brow. "Are you an archaeologist?"

"Close. I am a professor of Archeoastronomy." He chuckled at my expression. "Yes, it *is* a genuine area of study. It's the investigation of the astronomical knowledge of prehistoric cultures. Essentially, how people in the past understood the phenomena of the sky—and how this is reflected in their architecture and their cultural expressions, such as their myths and crafts. Some of the most common things we study are ancient structures built by man—such as this pyramid, and the circle at Stonehenge, for example," he said, gesturing to the replica model. "We can draw astronomical information from the alignment of ancient architecture and even landscapes—" He caught himself and gave a sheepish laugh. "I'm sorry, my dear. As my students will tell you, if you get me started on the topic I will never stop! I'm sure you didn't come here today to listen to me talk about Stonehenge and its astronomical significance. You were telling me what I can do for you?"

Bugger. Back to square one. And I still haven't come up with a good story. Then I suddenly remembered my ploy to get into Clifford House.

Using the catering connection had worked well enough with Rachel—maybe I could use it again.

I gave Professor Clifford a slightly anxious smile. "I was wondering if you knew if Mrs Clifford—your sister-in-law—had any food allergies? I've been worrying ever since I heard the news of her death. Having catered the event, you see, I'm concerned that something I provided might have inadvertently triggered a reaction and caused her to collapse."

He looked surprised. "As far as I know, Adele didn't have any food allergies," he said. "And in any case, I thought the police were treating it as a suspicious death? I heard that on the radio this morning. They believe she was deliberately poisoned."

"Ah... yes, right... I'd heard the rumours too. But I was still worried, you know..."

He smiled. "I don't think you have to worry, my dear. Her death was certainly not on your account."

"Er... have the police come to question you?"

"No, not yet—although they will get in touch soon, no doubt."

What is Inspector Pratt doing? I thought in exasperation. Aloud, I said, "Do you know if Adele had any enemies who might have wished her ill?"

Miles Clifford sighed. "Much as I hate to say it, my sister-in-law was not a particularly pleasant woman at times. She could be very ruthless—and quite insensitive too. So, unfortunately, she was never generally well liked in the village.'"

"Or in the family?" I gave him a crooked smile. "I couldn't help overhearing some of the conversation in the kitchen before the funeral on Saturday morning."

He grimaced. "Oh dear. I'm afraid we probably sounded like the most sordid stereotype of a family squabbling over the inheritance."

"Well, I have to say—I can see why Rachel would want to 'squabble'. It does seem very unfair to her," I said.

"Yes, it does, but at the end of the day, the money was my brother's to leave as he chose."

"Were you surprised, though, when you found that he had left everything to Adele?"

"Extremely so," he said. "I must confess—it was a whirlwind romance and I never saw my brother behave like that before. But I always thought that when it came to matters of the estate, he wouldn't let his heart rule his head. My brother was always a very shrewd businessman, Miss Rose, and a brilliant entrepreneur. He could sell snow to the Eskimos, as they say," he said with a whimsical smile. "He was ten years older than me, you know, and he always seemed more like a father than a brother to me..."

I gave him a sympathetic smile. "It must have been horrible for you to have his funeral eclipsed by Adele's murder. And especially after the shock of his sudden death—and that fight last week."

"Fight?" Miles Clifford had gone very still, like a

deer sensing a predator.

I gave him an innocent look. "Yes, Mrs Wiseman, the neighbour, told me about it when I popped in to see Rachel earlier today. She said she could hear you and your brother shouting. It seemed that he was very upset about something...?" I trailed off hopefully.

Professor Clifford didn't respond.

I continued doggedly, "And Mrs Wiseman thought she heard Rachel's name being mentioned several times...?"

"It seems to me that Mrs Wiseman heard a great deal from beyond the hedge," said Professor Clifford, his eyes guarded.

"Were Rachel and her father not close?" I asked.

"They had a good relationship," said Miles Clifford in a neutral tone.

"Well, I just wondered... you know... it does seem odd that he would cut his only daughter out of his will, so suddenly like that. Usually that kind of thing only happens if you find out something terrible about the person, which totally turns you against them."

He stiffened. "What do you mean?"

"Um... well, Mrs Wiseman mentioned that... um... Rachel might have made different... er... lifestyle choices to what her father had hoped for. I suppose for a man who is old-fashioned and set in his ways... well, I guess there must be a few... um... modern 'practices' that he might struggle to accept?"

Miles Clifford's expression turned frosty. "Miss Rose, while I understand your curiosity, especially given the current circumstances with Adele's murder, I would like to point out that these are private affairs of my family. I would appreciate if you could refrain from delving into matters that are none of your concern."

I flushed with embarrassment. Suitably chastened, I stammered, "I'm... I'm sorry... I was just curious... Um... Thank you for seeing me. I'll... I'll leave now..."

He made no move to stop me, watching me coldly from behind his desk as I scurried to the door and let myself out of his office. My face was still red as I came out of the college staircase and made my way back across the quads to retrieve my bicycle. I didn't think I'd ever been told to "Mind your business!" in quite such a polite and yet cutting way before. Miles Clifford was right, though, of course, and I had been unforgivably nosy and insolent with my questions. Now I felt ashamed.

Still deep in my thoughts, I collected my bicycle from the college bike shed and pushed off again, cycling rapidly down the street towards the river and Folly Bridge. Just before the road joined the bridge, I made a sharp right turn and cut across the opposite lane, heading for the shortcut that connected to the towpath which ran alongside the river. There was a car coming from the opposite direction and I put on a burst of speed, pedalling fast to cross the road before it reached me.

I shot off the road, yanking my handlebars around to slide into the shortcut path. But as I rounded the corner, I discovered to my horror that there was someone coming along the path in the other direction. I was going too fast to avoid a collision. I squeezed my brakes frantically and swerved, trying to avoid hitting the person. There was a flash of a pale face in front of me, the sight of hands flung out defensively, then I felt the thump of the impact and heard a cry.

But there was no time to think about it because, the next moment, my hands lost their grip on the handlebars and I gasped as I found myself suddenly careering towards the river.

CHAPTER ELEVEN

It took all my strength to grab the handlebars again and yank the nose of the bicycle around just in time before I shot headlong into the river. I skidded to a stop and sat, panting for a moment. Then I remembered the pedestrian I had hit. My heart in my throat, I jumped off the bike and ran back to the fallen figure.

"Oh my God! I'm so sorry—I didn't see you. Are you okay?" I crouched down beside the red-haired girl. She raised herself up on her elbows, slightly dazed.

"I... I think so..." she murmured, moving her limbs gingerly. She gave me a weak grin. "Nothing broken."

Whew! I exhaled in relief. "I'm so sorry—" I started to say again.

She waved a hand. "Please—don't worry about it. It was an accident. Could have happened to anyone." She started struggling to her feet and I hurried to help her.

As she straightened up and brushed herself off, I suddenly realised why she had seemed so familiar. She was the girl I had seen coming out of Miles Clifford's office.

"Oh! You're the—"

She smiled as she recognised me too. "I think we met just a while ago, didn't we? Back in St Frideswide's College. My name's Caitlyn." She held a hand out to me.

"I'm Gemma." I smiled and shook her hand, instantly warming to her.

I realised that she was actually very pretty. My brief glimpse of her in the college staircase hadn't done her justice. Perhaps it was also because she was the kind of girl you didn't notice at first glance, but I saw now that she had beautiful hazel eyes fringed by the kind of thick lashes I always envied, and creamy white skin marred only by a smattering of freckles across her nose. Her vivid red hair was caught up in a careless ponytail and she was dressed in faded jeans and a cotton peasant-style blouse, with her face scrubbed free of make-up. But in spite of her low-key outfit, there was still something about her—something almost *bewitching*—that I couldn't put my finger on.

Perhaps it was her accent, which was a strange

mixture of refined British with hints of American. I wondered who she was and what she was doing in Oxford. She didn't seem like the average tourist and yet she didn't come across like a student either.

"Where're you from?" I blurted. Then I realised how abrupt that sounded and added hastily, "Sorry, it's just that your accent is so unusual."

She laughed. "I get that comment a lot," she said. "I had an English nanny who brought me up and also home-schooled me, so I suppose I picked up my British accent from her."

"A nanny?" I looked at her curiously.

The way she spoke about it, it sounded like she had a modern-day governess and most people nowadays didn't have that kind of relationship with their "nanny". Not unless they were very rich or very famous. Surreptitiously, I looked her up and down again. She wore no jewellery other than some kind of stone pendant attached to a ribbon around her neck and there wasn't a designer label in sight. She certainly didn't *look* like a wealthy celebrity princess, but I knew that looks could be deceiving.

Before I could ponder further, Caitlyn put her weight down on her right foot, then yelped and staggered sideways. I grabbed her elbow and steadied her, looking at her in consternation.

"It's my ankle," she said, grimacing in pain. "I think... I might have sprained it."

I looked down and saw to my dismay that she was right. Her ankle was swollen and looked very painful.

"You'd better get some ice on that quickly," I said. "Listen, my house is just a couple of hundred yards down the towpath. If you like, we can go there and I can put some ice on your ankle, otherwise you might have trouble getting your shoe off later."

"Thanks, that sounds like a good idea," said Caitlyn, looking at me gratefully.

Leaning on me for support, she hobbled down the towpath and we made our way slowly back to my cottage. Muesli came running to greet us as soon as I opened the door and gave an inquisitive "*Meorrw!*" when she saw my new friend.

"You've got a cat!" said Caitlyn, breaking into a big smile. "Oh, she's absolutely gorgeous! What's her name?"

"Muesli," I said with a chuckle. "And don't let her hear you. She's very full of herself already as it is."

I settled my visitor on the couch, then hurried into the kitchenette to get some ice. I could hear Caitlyn having a conversation with Muesli, punctuated by chuckles of laughter and "*Meorrw!*"s every so often, and when I returned, I found that my little tabby cat had made herself very comfortable on Caitlyn's lap.

"Oh... shove her off if she's bothering you," I said.

"No, no!" she replied, laughing. "I love cats. I've always wanted one but my... mother was allergic to them. In any case, we were always on the road, travelling around a lot, so pets were really out of the question."

I noticed the slight hesitation before she said "mother" and I wondered what that was all about. And her mention of life "on the road" was intriguing too. My new friend was turning out to be quite a mystery!

"She's very friendly, isn't she?" said Caitlyn, rubbing Muesli's chin while the little cat purred with delight.

"Yeah, she's feeling a bit cooped up, poor thing, because she has to stay at home alone all day and she misses the company. She used to live near where I work and meet lots of people every day, so being alone is a big change."

"Where do you work?"

"In a village called Meadowford-on-Smythe, just on the outskirts of Oxford. I run a tearoom."

"Oh, like a traditional English teashop? I've been wanting to visit one of those!"

"Don't you live in the U.K.?" I looked at her quizzically.

"No, my... um... my mother was American and she was based in the States, although we travelled around a lot. I've visited England a few times in the past with her but we always just stayed in London. This is the first time I've come out into the countryside."

"Oh? First time to Oxford? What do you think?" I smiled.

She gave a dreamy sigh. "It's absolutely spectacular. Even more beautiful than the postcards, and I didn't think that would be possible. It's not just the buildings—it's the atmosphere here, the sense of history and... and scholarship, if that makes sense?" She gave a bashful laugh. "You probably think I'm being silly."

I smiled at her. "No, I know what you mean. I grew up here, you know, and went to university here—but I never really appreciated it until after I went to live in Australia for eight years and then returned. You're right—there's something timeless and magical about Oxford." I leaned forwards. "Hey, listen, when your ankle is better, you must come and visit my tearoom. It's called the Little Stables and it's on the high street in Meadowford."

"I will!" she promised. "And speaking of my ankle..." She lifted the bag of ice from her foot and gave it an experimental wriggle. "It feels a lot better. The swelling seems to have gone down."

"Good. Hopefully you didn't sprain it after all. You'd better stay off it for a few days, though. Where are you staying? I can call a taxi for you if you like."

"Oh, that would be great. Thanks! I'm staying at the Old Bank Hotel in the city centre."

I started to reach for my phone, then glanced at my watch and gave a gasp. "Oh, cripes, I'm supposed to be going to my mother's for dinner! I'll never hear the end of it if I'm late!" I glanced at

Caitlyn. "Do you mind if I share the taxi with you? I can drop you off at the hotel and go on to my parents' place."

"No, of course not."

There came a loud, indignant *"Meeoorrw!"* as Muesli jumped off Caitlyn's lap and sat at my feet, looking up at me expectantly.

I grinned. "Don't worry, Muesli, I haven't forgotten you. You'll get your dinner before we leave!"

CHAPTER TWELVE

I arrived at my parents' house, hot and flustered, to find a dark green Land Rover parked on the street outside. My heart sank slightly as I recognised the number plate and realised who must have been visiting: Lincoln Green, son of my mother's best friend, Helen Green, and also—as far as my mother was concerned—perfect future son-in-law material. The only problem was, I didn't share her views and it made for some pretty awkward moments.

Oh, it wasn't that I didn't like Lincoln—I liked him very much. He was kind, good-looking, the perfect English gentleman, and an eminent doctor to boot. In fact, you could say that he was most girls' dream guy. And I had to admit that if the situation had been different—if I hadn't met Devlin first—then perhaps something might have developed between us...

In fact, there were still times when I wondered if I had made the right choice. Lincoln might never have made my heart race the way Devlin did, but there was something very attractive about someone who was so... well, so *uncomplicated*. He came from the same background I did, moved in the same social circles, and had an open, easy manner, with no hidden secrets or turbulent past; he represented everything that was safe and familiar.

Devlin O'Connor, on the other hand, was complex, brooding, and enigmatic—and I didn't think that he was a man I would ever fully understand. I thought again of the angst over his recent behaviour: his mysterious evasiveness, his distant manner, the question of whether he was having an affair... None of those things would have worried me with Lincoln.

Then I caught myself, guilty for having these thoughts. *I've made my choice*, I reminded myself. Devlin was the man I wanted to spend my life with and I loved him, in spite of all the "issues". After all, every couple had troubles, didn't they? I was sure we would work through ours. Like I had told Cassie, I was just waiting for the right moment to bring up the subject—and once I'd finally asked Devlin about it, I was sure I'd find out whatever it was that had been bothering him and making him behave so strangely.

I thanked and paid the taxi driver, then hurried into the house. I was a bit late, in spite of my best efforts, and I braced myself for my mother's disapproval.

"Hi," I said, stepping in the living room.

"Gemma!" My mother looked up with delight. "We were just wondering what had happened to you."

Lincoln immediately sprang up and stood politely, waiting for me to sit down.

"Sorry," I said, coming in and dropping down on the sofa. "I had a bit of an accident. I ran into a girl with my bicycle. Oh, she's fine," I said quickly, seeing their looks of concern. "But she twisted her ankle so I took her back to my cottage to get some ice. And then I had to feed Muesli as well before I left."

"Oh, you should have brought Muesli with you!" said my mother. "You know how much we miss her. Your father keeps talking about her all the time—he would love to see her."

I smiled to myself. For two people who had claimed not to like pets, my parents had become completely besotted with Muesli and indulged her more than I did.

"Did you find my iPad?" my mother asked eagerly.

"No, sorry," I said. "I looked everywhere but it's not at my cottage."

"Oh." My mother looked crestfallen.

"Are you sure you checked everywhere you've been today?"

"Well, I suppose I could call the Debenhams Lost & Found and ask again—the girl I spoke to earlier was very distracted and didn't seem to make much effort to look. All right, I shall ring them again first thing tomorrow morning. Now, I'll just leave you two here to chat," said my mother, rising and giving us a coy look. "I need to check on the roast..."

She hurried out of the room, a complacent smile on her face, and I immediately wondered if Lincoln's presence had been engineered on purpose. I wouldn't have put it past my mother to find an excuse to get him here, once she knew that I was coming for dinner.

"So how's business?" asked Lincoln with a smile.

I returned his smile. "It's going really well! So much better than I'd dared hope for. You know, when I gave up my corporate career to come back home and open a tearoom, everyone thought I was crazy... and I was so scared that they might be right! It was a huge gamble for me. I'm just so relieved that it seems to be paying off. You know, I've even started taking on some catering orders? Just a few, so far, but it's a step in the right direction."

"You mean for weddings?"

"Oh, I'll do anything," I said with a grin. "Weddings, christenings, birthdays, reunions... even funerals! In fact, I catered a funeral yesterday morning, in Meadowford."

"A funeral in Meadowford?" Lincoln frowned. "That wasn't the Clifford funeral, by any chance?"

I looked at him curiously. "Yes. Why?"

"There was a woman rushed into Intensive Care yesterday morning—she had collapsed at a funeral in Meadowford."

I gasped. "That must have been Adele Clifford, the widow! I didn't realise that you looked after her."

"Well, there wasn't much I could do for her by the time she arrived," said Lincoln grimly. "We tried all the standard treatments but it was too late. She was in multi-organ failure by then. She'd been poisoned by a very high dose of arsenic."

I stared at him. "It was *you* who thought of testing her urine, wasn't it? The detective in charge of the case said the doctor who looked after Adele discovered that it was arsenic."

"It was just a hunch," said Lincoln modestly. "I could smell garlic very strongly on her breath and that's one of the classic symptoms of arsenic poisoning. Together with her other symptoms... well, it got me thinking." He laughed. "My Pharmacology professor at medical school will be pleased to think that I *was* listening during his lectures. It was a lucky guess, really, since one sees so few cases of arsenic poisoning these days."

"What do you mean?"

"Arsenic is rarely used for anything anymore as it is so toxic. Not like back in the 1930s and '40s

117

when it was easily available everywhere, in all sorts of solutions and products. You could practically buy it over the counter. It's why it was such a popular poison in those days—you know arsenic used to be called the 'inheritance powder'?"

I shook my head. "Really? Why?"

Lincoln gave me a cynical smile. "Because it was often used to get rid of 'inconvenient' relatives who stood in the way of an inheritance. One of the great benefits of arsenic as a murder weapon is that it is a cumulative poison—so you can use tiny amounts which can't be easily detected, but which would build up in the victim's body over time. And if they do show any symptoms of poisoning, these are usually mistaken as gastric problems, like stomach aches and diarrhoea. Nobody ever pays much attention to those—you just think you ate some dodgy food and had a bit of indigestion or food poisoning... But then, eventually, the arsenic reaches fatal levels and the victim succumbs."

"But Adele's case was different—"

"Oh yes, she had acute arsenic poisoning. She must have consumed an enormous amount a few hours earlier."

I frowned. "Yes, the police were saying that. They think that something she ate at the funeral reception was laced with a lethal dose of arsenic."

"Have they tested the food?"

"Well, the problem is—after Adele collapsed, there was total chaos in the parish hall. She fell against the buffet table and dragged half the food onto the floor, and then everyone stepped all over it. And of course, at that point, nobody realised that she had been poisoned. We all thought she'd had a seizure of some kind. So after she was rushed to hospital, we just cleared up as normal. Picked up all the spilled food, threw it all away, cleaned the floor... So the poisoned food was probably mixed up with the other food and tossed out with the rubbish. Even the Forensics team would have a hard time now tracing the source of the poison."

"Hmm... it sounds like it. And the police don't have any other clues? Did no one notice what Adele was eating?"

"Yes... actually, *I* did," I said. "She sampled several things from the buffet table. She had some treacle tart, some sticky toffee pudding—and then a piece of Victoria sponge cake."

Lincoln looked startled. "That's a lot of puddings."

"Well, she didn't actually get them all herself. She was served the treacle tart by Mabel Cooke at the buffet table, and then Rachel arrived with a plate of sticky toffee pudding, insisting that Adele have some... Rachel is Rex Clifford's daughter," I explained. "And she's got the most to gain because she inherits the entire estate in the event of Adele's death. She also hates her stepmother with a passion."

"She sounds like the perfect suspect already,"

said Lincoln.

"Ah... but she's not the only one! There was also a stranger who arrived at the funeral, knocked into Adele and made her drop her plate on the floor... and then insisted on bringing her a replacement: some Victoria sponge cake."

"You make it sound like he did that on purpose," said Lincoln, raising his eyebrows.

"He might have." I ignored Lincoln's puzzled look and hurried on, my mind buzzing. "But listen, the key question is *how* they could have got hold of the poison. You said it's not very easy to obtain arsenic these days?"

"No, mainly because it's hardly used in anything anymore. You'd have to be in a specialist field which uses arsenic compounds—for example, if you worked in a hospital, you could possibly get access to arsenic trioxide. It's used as a chemotherapy treatment for acute promyelocytic leukaemia."

"So you mean the average person wouldn't be able to buy something which had arsenic in it? I thought it was used in rat poison or something?"

"Yes, and it was used in a lot of pesticides as well—but not anymore. At least, not in the U.K. or most other developed countries. I think it might still be used in some Third World countries... and there have been terrible cases of mass poisonings in places like Bangladesh due to arsenic in the groundwater."

"What about China?" I asked eagerly.

"China?" Lincoln furrowed his brow. "I don't really know about China. I couldn't say... Oh!" He snapped his fingers suddenly. "I do know that it's used in TCM."

"T-C-what?"

"TCM. Traditional Chinese Medicine. It's a common belief in ancient Chinese medicine to use a poison against a poison, and arsenic mixtures are used to combat cancer. It's been a part of TCM remedies for centuries. But it's quite controversial, of course, especially in the West—as it often is with many TCM remedies, where there isn't the scientific evidence to support their safe use and yet they have been in use for hundreds of years..." He looked at me quizzically. "Why do you ask about China?"

"Because I know someone who recently came from China," I said excitedly. "Rex Clifford's long-lost love child, Tyler Lee!"

I explained about Tyler Lee's dramatic appearance at the funeral and his claim of being Rex Clifford's illegitimate son, which would also have made him Rachel's half-brother and an equal beneficiary of the estate.

"It gives him a very good motive to murder Adele... and now, if you're saying arsenic is easily available in traditional Chinese remedies, then that means he had easy access to the poison too..." I mused.

"Wow..." Lincoln blinked. "This is almost like a mystery novel. Do you seriously believe one of them poisoned Adele?"

"Well, they're both more likely suspects than Mabel Cooke!" I said, pulling a face. "Can you believe that the gormless detective in charge of the case thinks Mabel is the murderer?"

Lincoln looked at me in surprise. "Is Devlin not investigating this murder then?"

"No, he's been taken off the case. Some arrogant prat—who actually is called Inspector Pratt, believe it or not—has assigned himself to the investigation. And he's making a complete dog's dinner of it, if you ask me! He's fixated on Mabel and keeps trying to bend the facts to fit his belief, instead of the other way around." I gave an exasperated sigh. "I don't know how the guy ever got promoted to Detective Inspector. What happened to keeping an open mind and piecing together the evidence to find the real answers?"

"The lamb will be ready in a jiffy," my mother trilled, sailing back into the living room. "Lincoln, you *must* stay!" She shot a meaningful look in my direction and added, "I'm sure Gemma would *love* to have your company."

Lincoln gave her a regretful smile. "I would have loved to, Aunt Evelyn, but I've promised my mother that I'd go home tonight. She's cooking a big family dinner. My cousins are visiting from France and I haven't seen them in a long time. I only popped in quickly because you needed help with your DVD so urgently." He glanced across the room at the entertainment unit. "I'm still not sure why you had a problem, though, because it seemed to work fine when I tested it."

"Ah... ha-ha... well, you know what technology is like..." My mother gave an airy laugh. She looked very chagrined, though, at having lost such a rare opportunity of getting me and Lincoln together. "Well... another time, perhaps. You know you're welcome any day of the week!"

"Thank you." Lincoln rose to go.

"Oh! Wait...!" My mother gave a secretive little smile. "I've got something for you, Lincoln—and you, Gemma."

She grabbed both of our arms and dragged us into the hallway. From the depths of her handbag, she produced a long envelope and handed it to Lincoln with the flourish of someone announcing an Oscar winner. Lincoln pulled out two narrow cards with gold embossed writing and looked at them in puzzlement.

"They're tickets for the St Frideswide's charity gala ball on Thursday evening—the day after tomorrow," my mother explained eagerly. "It's all in a good cause and I thought it would be lovely if you and Gemma went together. There will be food and dancing and it will be such a wonderful evening!"

Lincoln gave me an embarrassed look. "Er... thank you, Aunt Evelyn. That's very kind of you, but Gemma might prefer to have another escort—"

"Oh nonsense—of course Gemma would love you

to take her—wouldn't you, darling?" My mother looked at me expectantly.

Grrr. I wanted to kill her for putting me on the spot like this. It wasn't that I minded going with Lincoln, but I resented the way my mother was still trying to play matchmaker. Devlin had been my "official" boyfriend for several months now and yet here she was still up to her old tricks. Nevertheless, I couldn't really refuse—it would have been embarrassing to Lincoln and the whole thing wasn't his fault...

"Of course, I'd love to go with you," I said, giving him a wan smile.

"Marvellous! That's arranged then!" said my mother, beaming.

As soon as the door had shut behind Lincoln, I turned to my mother, who was smiling like a cat who'd got a whole flock of canaries, and said, "Are you doing anything tomorrow night, Mother?"

"Tomorrow night, darling? No, not that I know of."

"So it'll be all right if I come for dinner again?"

"Oh, of course, darling—you know we always love to have you."

"And I'd like to bring someone with me."

My mother's eyes brightened. "Seth? I haven't seen Seth in ages! How is the dear boy?"

"It's not Seth, Mother. He's away at a research conference," I said, thinking of my second closest college friend after Cassie, who had remained in academia and was now a Senior Research Fellow at one of the Oxford colleges.

"Oh, is it Cassie then? It would be lovely to see her too. Has she got boyfriend yet?"

"No, it's not Cassie, Mother—it's Devlin."

"D-Devlin?"

"Yes, Devlin." I raised my chin. "My *boyfriend.*"

She winced slightly at the word. "Er... well, you don't really have to think of him like that, darling," she said quickly. "One can simply be *friends* these days with various young men and—"

"He's my *boyfriend*, Mother, and I'd like to invite him to dinner. To meet you and Dad. I mean, he's met you both, of course—but you haven't really spent much time with him so far. Since he's a part of my life now, wouldn't you like to get to know him better?"

My mother looked like she couldn't think of anything worse. But she gave a weak smile and said, "Er... yes, well... I suppose..."

"Good. It's arranged then. Shall I tell him to come around eight?" I gave her a nod, then turned and walked to the dining room, leaving my mother for once speechless behind me.

CHAPTER THIRTEEN

I paused on the steps outside the police station and hesitated, wondering if I was doing the right thing. It was Monday morning—my usual "day off"—and instead of catching up on emails, admin, and household chores, I had given in to an impulse and come down to Oxford Police Station.

I was hoping to see Devlin. I hadn't spoken to him properly since he left the tearoom yesterday morning with Mabel Cooke and that new inspector, and I was curious about developments on the Adele Clifford case. I could have called him but I didn't want another of our usual rushed conversations over the phone.

And okay, if I was being honest, I really just wanted to *see* Devlin, to hear his voice, see that familiar twinkle in his piercing blue eyes. I was slightly embarrassed to admit it but I missed his company. And this was what was making me hesitate now; I mean, coming to his workplace like this made me look like a clinging girlfriend and I always despised women like that. I'd always been proud of the fact that Devlin and I weren't the kind of couple who lived in each other's pockets: he had his life and I had mine, and I didn't expect us to need to "check in" with each other every day.

Still, with the way he had been acting so distant lately and the issue of the "mysterious blonde" still unresolved between us, I suppose I could be forgiven for feeling a bit insecure...

I took a deep breath and pushed through the main doors of the police station. The duty sergeant looked up as I approached the desk and gave me a grin.

"It's Gemma, isn't it? O'Connor's girl."

I smiled. *O'Connor's girl.* I liked the sound of that. Blushing slightly, I laughed and said, "Yes, I suppose I am... Is Devlin around?"

He nodded his head down the corridor, in the direction of the CID offices. "He was out this morning, but I saw him come in just a short while ago. He should be at his desk."

"Is it okay if I pop down to see him?"

"Well... I suppose you should really have an official reason. But I'll make an exception for you," he said with a wink.

I gave him a grateful smile. Most of Devlin's

colleagues knew me and liked me, partly because I was his girlfriend but also because I had helped the police solve quite a few murder cases recently and they had developed a grudging respect for my amateur sleuthing abilities.

"Just be a bit careful..." the sergeant warned. "Keep an eye out for Dylan Pratt. He's on the warpath and you wouldn't want to run into him, especially after yesterday."

"What happened yesterday?"

The duty sergeant roared with laughter. "Pratt made the mistake of bringing your friend, Mrs Cooke, in for questioning. Best show we'd seen in years!"

I grinned. I could just imagine Mabel causing havoc at the station. "I'm sorry—was she terrible?"

He chuckled. "Oh no, we loved the old girl. She was saying all the things we'd been itching to say to young Pratt, but out of professional courtesy, none of us had wanted to say it to his face! Between you and me, Dylan Pratt has been nothing but a pain in the backside ever since he transferred from London. Thinks he knows everything and that we're all a bunch of country plods!"

"He did seem very full of himself," I agreed, thinking back to the young detective's attitude in the tearoom.

"Oh, he's the product of some graduate fast-track programme, where they spend all their time with their heads stuffed in books and computers, learning fancy-shmancy things like criminal profiling. Well, I don't care what they say—there's nothing to substitute for hands-on police work and the experience of a good old-fashioned copper." The duty sergeant gave an emphatic nod. "It was good to see him taken down a peg or two!"

He gave me a sympathetic look. "But I think anything to do with Mrs Cooke is a bit of a sore point at the moment, and since you're her friend, you probably wouldn't be on his list of favourite persons either. Best to keep out of his way."

I smiled. "I'll keep that in mind. Thanks for the warning!"

I made my way to the CID department and found Devlin at his desk, frowning over a report.

"Hi..." I said softly, poking my head around the partition that separated his desk from the main area in the open-plan office.

Devlin looked up and his blue eyes warmed instantly as he broke into a smile.

"Gemma." He sprang up, coming towards me. "This is a nice surprise. What are you doing here?"

"Well... Mondays are my day off, you know, and I was... er... sort of passing. I just thought... well... I missed you," I said in a small voice, looking down and flushing in embarrassment.

Devlin smiled, his eyes tender, and raised a hand to brush my cheek gently with the back of his knuckles.

"I've missed you too," he said, low. He glanced

quickly around. The office was fairly empty at the moment—there was just one studious detective constable poring over a pile of spreadsheets in the corner—but with the open-plan design, there was very little privacy.

"Come on, we'd better not talk here..." Devlin nodded to the empty desk opposite his. "Pratt went down to the canteen to grab a coffee but he could be back any moment."

He took my arm and led me out of the office and down the corridor, stopping at a door marked "INTERVIEW ROOM 2". Quickly, he opened the door and stepped inside, pulling me after him. It was a snug space, with nothing other than a table along one wall, two chairs opposite each other, and a tape recorder on the surface between them.

"Sorry, I know it's not the nicest environment, but at least we won't get disturbed in here," said Devlin, shutting the door firmly behind us.

"How do you know I haven't had fantasies of being questioned by you in an interview room?" I teased.

Devlin raised a sexy eyebrow. "That can be arranged..." he murmured.

I felt my heart give a little jump and my pulse quickened, but I hastily reminded myself that I was here on business. Clearing my throat, I said, "Um... I heard that Mabel caused a bit of a stir here yesterday..."

Devlin choked back a laugh. "That would be the

understatement of the year. I almost felt sorry for Pratt. By the end of it, I thought he was going to burst a blood vessel. He even got the Detective Chief Constable to come in and try to scare the indomitable Mrs Cooke."

"What happened?"

Devlin laughed again. "Well, my money would have been on Mabel—and I was right. She sent the DCC off with a flea in his ear after ten minutes. I don't think I'd ever seen my boss so traumatised. The poor man was scared to come out of his office again until he was certain that Mabel had left the building!"

I laughed, feeling ridiculously proud of Mabel.

Devlin sobered. "The only thing is, Gemma, it's made Pratt even more determined to charge her. A man like that doesn't take well to humiliation. His pride is at stake now and he'll do anything to prove that Mabel's the murderer."

"But that's ridiculous!" I said angrily. "He could be letting the real murderer get away while he's busy trying to frame Mabel. You need to speak to him and convince him he's wrong!"

Devlin shrugged. "Sometimes it's best for people to learn from their own mistakes. In any case, I don't think anything I say would hold much sway. Pratt thinks he's above the rest of us—and it's not helped by the fact that his uncle is one of the DCC's oldest friends. It's why he's been allowed to get away with so much already, like assigning himself

131

to the case and conducting the investigation without following any of the usual protocols. It's a bit of good ol' nepotism in action."

"Can't you ask to be put back on the case?"

"Well, to be fair, I probably do know Mabel too well now to be considered an unbiased investigator—"

"But that's irrelevant, anyway, because it's obvious that she is not the murderer!"

"Gemma," said Devlin with a sigh, "you know the police can't work like that. We have to consider every lead, even those that seem most unlikely. In the eyes of the law, Mabel Cooke is a potential suspect, based on her behaviour at the funeral reception and her prior hostile relationship with the victim."

"What 'prior hostile relationship'?" I asked scornfully. "You're not referring to Mabel and Adele's little tiffs at bingo? Oh, for goodness' sake!" I rolled my eyes. "Don't tell me Pratt has been wasting his time investigating that? There are far more important things than who got the best chair in the bingo hall!"

Devlin looked at me curiously. "Such as?"

I told him what Mrs Wiseman, the Cliffords' neighbour, had seen and heard last Tuesday.

Devlin whistled. "That does put an interesting perspective on things..."

"I think whatever caused this 'fight' also led Rex Clifford to change his will in Adele's favour. And I think it was something to do with Rachel. From what Mrs Wiseman was hinting, it's possible that Rachel's friend, Kate, may be her lover."

Devlin raised his eyebrows.

"It's not a fact," I said quickly. "You know what these village gossips are like. The minute two women start spending a lot of time together, tongues start wagging—especially if Rachel is showing no interest in settling down with a nice young man and a baby on her knee."

"But what you're suggesting is that Old Man Clifford wouldn't have been happy to find out that his daughter might be lesbian?"

"Yes, according to Mrs Wiseman, Rex Clifford was a very traditional man. He would have been horrified—or furious—or both, probably."

"Enough to cut her out of his will?"

I shrugged. "It had to be something pretty major. I mean, he sent for the lawyer almost immediately after and changed his will that night. At least, that's what it looks like."

"I'm surprised the nosy neighbour can't tell you for certain. She probably knows their annual tax deductions, how much toilet paper they have left, and what everyone had for tea!" Devlin gave an exasperated laugh. "I'm beginning to wonder why we bother training new detectives—we should just recruit the senior citizens of Meadowford-on-Smythe into the CID."

"For heaven's sake, don't let Mabel hear you say

that!" I said, grinning. "You'd be overrun with
O.A.P.'s sticking their noses into everything!" Then I
grew serious again and said:

"I think Miles Clifford knows more than he's
letting on. He obviously dotes on his niece—I think
his more liberal views make him more sympathetic
to her—and he was also very close to his brother.
He's the best person to pump for more information.
I actually went to St Frideswide's yesterday to speak
to him—" I darted a guilty glance at Devlin;
normally he'd be telling me off for meddling in the
investigation, but this time he said nothing, "—but
when I tried to ask him personal stuff about the
family, he froze me out. I didn't really have the
authority to push him further. But the police would!
If you can get Inspector Pratt to go and question
him—ask Professor Clifford what that fight was
about—I think you'd make real progress on the
case."

"I'll try my best," Devlin promised. "But don't get
your hopes up, Gemma. Right now, Pratt wouldn't
listen to me if I told him the winning numbers for
the lottery! In fact... I wouldn't normally suggest
this, but for once, it might be worth us doing some
investigating ourselves first. Unofficially, of course.
Just until we can get enough evidence to take to
Pratt and force his hand. I've already made a start—
"

"But I thought he wouldn't let you see the case
notes."

"No, he's not sharing anything with me at the moment. But there are other means. I've got a good contact at Interpol, for instance, and I've already asked him to look into Tyler Lee's background."

"Yes, and?" I asked eagerly.

Devlin laughed. "I only asked my contact this morning! Give him some time, Gemma. I'll let you know as soon as I hear back from him. Oh, but I did also call my mate down at Heathrow Airport Border Control. It seems that Lee *did* enter this country the night before the funeral, on a flight that arrived from Hong Kong. So that part of his story does seem to check out."

"Well, far-fetched as the story may sound, maybe he *is* telling the truth—maybe he really *is* Rex Clifford's long-lost love child from China," I said.

Devlin inclined his head. "Yes, and it's possible that he really did just happen to arrive in the U.K. at the same time as his father's funeral, without any knowledge of it. It's a strange coincidence—but coincidences do happen in real life, more often than people realise."

A sound in the corridor outside made us both tense and look towards the door.

"We'd better not stay in here any longer," said Devlin, rising. "And I need to get back to work."

I nodded, feeling slightly wistful. It had been so nice to spend time with him, even if it wasn't exactly the romantic meeting I had envisaged. As if sensing my thoughts, Devlin reached over suddenly and drew me close. He lowered his head and gave me a brief hard kiss which left me breathless.

"Devlin..." I said as we broke apart.

"Hmm?"

I hesitated. The kiss had stirred up all my troubled thoughts and feelings again, and I could hear Cassie's voice in my head saying: *"...you can't keep brushing it under the carpet forever. It won't go away, you know. It'll fester inside you and destroy the trust in your relationship. You've got to have it out with Devlin."*

I opened my mouth to ask him about the mysterious blonde woman he had been seen with, but once again, as I looked into his vivid blue eyes, the words died on my lips. I lost my nerve. Anyway, I told myself, this wasn't the right place to have that discussion, in the middle of the CID offices.

"Um... Are you free this evening?" I asked instead.

He smiled. "Yes, I'm determined to get out of here at a reasonable time for once. I was going to ring you and see if you'd like to go out for dinner. It probably won't be until eight, though."

"I've got a better idea. Would you... would you like to come over to my parents' for dinner?"

Devlin raised his eyebrows. "Are you sure that's a 'better' idea?"

I swallowed. "Yes. I... well, it's time they met you properly. I mean, of course they've met you but... well... I'd like you to get to know each other better."

Devlin brushed my cheek again gently with his fingers. "Sure, Gemma. I'd like to get to know them too."

"Great. Okay, shall we say... eight o'clock?"

"Sounds good. I'll look forward to it."

CHAPTER FOURTEEN

I came out of the police station and stood, undecided, on the street for a moment. I knew that I should have really been heading home to catch up on emails and other chores, but I had to admit the prospect didn't fill me with enthusiasm. Then I brightened. I would pop over to Meadowford-on-Smythe and see how Mabel was doing, I decided. After all, I hadn't seen her since yesterday morning when she had been frogmarched away by Inspector Pratt, and with the tearoom closed today, I wouldn't have my usual "catch up" with the Old Biddies.

Mabel Cooke lived in a large cottage on one of the main streets in Meadowford, although as far as I could tell, she seemed to spend most of her time out and about. And though she frequently mentioned her husband, Henry, I had yet to ever see the man. Sometimes I wondered if he really did exist—or, if he did, whether he was just a mouse of a man huddled in a corner, obediently taking the high fibre supplements that Mabel handed out to him.

Even before I rang the bell, I could hear the sounds of excited conversation coming through the windows. From the familiar voices, it seemed like all the Old Biddies were here. When I was let in, I discovered that I was right.

"Gemma! Just the person we were hoping to see!" said Glenda delightedly as Mabel ushered me into the sitting room.

I sat down on a sofa which nearly swallowed me up in chintz cushions and tried not to go cross-eyed from the cabbage-rose wallpaper circling the room. A colony of lace doilies fought for space on the coffee table in front of me and a row of scary-looking porcelain animals stared down at me from the mantelpiece.

"You're looking a bit skinny, Gemma—are you sure you're eating enough?" asked Florence, peering at me closely. "Yes, your face looks thinner than usual." Plump, easy-going Florence loved her food and spent a lot of her time worrying that others weren't being fed enough. "Would you like me to make you a sandwich, dear?"

"Oh no... no, thank you," I assured her. "Trust me, I do not have a weight problem. At least, not in that direction," I said ruefully, looking down at my waistline.

One thing I hadn't anticipated when I opened my tearoom was the occupational hazard of having too much delicious baking available around me, all the time, every day. If it wasn't for all the cycling I did— as well as being blessed, I suppose, with a naturally athletic figure—I would have probably been the size of a whale from all the cakes, scones, and buns I consumed.

Glenda tutted. "Women shouldn't be too thin. It's so very *ageing*. Besides, gentlemen like to have something to get a hold of, you know."

"Yes, I was wondering if you might have worms, dear," said Florence, continuing to look at me with concern. "I mean, you do seem to have a healthy appetite, so it seems strange that you're not plumper."

"It's poor digestion," Mabel declared. "Young people nowadays just don't get enough fibre in their diets. It's no wonder they can't concentrate and always find everything too much of an effort. Did you know that constipation can lead to headaches, haemorrhoids, and even hysteria?"

According to Mabel Cooke, all the world's problems arose from not enough fibre in the diet. World War II could probably have been avoided if Hitler had got more bran in his cereal.

"Don't worry, I've got just the thing for you!" said Mabel suddenly, rising and hurrying from the room. She returned a few moments later with a cardboard box under one arm and a glass of murky brown liquid in the other hand.

"Here, drink this." She thrust the glass at me.

"Wh-what is it?" I asked nervously, taking the glass.

"My daughter just sent it to me from Australia. Powdered super fibre psyllium husk. A spoon dissolved in water and it'll clear you out like a scouring brush!" She beamed at me.

I eyed the glass in my hand with horror.

"Go on, drink it up!" Mabel urged.

With four pairs of beady old eyes watching me eagerly, I had no choice but to raise the glass to my lips and take a fearful sip. I blinked in surprise. Actually, it wasn't that bad—it had obviously been artificially sweetened—although Mabel's words about the liquid scrubbing my intestines still had me wincing.

"It's... it's quite nice," I said, taking another cautious sip.

"Oh, it's marvellous stuff! I've been giving my Henry a glass every morning," said Mabel, nodding emphatically. She set the cardboard box on the coffee table next to me, pulled back the flaps, and happily began taking out its contents, showing each to me proudly: "My daughter sent me a range of other natural remedies too—all guaranteed to boost the digestion and improve bowel function! There's raw liquorice root tea, milk thistle capsules, tincture of arsenicum album, slippery elm lozenges, and some probiotic supplements!"

"Don't forget raw ginger," Ethel piped up. "Steeped in some hot water—I find that very soothing."

"Would you like to try one of these remedies, dear?" asked Mabel eagerly.

"NO! Er... no, thank you," I said. Then quickly, to distract her, I said, "I've just been to see Devlin at the police station. I wanted to ask him about Adele Clifford's murder investigation."

It worked. Mabel looked up from the box, the digestion remedies forgotten in favour of her other favourite hobby.

"Is he in charge of the investigation now?" she asked hopefully.

"No, officially Inspector Pratt is still in charge— but Devlin has been doing some investigating of his own. For example, he's checked to see when Tyler Lee arrived in the country."

"Aha! I'm glad someone is finally investigating that young man," said Mabel.

"So very handsome!" Glenda sighed dreamily.

"A trifle thin, though, don't you think?" Florence frowned. "He could do with a bit of fattening up."

"What the police need to do is search his room at the Cotswolds Manor Hotel," declared Mabel.

I stared at her. "How did you know where he was stayin—Never mind," I sighed, not sure I wanted to know. The village grapevine was frightening sometimes. "You know the police can't just barge in and search his room. They need a good reason and a search warrant."

"There are plenty of good reasons," said Mabel tartly. "And if that fool of an inspector can't think of a way, then we might just have to step into the breach. In any case, I always think that if you want anything done properly, you have to do it yourself."

I eyed her warily. "Mabel, please don't do anything rash! Devlin isn't handling the case this time and if you do something... er... illegal and get caught, there won't be anyone to take a lenient view on things. In fact, I think Inspector Pratt would like nothing better than to have an excuse to arrest you." I glanced at my watch. "Oh, gosh—I'd better go. Thank you for the... uh... drink." I started to rise from the sofa.

"Oh, wait, Gemma—we still haven't told you about Pricklebum yet!" cried Glenda.

I looked at her quizzically. "Pricklebum?"

Ethel got up and hurried to the far corner of the sitting room, returning a moment later with another cardboard box punctured with holes. What strange herbal remedy were they inflicting on me now? I wondered as I watched her reach inside the box and carefully lift something out.

"This is Pricklebum! Isn't he just precious?"

I jumped in alarm as something brown and spiky landed on my lap. Then I realised that it was a little hedgehog, curled up into a ball of prickles. Gingerly, I lifted him up with two hands. He was about the size of a tennis ball, with a tiny pointed nose and two bright black eyes that peeked out at me from above a fold in the centre of the prickles.

"Mabel just picked him up from Happy Hedgehog Friends HQ," Florence explained. "He fell into a drain, you see, and hurt one of his back legs, but he seems to be recovering well. He just needs a bit of TLC before he can be released back into the wild."

"Uh... he's lovely," I said lamely, holding the ball of prickles out to Ethel. "You can have him back now."

She made no move to take him. "Yes, and we wanted to ask you, Gemma, if you would look after him for a while."

"Me?"

Mabel's chest swelled importantly. "You see, I would normally volunteer to foster him, but since I am the victim of police prosecution now, I might be hauled back in again for questioning at any time—or even arrested!" she said with relish. "With all this uncertainty, I'm worried about having full responsibility for Pricklebum—I'd like him to stay with someone 'safer' until things have settled down."

"What about your husband, Henry?" I asked.

"Oh, Henry...!" said Mabel with a dismissive wave, which made it clear what she thought of her husband's abilities in hedgehog husbandry.

"But I'm at work all day," I protested.

"Ah, that's no problem! Hedgehogs are nocturnal

anyway so Pricklebum would be asleep during the day when you're at work. You would simply need to give him a bit of attention in the evenings, change his water, food, and bedding for him—that sort of thing."

I sighed. "Oh, very well. I suppose I could take him for a bit—but I don't know how Muesli will react to him. She might hurt him or something."

Glenda chuckled. "I think once she's had a taste of his prickles, she'll leave him well alone!"

***

So somehow, against my better judgement, I found myself cycling back to Oxford with a hedgehog tucked in my bicycle basket. As I was passing the main pedestrianised shopping street in the city centre, I spied the sign for a local pet store and slowed my bike. Although the Old Biddies had assured me that Pricklebum would do fine in a converted plastic storage container, I wasn't very comfortable with that idea. I decided to pop into the pet store and pick up a proper cage.

The pet store was housed in the eighteenth-century historic Covered Market: a collection of unique shops and stalls—from traditional cobblers and butchers to artisan jewellers and cake makers—which was a favourite destination for locals and tourists alike. I wheeled my bicycle to one of the arched entrances and propped it against the wall, then looked hesitantly at the cardboard box in my basket. I couldn't leave the hedgehog out here unattended, but the box was too big and bulky to carry.

I reached inside the box and lifted the ball of prickles out, then placed it gently inside my tote bag. *Pricklebum should be safe enough in there for the short time I'll be in the pet store*, I decided. Then I hurried into the market and navigated the warren of alleyways until I came to the pet store. It seemed to be a busy time, with several people waiting to be served, and I had to wait in line for a while before I could finally step up to the counter.

"Can I help you, miss?"

"Yes," I said, placing my tote bag down next to my feet and leaning across the counter. "I'm looking after a hedgehog for a few days and I want to make sure I have a safe place to keep it. Do you sell a small rabbit cage or something like that?"

"Certainly. In fact, we have a beginners' starter kit for our new guinea pig owners which would be ideal. It includes a large cage with a plastic tray bottom, a water dropper, and a food bowl."

"Oh, that sounds perfect," I said.

"Would you like some bedding with that?"

"Um... I suppose so. What do hedgehogs normally use for bedding?"

"Well, in the wild, they'd be using dead leaves," said the shop owner with a laugh. "But I think yours will be quite happy if you provide it with some hay or straw. They like to have something they can burrow into. Put lots of newspaper on the bottom of the cage first, though. And have you got any hedgehog food?"

"There's special hedgehog food? I never realised."

"Yes, there are actually commercial preparations now, probably due to the fact that the African pygmy hedgehog has become a very popular pet in the Unites States. Of course, the native English hedgehog is a different animal and they shouldn't be kept as pets—but they can still benefit from the foods. Otherwise, you can also give dry cat biscuits and some tinned cat food, although stay away from the fish flavours. Oh, and they also like dried bananas, sultanas, a bit of cooked potato or rice, peas, and other fruits and vegetables. We also sell live crickets, beetles, and mealworms which can be used to supplement their diet, if you'd like to have some."

"Er... I think I'll stick with the cat biscuits and dried fruit for now," I said hastily.

I waited as he rang up my purchases, giving me a nice discount as a bonus, then pushed the cage across the counter. *I'll put Pricklebum in his new home*, I thought, bending down to pick up my tote bag. My hand groped empty air and I looked down quickly. To my dismay, my tote bag had tipped over sideways. With a sinking feeling, I crouched down and opened the bag to peer inside.

The hedgehog was gone!

CHAPTER FIFTEEN

"Oh no! He's gone!" I cried, straightening up and looking frantically around the shop.

"Who's gone?" asked the shop owner.

"Pricklebum! My hedgehog! I had him in my bag and he must have rolled out when the bag tipped over. Oh God, the Old Biddies will never forgive me!"

I rushed around the store, looking under display units and behind shelves. There was not a spine to be seen anywhere. Then I saw the wide open door and my heart sank even further. Could Pricklebum have gone outside?

"Listen, can you keep my stuff for a moment? I'll be right back!"

Leaving the shop owner gaping after me, I grabbed my tote bag and rushed out into the main market. Then I stopped and looked around in despair. The Covered Market was a warren of interconnecting lanes and alleyways, all filled with tourists and locals milling about. *Where should I start searching?*

I picked an alleyway at random and began pushing my way through the crowd, desperately scanning the floor. Many of the shops had their wares displayed on benches and stands outside their premises, and I had to keep stopping to crouch and look underneath them.

"Are you all right, miss?" asked a man as I crouched down next to him.

"Yes," I said distractedly, lifting the edge of the canvas covering the bench and peering underneath. "Have you seen a hedgehog anywhere?"

"A hedgehog?" he said, looking at me a bit funny.

"Yes, I've lost my hedgehog. Have you seen him? About the size of a tennis ball, brown with cream-tipped prickles. His name's Pricklebum."

"Er... no, I haven't seen any hedgehogs," said the man, edging away.

I turned away in frustration, then my heart leapt as I suddenly spied something moving in the distance. *Yes!* A little prickly ball ambling across the open space up ahead, where several of the alleyways criss-crossed and intersected. It was Pricklebum and he was heading determinedly for the butcher's stall down one of the other alleyways. I wondered if the smell of fresh meat might have attracted him. He was sure moving with surprising speed for such a small creature!

I rushed towards him but, before I could reach the open space, a group of schoolchildren swarmed across the intersection in front of me, led by a harassed-looking teacher. They were obviously on a school outing and the kids were boisterous and excited.

"Noooo! Be careful!" I cried, closing my eyes in horror as the school group swept over Pricklebum in their path. I thought he would be squashed for sure but the little hedgehog sensed the danger just in time and curled up protectively. One of the children kicked him by mistake and he went rolling away like a football.

"Aaarrghh!" I cried, pushing my way through the children and rushing after him.

Pricklebum bounced against the wall, rolled across the cobblestones, and came to rest next to a bespoke shoe store. A moustachioed gentleman who had been examining a pair of brogues looked up in surprise as a ball of prickles rolled to a stop next to his foot. I hurried up and knelt down to retrieve the hedgehog.

Please be all right, please be all right... I prayed as I gently picked Pricklebum up. To my relief, I saw the prickles unfold slightly and a little pointy nose poke out, quivering, to sniff the air. This was followed a moment later by a pair of bright black eyes as the hedgehog's tiny furry face came into view. My heart melted. He really was adorable. He made little huffing and puffing sounds, as if scolding me for his recent mishap, and I laughed.

"I'm sorry, Pricklebum. You're right—it was all my fault and I shouldn't have been so careless. But you shouldn't have been so inquisitive either! Anyway, you're safe now and hopefully none the worse for wear after your adventure."

I pulled a scarf out of my tote bag, carefully wrapped the hedgehog in its soft folds, and tucked him securely into the bottom of my bag. Then I rose to my feet and—ignoring the strange looks from the gentleman who was still holding the pair of brogues—I turned to go. But as I swung around, I caught sight of someone inside the shoe store and I froze.

It was Tyler Lee.

I hadn't seen him since the day of the funeral. He was still as sleek as ever, fashionably dressed in a tight polo shirt and designer jeans, but without his trench coat today. He was bent over a shelf in the store, examining a pair of men's leather loafers. I hesitated. It was too good an opportunity to miss.

I slipped into the store and picked up a shoe at random, then sidled up to the handsome Eurasian. Pretending to knock against him by mistake, I turned around and did an exaggerated double take.

"Hey! It's...Tyler Lee, isn't it?"

He regarded me warily.

"You were at the funeral!" I said with all the enthusiasm of someone meeting their old chum at a high school reunion. I thrust my hand out at him. "I'm Gemma Rose!"

Reluctantly, he took my hand, although I saw him shift restlessly and his eyes dart to the shop doorway, as if looking for an escape.

"I was the caterer who provided the food for the reception," I explained.

The guarded expression in his eyes eased and I saw him relax slightly. Scones and home-made jam tend to give an image that doesn't make people suspicious.

"Oh yeah. The food looked awesome. I didn't get to taste anything but it looked really good." He spoke with an exaggerated American accent, like someone who had learned English as a second language from Hollywood movies.

"It must have been a really horrible experience for you at the funeral," I said, my voice dripping with false sympathy. "Coming such a long way to meet your father at last and then not only discovering that he was dead but finding yourself involved in a murder investigation too!"

The wary expression was back on his face. "Hey, the murder investigation's got nothing to do with me!"

I looked at him innocently. "Oh, but I thought—as Rex Clifford's son—you'd be entitled to a large share of the estate if Adele died. So wouldn't the police naturally have you as suspect?"

"I didn't know anything about the will," said

Tyler Lee quickly. "So I couldn't have wanted to kill her."

"But wasn't the will the reason you came to England?"

"No, no," he said, shaking his head vehemently. "I told you—I came to England to find my dad."

"So how did you know to come to the funeral? I mean, people who aren't close friends of the family usually only find out about a death when they are one of the beneficiaries in the will and are contacted by the solicitors."

"I..." He licked his lips. "There was... a letter... yeah, a letter that my dad sent my mother. Like, a couple of weeks ago. He knew he was sick, you see, and maybe he was thinking he might die soon—so he wanted to tell her that he always remembered her. I got the letter and saw the address... and decided to come."

"Oh? So you hadn't contacted the lawyers beforehand? Because I thought you knew the Cliffords' solicitor—"

"No, no, I didn't know anybody at the funeral—"

"But I saw you talking to him? At the funeral reception."

"Uh... oh, yeah, that guy." He shifted uncomfortably. "Yeah, I talked to him for a bit."

"You looked like you were having an argument."

He gave an uneasy laugh. "Argument? No, no, you must have got things wrong. He just... asked me... um... where the toilets are. I told him I didn't know." He shifted from foot to foot again. "Look... uh... I have to go now."

He put the loafer back on the shelf, turned, and hurried out of the store before I could say anything else. I watched his retreating figure. Now if that wasn't the behaviour of a guilty man, I didn't know what was.

CHAPTER SIXTEEN

I stood in front of the mirror in my bedroom, examining my appearance critically. Normally I wouldn't have fussed so much for dinner at my parents' house, but tonight seemed crucially important. It was silly, but I felt like if I could make sure I looked perfect, I could somehow influence my parents to like Devlin more too.

I sighed. I didn't want to admit it but my stomach was tied up in knots and I was beginning to wonder if I had made a terrible mistake insisting on taking Devlin home to "meet the parents" tonight. I knew my mother would be constantly comparing him to Lincoln Green and probably find him wanting—and suddenly, it was desperately important to me to have her approve of Devlin.

I made a sound of impatience, annoyed at

myself. I thought I had left all that behind. It was my fear of disapproval that had led me to reject Devlin's proposal eight years ago, and caused all the pain and bitterness that followed. After the years of independence Down Under, away from the apron strings, I was sure that I had grown beyond needing or wanting my mother's approval. But tonight it was as if I had regressed to my younger self again, just as nervous as those early student days when my relationship with Devlin O'Connor had been a guilty secret.

"*Meorrw!*" said Muesli from the corner of my dressing table where she was sitting, watching me get ready. She reached out and batted a lipstick with one paw, prodding it until it fell over the edge of the table and onto the floor.

"Muesli, don't do that..." I frowned at her, bending over to pick up the lipstick and put it back on the table.

The little tabby gave me a look, then batted the lipstick again, making it roll off the edge of the table once more.

"Muesli! Stop it!"

I picked up the lipstick again, putting it on the other side of the table this time and out of her reach.

"*Meeorrwww,*" said Muesli petulantly, turning to glare at the other side of the room where snuffling sounds could be heard coming from a cage tucked into the corner.

I smiled to myself. So *that* was why she was in a temper! When I'd finally got home from the Covered Market and introduced Muesli to Pricklebum, the little cat had not taken kindly to the suggestion of sharing her home with a houseguest. She had let me know in no uncertain terms all evening, stalking around with a scowl on her whiskered face and a hiss on her tongue. After examining the hedgehog suspiciously through the bars of the cage, she had proceeded to ignore him—except to occasionally give him a glare when the sounds of him happily munching *her* cat biscuits got too loud for her liking.

"It's only for a few days, Muesli," I promised her. "He's not moving in with us permanently."

"*Meorrw!*" Muesli shot the hedgehog cage another dirty look, then jumped off the dressing table and stalked from the bedroom, the tip of her tail twitching.

I hastily finished getting ready, then scooped up Muesli, put her in her cat carrier, and set off. A short while later, I found myself pacing the hallway in my parents' house as I waited for Devlin to arrive, hoping nervously that he wouldn't be late. According to my mother, tardiness was the eighth deadly sin. Devlin was normally very punctual but I knew that sometimes work could delay him.

The bell rang and I sprang forwards to open the door, then fell back in dismay as I saw who was standing on the threshold. It was Lincoln Green and his mother, Helen.

"Lincoln! Er... Aunt Helen..." I greeted them in surprise.

"Your mother invited us around to dinner this evening," Lincoln explained, looking very embarrassed. He darted a look at his mother. "I... I thought it would be better if we came another time but... Mum insisted."

"Hello, Gemma," said Helen Green in a cool tone, her manner very stiff.

Recently, things had been particularly uncomfortable with my mother's closest friend, who couldn't quite conceal her angry indignation at my audacity for choosing Devlin over her beloved son. She had been decidedly frosty towards me every time I saw her since, and it had made for a lot of awkward moments. Now I groaned inwardly as I imagined having Helen's disapproving presence looming over us all evening.

"Um... come in..." I ushered them into the house.

But before I could shut the door, a tall figure appeared on the threshold, carrying a bottle of wine and a large bouquet of yellow roses. It was Devlin. He stepped into the house, pausing in surprise as he saw Lincoln and Helen Green.

The two men shook hands, then Helen looked Devlin up and down and sniffed.

"So... this must be your new young man?" she said to me.

I squirmed slightly, wishing that Devlin hadn't changed. Instead of his usual beautifully tailored suits, he was wearing dark jeans and a simple, open-necked cotton shirt. He looked broodingly handsome but not as suave and elegant as he did during the day in his work wardrobe.

"Yes, this is Devlin. Devlin O'Connor."

"I remember you," said Helen, looking down her nose at Devlin. "You were at college with Gemma, weren't you? You used to have *long hair*," she added, in the tone of someone suggesting he used to have leprosy.

"Darling! Why didn't you tell me that everyone had arrived?" My mother sailed into the hallway, resplendent in a mauve silk dress and a string of pearls.

"Mrs Rose." Devlin stepped forwards and presented the flowers to her. "It's good to see you again."

"Oh... er... how nice." My mother looked very flustered. She accepted the flowers and the bottle of wine. "Oh... a *Château Léoville-Las Cases*," she said with some surprise as she examined the label.

"Oh? So you know a bit about wine?" said Helen, looking at Devlin haughtily.

"A bit," said Devlin with an amused look.

"Yes, well... let's not stand around in the hall..." My mother gave a trill of nervous laughter and escorted Helen into the living room.

Lincoln gave Devlin an apologetic look. "Sorry

about my mother... She's..." He seemed at a loss for words.

"Don't worry, mate," said Devlin with a grin. "We've all been there."

Lincoln gave him a grateful smile, then, with a nod to both of us, he turned and hurried into the living room. As soon as he was out of earshot, I turned to Devlin and hissed:

"I wish you hadn't gone home to change."

He raised an eyebrow. "You wanted me to come to dinner in a three-piece suit?"

"Well, it's just that... you look so nice when you're dressed for work."

"I thought it would be nicer for your parents to see me in 'off duty' mode, instead of being reminded of my role as a detective. I thought the whole idea of this dinner was to get to know each other on a more personal basis."

"Yes, I suppose you're right..." I sighed, twisting my hands. "Um... Devlin, you *do* know about the right forks and spoons to use, don't you?"

He gave me a funny look. "Of course. Why do you ask?"

"It's just... well, my mother cares a lot about proper table etiquette. You know, making sure you don't use the fish knife with the dessert fork—"

Devlin made a wry face. "Gemma, in case you'd forgotten, we were at Oxford together. I think I've been to enough Formal Halls and guest dinners to know the table etiquette required."

"Sorry," I said sheepishly. "I'm just a bit... I just wanted you to make a good impression."

Devlin opened his mouth as if to say something, then changed his mind. "Shall we go in? Skulking here in the hallway when everyone else has gone inside definitely isn't going to make a good impression."

"Yes, sure..." I started down the hall, then stopped and turned around again. "And when we're having the soup, you will remember to scoop the spoon *away* from you and not towards you, won't you? My mother is very particular about that."

Devlin rolled his eyes. "Yes, I will make sure I drink the soup the correct way."

"I... I know it seems stupid. But you know how some things just matter a lot to mothers? Your mother probably has some silly things that she cares a lot about too, right?" I gave him a tremulous smile and turned away but Devlin put a hand on my arm.

"Gemma..."

"Yes?"

He hesitated. "There's something important I've been wanting to tell you."

I looked at him in surprise. He sounded so serious. "Yes?"

He hesitated again, then said with a rueful smile, "Well, we can't talk about it now. Maybe after dinner."

"Okay." I looked at him curiously but he didn't

offer any more information.

We went into the living room and joined the others, making stilted conversation until my mother announced that dinner was served. Even Muesli's mischievous presence didn't really help to lighten the mood. Conversation at the dining table wasn't much better. Helen spent most of her time shooting daggers at Devlin across the table whilst my mother served him with exaggerated politeness, eyeing him a bit like a wild animal that had strayed into her home. My father, thankfully, was his usual absent-minded self and made vague attempts to engage Devlin in conversation, while Lincoln also did his best to keep up a cheerful flow of comments. I sat on the edge of my chair, jumping and twitching every time Devlin lifted a fork or raised his glass, terrified that he would do something "the wrong way". By the time dessert arrived, my nerves were frayed to pieces and I had a pounding headache.

"So, Devlin... which cricket team do you follow?" asked my father as my mother served the rhubarb crumble accompanied by double cream.

"I don't actually watch cricket, sir," said Devlin apologetically. "Football's my game."

My mother gave a gasp and put a hand to her throat. "You're not one of those football hooligans, are you, Devlin?"

Devlin chuckled. "Well, I don't know what my friends would call me—I can certainly get very heated, especially when England is playing in the

World Cup."

"Haven't you played cricket at all?" asked my father, looking at Devlin in deep disappointment. "Not even at school?"

"I would probably have got beaten up if I tried to play cricket at *my* school," said Devlin with a wry laugh.

I winced. Cricket was considered the "gentleman's game", favoured by the upper classes, whereas football was traditionally seen as a working-class sport. Oh, it was never spelled out as such—and of course, nowadays, the lines were blurred, especially with celebrity football stars like David Beckham—but still, that subtle class distinction was there.

"Lincoln played cricket at Eton—and for the university team," Helen said proudly. "He's a wonderful batsman and once scored a six off the last ball to win a match!"

"That was probably just luck, Mum," said Lincoln quickly, coughing with embarrassment.

"Nonsense, darling! You were fabulous! Of course, everyone knows that cricket is a game which requires a certain level of intelligence and education to understand and play." She shot a meaningful look at Devlin. "Unlike some other sports, which simply involve a lot of mindless violence and are really just for working-class yobs."

"Mum, that's not really true," said Lincoln uncomfortably, torn between not wanting to disagree with his mother in front of company and being aghast at her condescending generalisations.

"Of course it's true!" she said. She turned to my mother. "Evelyn, didn't we see an article in your Times Online newspaper all about England's disgraceful football hooligans and what a menace they were? Haven't you got it on your iPad?"

"I would have—except that I still can't find my iPad," said my mother, looking distressed. "I've called every place I could think of, where I might have left it, and no one has seen any sign of it. The only place I haven't checked yet is Sexton, Lovell & Billingsley. Although I was there on Friday morning so I don't think—"

"Oh!" I stared at my mother. "I'd completely forgotten that you and Dad are with Sexton, Lovell & Billingsley as well."

"As well?" My mother looked at me, puzzled.

"As well as the Cliffords—you know, Adele Clifford was that woman who was murdered by poisoning at her husband's funeral."

My mother gave a little scream. "Gemma! Is this really appropriate conversation for the dinner table?"

"This is what happens when one spends too much time among those with criminal interests," murmured Helen, shooting a look in Devlin's direction.

"Sorry, sorry—I'll get off the subject." I ducked my head. "But Mother, listen, I'll pop into Sexton,

Lovell & Billingsley for you tomorrow and ask about your iPad, okay?"

"Oh, that's very nice of you, darling, but surely there's no need to go in person? I could simply give them a ring—"

"No, no, I don't mind stopping on my way to work tomorrow morning," I said. "It's better to ask these things in person sometimes—people might make more of an effort to look, rather than if you just ask them on the phone. And this way, if your iPad is there, I can pick it up right away and keep it safe with me during the day at the tearoom."

"Oh, would you, darling? That would be marvellous. I've been so bereft without my iPad—I really don't know how I managed before without it," my mother said with a tinkling laugh. "Now, shall we have tea and coffee in the living room?"

Obediently, we all moved back to the sofa suite and my father settled happily in his favourite armchair with Muesli on his lap, purring contently, her eyes narrowed to slits. My mother brought in a silver tea service and I helped her pass around tea, coffee, and gourmet chocolates.

"So... where do you live, Devlin?" asked Helen, balancing her teacup on her knee.

"In a converted barn out in the Cotswolds, just on the outskirts of Oxford."

"And I presume that you're renting?"

"No, in fact, I bought the place."

Helen's eyebrows shot up. "Really? Given the

prices of houses in the Cotswolds, I can't imagine how you could have afforded it on a policeman's salary!" She looked at him suspiciously, as if suspecting Devlin of having gained his house through illegal means.

Devlin smiled. "It *would* have been difficult on a policeman's salary. But luckily, I didn't have to rely solely on that. I had some investments which gave me the necessary capital."

"Devlin's a whizz with numbers and brilliant at investing money," I said quickly. "I remember, even when we were at college, while the rest of us were still juggling our weekly allowance, Devlin was already putting his savings on stocks and shares, and speculating on the currency exchange." I smiled at him proudly.

Devlin looked embarrassed. "I got lucky a few times, that's all."

"It's much more than luck," I insisted. "You don't make those kinds of returns just on luck. That requires serious talent with money and a knack for investments."

"Well, I'm just grateful that Lincoln is in a highly specialised profession with an assured income, so he never has to rely on risky investments," said Helen pointedly. She turned to my mother and said airily, "Did I tell you, Evelyn, that Lincoln was named the Top Intensive Care Specialist at the hospital?"

Lincoln coughed again in embarrassment and

said hurriedly, "These are smashing chocolates, Aunt Evelyn. I don't think I've ever tasted anything like these before. Where are they from?"

"Oh, they're from a Cotswolds village called Tillyhenge. My friend, Eliza Whitfield, was out that way last week. She said she found a delightful little chocolate shop—owned by a rather strange old woman, mind you—that sold the most incredible chocolates. She bought a few boxes and brought one back for me. Wasn't that lovely of her?"

My mother offered the box of chocolate truffles around. I helped myself to one, popping it into my mouth and closing my eyes briefly to savour the flavours. Lincoln was right—the chocolate was *amazing*: rich and velvety, with a soft caramel centre and a crisp coating of smooth, dark chocolate. The creamy, bittersweet flavour lingered on my tongue and the rich cocoa fragrance filled my senses, making my headache lift slightly.

I opened my eyes again to see everyone enjoying their piece of chocolate in a contented silence and, for the first time that evening, a feeling of congeniality settled over the group. Even Helen Green seemed to have mellowed slightly, her expression no longer belligerent as she thanked Devlin for handing her a napkin. The change was startling and I smiled to myself. You could almost believe that the chocolates were enchanted! Okay, that was a silly idea, but whatever it was, I was grateful that the chocolates had somehow helped the evening end on a happier note.

Lincoln and his mother left soon after and my parents also retired early to bed, leaving me and Devlin alone in the living room, pretending to watch TV whilst trying not to talk about the dinner.

"I'm sorry about Helen Green tonight," I said at last. "I've never seen her like that before. You know, she's my mother's best friend and I've known her practically all my life. She's normally such a mild-mannered, friendly woman—and she's not much of a snob—I don't know what got into her tonight!"

Devlin gave a cynical laugh. "Maternal instincts."

"Huh?"

Devlin shrugged. "Watch any nature programme: parents always get very protective when defending their offspring. It's the one time they can act totally out of character and become completely irrational."

"Still, there was no need for her to keep trying to put you down! And you let her too," I said accusingly.

"What do you mean?"

"Well, you just let her say things all the time— you made no effort to defend yourself or anything." I gave him a peevish look. "Like when I was telling them about your investments—why did you make it sound like it was just luck? You know it's true that you're a whizz with money! You could have really impressed everyone."

"Do I need to? You don't think I could have just impressed everyone as myself?"

"But that *is* you! It's not like you're presenting a fake image—you *are* a financial genius. Why hide it?"

Devlin gave a weary sigh. "Gemma, why don't we face what this is really about? At the end of the day, no matter how much of a financial genius I am, I will still always be the working-class boy who went to the wrong school, speaks with the wrong accent, plays the wrong sport, and who isn't really good enough for you. Isn't that what the real problem is? And nothing is ever going to change that—no matter what I say or how I dress." He leaned forwards and looked at me, his blue eyes serious. "Does that bother you? Are you ashamed of me?"

"No, of course not!" I said quickly. "It's just..."

An awkward silence fell between us.

Finally, I cleared my throat and said, fiddling with the tassel on a cushion, "What was it that you wanted to speak to me about earlier? You said there was something you wanted to tell me."

Devlin hesitated, his expression uncertain. "I... I'm not sure now... Look, forget it, Gemma."

"But you said it was important—"

My phone rang, startling us both. I answered it hastily.

"Gemma? Gemma, are you there?" hissed a familiar voice.

"Mabel?"

"Oh good. Listen, dear, we need your help."

"I'm not looking after any more hedgehogs," I

said.

"We seem to have got ourselves into a sticky situation," Mabel said in an urgent whisper. "We're trapped. You have to help us. Cotswolds Manor Hotel. Second floor. Fifth balcony on the car park side."

"*What?*" I glanced nervously at Devlin and turned slightly away from him, lowering my voice. "What do you mean—what's going on?"

"No time to explain, dear. Just get here as soon as you can."

The line went dead.

I lowered my phone and stared at it.

"What is it?" asked Devlin.

"Um... nothing. It's the Old Biddies." I gave him a wan smile. "You know what they're like... Um... listen, Devlin, I hope you don't mind but... uh... I think I might have an early night..."

He raised his eyebrows slightly but, to my relief, he didn't question me further, simply saying, "I've got an early start tomorrow too. In any case, it's been a long evening," he added sardonically.

He started to rise but Muesli—who had transferred from my father's lap to his and had been happily snoring—woke up and gave an indignant "*Meorrw!*"

"Sorry, sweetie," said Devlin as he eased her gently off his lap.

He gave her head a quick pat, then stood up and followed me out to the foyer, where he gave me an equally quick kiss before getting into his Jaguar XK and driving away.

I waited until his car was safely out of sight, then grabbed my mother's car keys and slipped out of the house. Hoping that my parents were sleeping too soundly to hear, I started the engine, slid the car out onto the street, and started on my way to the Cotswolds Manor Hotel.

CHAPTER SEVENTEEN

The Cotswolds Manor Hotel was the kind of genteel country resort where wealthy executives went for golf retreats and their pampered wives and daughters enjoyed spa weekends. At this time of the night, it was quiet, with most of the middle-aged guests already tucked up in bed and the rest having a quiet drink in the lobby lounge bar.

I pulled into the car park around the side of the main building, which was overlooked by the cheaper guest rooms. As I walked from the car towards the front entrance of the hotel, I was astonished to hear my name being called from somewhere above my head.

"Psst! Gemma!"

I stopped and looked up. From the second floor upwards, each of the rooms on this side had a balcony terrace with outdoor seating and a little table. In the one directly above my head, I could see four small figures huddled together. *The Old Biddies!*

I had thought that Mabel was joking when she said they were on a balcony. I sighed. *I guess not.*

"What on earth are you doing up there?" I demanded.

"Never mind that now," said Mabel. "You need to help us. We're stuck on this balcony."

"Can't you just go back in the room?"

"We're locked out," Glenda supplied helpfully.

"Well, I suppose I can go to Reception and ask them for help, although I don't know why you couldn't have just called them yourselves—"

"No, no! You can't do that!" said Mabel. "The hotel reception doesn't know that we're here."

I stared at her. "What do you mean they don't know?"

"We're undercover!" said Florence proudly.

"You're *what*? Look, you need to tell me what's going on—"

"Really, Gemma, if we knew you were just going to come and ask us a lot of silly questions, we wouldn't have called you," said Mabel. "We thought you would be more resourceful than that. But if you can't figure out a way, I suppose we'll have to think of something ourselves."

"Do you think it's too far to jump?" asked Ethel, peering over the edge of the balcony.

"No, no, don't even think of doing that!" I cried, visions of four little old ladies landing in a heap of broken bones filling my head. I took a deep breath. "Okay. I'll try and think of something. Just... wait there for me and don't do anything crazy, please?"

I started to hurry away, then remembered something and turned back. "By the way, which room is it?"

"Room 208. Tyler Lee's room."

I gaped at her. "*What?* What were you doing in Tyler Lee's room?"

"There's no time to explain now," said Mabel briskly. "Just get us out before he comes back."

I took another deep breath, swallowed my exasperation, and said, "Okay, fine. But I want a full explanation later!"

Muttering to myself, I hurried into the hotel and paused in the lobby. The Cotswolds Manor Hotel had only opened a short while before I returned to England. In fact, the last time I'd been there was when I first arrived back in the country and had become embroiled in the murder of a young woman I'd met on the plane. I grimaced at the memory now and felt a pang again for the girl who had been killed. I'd liked her a lot. And although her killer had been brought to justice, it was still a terrible tragedy and the loss of a potential friendship.

The lobby was just as I remembered, with the reception counter on one side and the lounge bar on the other. There were still quite a few people sitting in the lounge, sipping drinks. I wandered over to a stand displaying promotional flyers for various Cotswolds tourist activities and randomly plucked a leaflet out of the stand. Opening it, I pretended to read whilst my mind worked feverishly, trying to figure out how I was going to get upstairs and into Tyler Lee's room.

If I'd been in a movie, perhaps I could have simply swanned upstairs and picked the lock on the door. But I had no idea how to pick a lock—and even if I had, I wasn't sure I would've wanted to risk doing it in the middle of a public hotel hallway. I'd probably end up getting caught by security and—together with the Old Biddies—marched down to the local police station! I shuddered to think of what Devlin would say, not to mention that supercilious Inspector Pratt. I knew he would've liked nothing better than to arrest us all for "breaking and entering".

No, I couldn't pick the lock. Or even attempt it. So how else was I going to get into the room? My eyes drifted to the opposite wall where a large poster, showing a woman in a towel and turban, advertised the hotel's spa services.

Suddenly, I had an idea.

It was a crazy idea and probably wouldn't work—but it was worth a shot. In fact, I remembered reading somewhere that some hotels were so used to this sort of thing happening, the staff hardly batted an eyelid. Well, I was going to find out.

Stuffing the leaflet back in the stand, I hurried past the reception counter and turned down the hallway leading towards the spa. This would be closed now, I knew, but the spa was also connected to the gym, which was open twenty-four hours for guests to use, and they shared a changing room and shower area.

I stepped into the network of corridors connecting the toilets, sauna, showers, and lockers, and quickly found the central communal area, surrounded by vanity tables and mirrors. Like a lot of posh spas, each mirrored cubicle was supplied with various toiletries like moisturiser, wipes, cotton buds, and tissues. Next to them stood a large laundry basket for used towels, with a stack of clean towels on top.

I grabbed a fluffy white towel and hurried into a changing cubicle. There I stripped off my clothes and shoes, and wrapped the towel around me. Then I locked my things away in a locker and hurried over to a sink. Turning on the taps full force, I tipped my head over and dunked my hair in the water, then cupped my hands and splashed some water over my face and neck as well.

I straightened and inspected myself in the mirror. I looked like a drowned rat, with water running off my short hair to drip onto my bare shoulders, and major "panda eyes" from the impromptu face wash. Just the way someone would look halfway through their shower, I hoped. It probably wasn't necessary—I could have tried my ploy just in my normal clothes—but I was sure that by looking this way, I was more likely to be believed and pitied.

Taking a deep breath, I left the changing rooms and headed back to the lobby. I paused at the end of the hallway and waited around the corner until I was sure no one was looking, then I stepped out and walked towards the reception counter, making sure to walk in an arc so that it looked like I had come from the direction of the lifts.

I saw several people in the lounge bar glance up, then stare as I walked across the lobby in just my towel and bare feet. Flushing, I clutched the towel tighter to me and fought the urge to turn around and run back to the changing rooms.

If this doesn't work, I'm going to kill the Old Biddies, I thought, gritting my teeth. *In fact, even if it does work, I just might kill them anyway.*

I went up to Reception and cleared my throat. The girl behind the counter looked up, startled, and her eyes widened as she took in my appearance—clad in nothing but a towel, with dripping hair and a wet face.

"Hi..." I said with a sheepish smile. "I've... uh... locked myself out of my room. Can you please give me the spare key?"

The girl hesitated. "Well, normally we're supposed to ask for ID... but I don't suppose you'd have any ID on you?" she said with sympathetic smile.

"No, I didn't think of showering with my passport," I said with a droll smile.

She laughed. "Oh, I guess it's all right. To be honest with you, I've always had a fear of locking myself out of a hotel room like this. Which room is it?"

"Room 208," I said. I beamed as she handed me the key. "Thank you so much! I can't tell you how much I appreciate it."

The girl smiled. "No problem. These things happen. Can you bring back the spare key tomorrow? Guests are only really supposed to have one copy."

"Sure. Thanks so much again."

Clutching the precious key, I turned and hurried to the lifts, avoiding the curious gazes of the guests in the lounge who were still staring at me. The lift seemed to take ages to come—I groaned inwardly as I remembered my frustration the last time I was at the Cotswolds Manor Hotel and had to wait forever for the lifts. Finally, just as I was thinking of taking the stairs instead, the lift doors opened with a soft *ping!*

I stepped in, relieved that there was no one else waiting with me, and was about to push the button for the second floor when I caught a glimpse of a figure coming through the main lobby doors. I froze in horror. It was Inspector Pratt. What was *he* doing here?

The lift doors slid shut before I could think any further. I hesitated, then jabbed my finger on the button for the second floor and tried to calm my breathing as I began to ascend smoothly. *It's okay, he didn't see you*, I reminded myself. Then another thought struck me and I felt my heart jerk in alarm. *Oh bugger, I hope he's not here to search Tyler Lee's room or something!*

I arrived outside Room 208 with my heart already pounding uncomfortably. I inserted the key in the lock and let myself in, glancing around. The room was in darkness and obviously empty. I breathed a sigh of relief. Quickly, I crossed over to the balcony doors and pulled back the curtains.

"*GAH!*" I jumped in fright as four wrinkled old faces suddenly loomed at me through the glass. Mabel beckoned impatiently. I unlocked the glass door and let the Old Biddies back into the room.

"About time," grumbled Mabel. "It was getting quite nippy out there."

"How did you get into the room without a key?" I demanded. "And how did you end up locked on the balcony?"

"Oh, it was very exciting," said Glenda with a giggle.

"It was my idea!" said Florence proudly. "We called Housekeeping from the extension in the lobby and told them that Room 208 needed extra towels. Then we came up here and waited down the hallway until the maid came. When she opened the door, we slipped in after her."

"What—all four of you? Didn't she see you?"

"We may be old but we're quick on our feet," said Ethel indignantly. "Anyway, she was busy putting the towels in the bathroom."

"We thought we'd wait on the balcony and then come back into the room after she'd gone," Glenda explained. "We left the glass door open a crack so we could get back in."

"If only the girl hadn't noticed the curtains blowing in the draught and come over to shut the balcony door, we would have been fine," lamented Ethel.

"Well, you have to admit, that was very conscientious of her," said Florence.

"Anyway, it doesn't matter," said Mabel briskly. "We're in the room now and we can begin our search." She began moving purposefully around.

"Wait, wait... you can't just come in here and search through Tyler Lee's things!" I protested. "Even the police need a search warrant to do that!"

"Oh tosh," said Mabel, waving a dismissive hand. "We're only having a little nosy. There's no harm in that."

She bent over Tyler Lee's open case and rummaged through his clothes. I watched in horror as her elbow knocked over a travel bag, spilling the contents on the floor.

"Oh dearie me."

She bent and hastily scooped up the disposable

razors, toothpaste, soap, and aftershave, shoving them back into the bag anyhow. I winced, then told myself that hopefully Tyler Lee would never notice. From the look of the room, tidiness wasn't one of his virtues anyway. The place was a mess, with clothes tossed on the bed, shoes everywhere, and earphones, cables, cigarettes, and papers scattered across the desk.

I stepped forwards and caught Mabel's arm. "There's no time—I saw Inspector Pratt downstairs," I said. "He might be coming up to search Tyler Lee's room himself and we can't be found here!"

Even as the words left my mouth, I stiffened. The sound of male voices drifted from outside in the corridor. I ran to the door, opened it a crack, and peered out. My heart lurched as I saw two figures at the other end of the hallway: Inspector Pratt and, with him, Tyler Lee. They had obviously just got out of the lifts and were standing there arguing.

"… but I know nothing about the murder!" Tyler Lee was saying in a panicked voice. "I told you—I came to England to find my dad; I didn't even know Adele—"

"We'll see about that. If you'll take me to your room, Mr Lee, we can have a private chat there," said Pratt.

I jerked back from the door and looked at the Old Biddies frantically. "Inspector Pratt's coming with Tyler Lee!" I hissed. "We've got to get out of here!"

"But we can't just go out into the hallway and

walk down to the lifts—we'll walk straight into them!" cried Glenda.

"Maybe we ought to go back out on the balcony?" Ethel suggested.

Oh heavens, no, I thought. We couldn't be trapped out there while Pratt was in the room, waiting, hoping for him to leave. And even after he left, how could we explain ourselves to Tyler Lee? We couldn't stay out on the balcony until morning, waiting for him to leave too!

In desperation, I peeked out through the crack in the door again. The men were still arguing by the lifts. Then I saw the door to the room next to ours open and a couple step out into the corridor. My eyes widened as I recognised them. It was the American couple who had come to my tearoom!

This was our only chance.

"Quick, follow me!" I said to the Old Biddies, then stepped out into the corridor.

I rushed up to the couple, shoving a foot against their door to stop them from shutting it.

"Hello! Fancy seeing you here!" I said brightly, pinning a manic smile to my face.

They turned and stared at me. Belatedly, I remembered that I was still only wearing a towel, with wet hair dripping water down my neck and shoulders.

"Er..." The husband looked at me warily. "Do we know you?"

"You were at my tearoom in Meadowford-on-

Smythe, remember? So how was Upper Slaughter? And Stow-on-the-Wold? Did you do any shopping while you were there? There are some fabulous antique shops out there, you know!" I gabbled as the Old Biddies joined me. From the corner of my eye, I saw Inspector Pratt and Tyler Lee start to walk this way.

I turned to the wife. "Um... why don't we go in your room? So silly standing around in the corridor, isn't it?"

"But—"

Not giving her a chance to speak, I hustled the poor bewildered couple back into their room, with the Old Biddies pushing and shoving frantically behind me. We slammed the door just as the two men reached us. I froze, holding my breath. The footsteps went slowly past, then we heard the creak of hinges as Tyler Lee's room door opened, then closed.

I sagged against the door, weak with relief. *Whew.* Safe for now. Then I looked up to see the American couple huddled together by the bed, eyeing me and the Old Biddies uncertainly.

"Oh, my goodness—look at the time! I didn't realise how late it was! Well, I suppose we'd better chat another time," I said, giving them a breezy smile.

The couple gaped at us as I opened their door again and waved the Old Biddies out into the corridor again. I backed out after them, leaning around the door to give the couple a parting smile. "Have a lovely evening. Cheers!"

CHAPTER EIGHTEEN

I woke up the next morning, bleary-eyed and exhausted, and, for a moment, thought it had all been a bad dream. Then I groaned and turned over as it all came back to me. No, it hadn't been a nightmare—I really *had* been skulking around the Cotswolds Manor Hotel dressed in nothing but a towel, and nearly *had* got arrested with the Old Biddies for unlawful trespassing. It was a miracle that we had managed to escape Inspector Pratt's notice and then get down to the lobby and out to my car with no further mishap. I'd half expected the American couple to call Reception and complain about being harassed by a crazy girl in a wet towel and four nosy old ladies.

Sitting up wearily in bed, I yawned and rubbed my eyes. I wondered why Muesli's warm little body wasn't curled up next to me, then I remembered that I had left her at my parents' house last night. It would probably be nice for her to spend the day there anyway, and enjoy being spoiled by my parents.

Thinking of my parents reminded me suddenly that I had offered to stop off at the lawyers' offices this morning to ask about my mother's iPad. I sighed, regretting my impulsive offer—I could have had another hour in bed!—but I forced myself to get up and head to a hot shower and breakfast. An hour later, feeling a lot more human, I entered the offices of Sexton, Lovell & Billingsley and went up to the receptionist.

"Can I help you?" She gave me a cool, professional smile.

"My mother was in here last Friday to see Gavin Sexton. She thinks she may have left her iPad here. I was wondering if you might have seen it?"

The girl frowned. "I haven't seen anything out here..."

"Oh, she might have left it in his office. Is Mr Sexton in yet?"

"Yes, he has just arrived in his office."

I put on my best imitation of my mother and said breezily, "I'll tell you what—I'll just pop along to his office and ask him, shall I?"

"But—"

"Don't worry, I won't be a moment," I said gaily. Before she could argue further, I hurried down the hall and knocked on the door with the sign: "GAVIN SEXTON".

"Come in!"

I stepped into the office and found the lawyer at his desk, perusing some documents. He glanced up in surprise as I entered and I saw that he recognised me.

"I hope you don't mind me popping in," I said, giving him a bright smile. "My mother has lost her iPad, you see, and she thinks that she might have left it here when she came to see you last Friday...?"

"Hmm... an iPad? No, I don't think so..." He looked around distractedly at the piles of foolscap folders, stapled documents, and legal books stacked on his desk.

"Oh, that's a shame..." I pretended to look around his office. "Well, I suppose she must have left it somewhere else."

He said nothing, just stood politely, obviously waiting for me to leave.

"Um... so did you enjoy the food at the Clifford funeral reception?" I asked. The mention of my catering and the delicious baking had done wonders to make Rachel, her uncle, and even Tyler Lee relax—perhaps it would work on Gavin Sexton just as well.

But the lawyer's face remained impassive. "I'm afraid I didn't get a chance to sample any of the food."

"What, not even the treacle tart?" I made a moue of disappointment. "I was so hoping to restore your faith in your childhood favourite treat."

This got a ghost of a smile from him. "Yes, that treacle tart did look delicious, I must say."

"I'll tell you what—I'll make one up especially for you and bring it in later this week," I said warmly.

"Oh, no... I wouldn't want to put you to any trouble," he started to protest but I waved him away quickly.

"It's no trouble at all. It would be my pleasure. And it's the least I can do in return for you looking after my parents' legal affairs so well. My mother speaks so highly of you, you know," I gushed. "She says she's never seen anyone handle things with such... er... clarity and expertise."

"Er... thank you." He flushed, looking embarrassed but also flattered.

I pressed my advantage. I glanced sideways at him and said casually, "By the way, I was wondering if the police had come to question you about Adele Clifford's murder?"

His expression changed, the pale blue eyes suddenly becoming alert and guarded. "No, why should they?"

"Well, you were her lawyer, so I thought—"

"Correction, Miss Rose, I am the Clifford *family* lawyer."

"Oh, but that's what I mean. Adele's murder is probably linked to the change in Rex Clifford's will, isn't it? So as the family lawyer, you must be in the best position to shed some light... I mean, don't you think it's strange that her husband should change the will in her favour, a day before he dies—and then she herself is murdered at his funeral?"

"How do you know about him changing his will?" asked Gavin Sexton sharply.

I gave an innocent shrug. "Oh, you know... village gossip."

"I wouldn't put too much stock on gossip, Miss Rose, if I were you."

"Do you mean it's not true? I thought Rex Clifford called you to his house last Tuesday specifically to make a new will?"

"How did you know about last Tuesday?" he said, looking slightly alarmed.

I shrugged again. "I told you—it's all over the village grapevine. Everyone knows," I lied.

He hesitated, then finally said, "Well, if it's common knowledge... I don't suppose there's any harm in telling you... Yes, Rex Clifford did ask me to visit his house last Tuesday to help him make a new will."

"Were you surprised?"

"Not initially," he said. "Obviously, clients do often change their wills, especially as time passes. But it's rare for things to change so drastically. When he told me that he wanted to make the entirety of his estate over to Adele and cut his own child out..."

"Do you think he was aware of what he was doing?"

"Oh, yes," said Gavin Sexton. "There was no doubt of that. He was always sharp, Rex Clifford, and age and illness hadn't changed that. He knew what he was doing. If there was anything, it was just that..."

"What?" I asked eagerly.

He sighed and shook his head. "I shouldn't really be talking about this."

I pretended to look understanding. "Oh, of course—you want to save it for the police interview."

Mention of the police brought the look of alarm back into his eyes again.

"No, no, it's nothing for the police to concern themselves with," he said hastily. "Nothing to do with the murder. In fact, it was probably nothing, full stop—it was just that Rex didn't seem his usual calm self. I'd seen him in various business negotiations before and he was always a steady opponent: shrewd, calm, very hard to ruffle... it's what made him such a successful businessman. But last Tuesday night... well, frankly, he seemed to be very distressed about something."

"About what?"

Sexton shrugged. "I don't know, exactly. He kept muttering to himself as we were going over the papers—something about everything being a lie and how he had been fooled all his life."

"'Fooled all his life'?" I frowned.

"Look, I'm probably remembering wrong. It might just have been his illness—he did look quite frail and I wondered about his heart condition. Anyway, I counselled him not to act too rashly—to sleep on it and think things over—but he was adamant. The new will was written, signed, and witnessed—and I took it with me when I left."

"And the next morning, Rex Clifford was dead," I mused.

"There was nothing suspicious about that death," he said. "It was a straightforward heart attack—which was not surprising, really, given his heart condition."

"I thought he was getting better after his operation?"

"People can have setbacks."

"And what's happening with the estate now? I mean, with Adele dead, it goes to the next of kin, doesn't it?" I leaned forwards suddenly. "That guy who turned up at the funeral—is he going to have an equal claim?"

Gavin Sexton stiffened, his eyes sliding away from mine. "I'm sorry, Miss Rose, I'm afraid I can't talk any more—I am very busy this morning. In fact, I have to go to a meeting with a client now," he said, standing up and shuffling some papers importantly.

He stuffed the papers into his briefcase, fumbled with the locks, then hurriedly grabbed the handle to go. But his haste was his undoing, because as he lifted the briefcase, it opened suddenly—the locks obviously not having clicked in properly—and a flurry of papers and stationery came tumbling out.

Sexton cursed under his breath and began frantically picking things up. I crouched down beside him to help.

"No, no... I'm fine," he said irritably, pulling things out of my grasp.

It would have been almost rude if it hadn't been for the fact that I could clearly see that he was scared. He was desperate to get away from me. Why? What had I said?

Then I spotted something yellow which had fallen out and been knocked under one corner of his desk. I reached underneath and pulled out a half empty packet of cigarettes. I stared at it, frowning. It looked so familiar... the bright yellow packaging with the emblem of a dragon on one side and Chinese characters on the other. Where had I seen a similar packet recently? Then it came to me: on the desk in the hotel room last night.

"I'll take that," said Gavin Sexton, snatching the packet out of my hand and stuffing it quickly back into the briefcase.

"Do you prefer foreign cigarettes over English ones?" I asked.

"Er... I don't really smoke much at all," said Sexton with a nervous laugh. "Filthy habit really. This was just... um... something I got from a friend."

"Really? A friend from China?" I grinned at him. "This friend wouldn't be Tyler Lee, by any chance?"

He jerked back and said, "I... I don't know who you're talking about."

I raised my eyebrows. "For someone who is the Clifford lawyer and in charge of the estate, you don't seem to be very familiar with the key players. I would have thought that you'd be familiar with Mr Lee? He's the guy I mentioned who turned up at the funeral, claiming to be Rex Clifford's son. With Adele dead, he would be a beneficiary of the will, wouldn't he? The same as Rachel?"

"Yes, well, nothing has been decided yet... what with Adele Clifford's murder and such... things will be in limbo for a while."

"Had Mr Lee made contact with you before the funeral?"

"No, certainly not," he snapped.

"Oh... because I thought it looked like you knew him. I saw you talking to each other at the funeral reception."

A muscle ticked in his jaw. "You must have been mistaken."

"I'm sure I wasn't. He was standing by the table with Rex Clifford's photo and you walked across to talk to him—"

"Oh, that... er... haha... yes, that's right. I'd forgotten," Sexton gave me a tight smile. "I noticed him and wondered if he was... er... gate-crashing the reception. So I... I felt that it was my duty as the

Cliffords' lawyer to... er... ask him what he was doing there. And now..." He made an impatient gesture with his hands. "I'm afraid I really must ask you to leave..."

This time I let him hustle me out of his office, but I was smiling as I left the building. Gavin Sexton was rattled, that was for sure—and the man was also a terrible liar. However he might prevaricate, it was obvious that he knew Tyler Lee. The question was, what was their relationship? Had Lee contacted the Cliffords' lawyer before he arrived in England and found out about the terms of the will? Perhaps Lee had bribed Sexton to give him information?

But how was any of that relevant to Adele's murder? My instinct told me that there was a connection, although at the moment I couldn't see it. After all, Gavin Sexton was a lawyer and he made his money in legal fees, which meant that it was actually in his interest to have the will contested and things dragged out. With Adele dead, there would be no appeal, no challenge to the will, no messy family drama to wade through, and no long court process to earn legal fees on... so surely the last thing a lawyer would want was Adele's death?

But I had definitely not imagined his fear. And now I realised that his whole demeanour had changed when I had mentioned Tyler Lee. He had been happy enough to talk about Rex Clifford and the sudden change in his will, but it was when I mentioned the stranger at the funeral that Sexton became very nervous and tried to cut our conversation short.

So Gavin Sexton obviously didn't want to talk about Tyler Lee. The question was—why?

CHAPTER NINETEEN

Cassie was already at the tearoom when I finally arrived at work. She was in the kitchen, standing at the big wooden table, attempting to make scones, with Dora looking on.

"Don't push so hard... you mustn't overwork the scone dough, otherwise the scones will come out hard and tough," Dora scolded, standing behind Cassie and watching over her shoulder.

Cassie sighed and gave the lump of dough in front of her another clumsy prod.

"Just fold over and push with the heel of your hand, fold over and push..." Dora demonstrated as she expertly kneaded the dough on the table.

I grinned to myself. Cassie might have been a whizz at the marketing and graphic design side of the tearoom business, but when it came to producing the actual baking, she was a disaster. During her short stint in the kitchen—when we were still looking for a permanent chef—she had managed to burn more scones and ruin more cakes than I could remember.

"Morning! Can I help?" I asked as I walked into the room.

"Oh good, Gemma, you're here," said Dora briskly. She pointed at a large bowl in which another ball of dough was resting. "That one has been resting for an hour now—it just needs to be rolled out and cut into rounds."

I washed my hands, donned an apron, and sat down at the table next to Cassie. While I certainly wasn't in Dora's league, I was better than my best friend and could manage some passable baking if I put my mind to it. In fact, I enjoyed the soothing rhythm of working the dough, feeling the mixture becoming smooth and pliant under my fingers as I kneaded it gently and then rolled it out into a thick slab.

Dora handed me a cutter and I carefully stamped out circular rounds from the flattened dough, laying the discs out on a greased baking tray. Even though they hadn't been baked yet, there was already a lovely buttery smell rising from the scone dough.

As Dora went into the pantry to get some supplies, Cassie leaned over and said, raising her eyebrows, "Well? How did the 'meet the parents' dinner go last night?"

I pulled a face. "Oh God. Don't ask."

"Why? What happened?"

I sighed. "Just... it seemed like everything that could go wrong, went wrong! First of all, Helen Green and Lincoln turned up just before Devlin arrived—and you know she's been really funny with me ever since Devlin and I got back together again."

Cassie chuckled. "Well, you know why. She can't believe that you chose Devlin over her darling Lincoln. Of course she'd be hostile."

"Yes, but... well, her behaviour was ridiculous! She was horrible to Devlin, cutting him down at every opportunity, and the thing is—" I made a sound of frustration, "—Devlin didn't help either! I mean, he's got all these amazing talents and achievements, and yet he won't talk about them!"

Cassie looked amused. "Gemma, you know Devlin is the quietly confident type. He doesn't feel the need to brag about things. I thought that's one of the things you love about him."

"I guess... it's just that I really wanted him to make a good impression on my mother, so that she would approve of him at last and—"

Cassie laughed. "I think you're on to a loser there, Gemma. As far as your mother is concerned, Devlin will *never* be good enough for you and he will never match up to her blue-eyed boy, Lincoln Green." She reached out and patted my arm consolingly, leaving a smear of flour on my sleeve. "I think you've got to let it go. Give it time, let them get to know him naturally. Devlin is a fantastic bloke. Your parents will learn to love him for who he is... eventually."

I sighed. I knew Cassie was right about not forcing things but it was hard to share her confidence. She came from a family of artists where everyone was encouraged to embrace their individuality and take pride in being "different"; she never had to worry about "fitting in"—whereas I came from the kind of repressed middle-class upbringing that was obsessed with what the neighbours think and gaining social approval from your peers.

"Anyway, don't tell me you let Helen Green ruin your whole evening?" said Cassie.

"No, it wasn't just her. The whole dinner was just stiff and awkward... and then I thought I might get a chance to speak to Devlin afterwards about... you know... the blonde woman thing... but he looked like he was in a bad mood—"

"I'm not bloody surprised," said Cassie dryly. "A lesser man would probably have developed an inferiority complex by then, with you and everyone hounding him."

I winced, remembering the hurt look in Devlin's blue eyes as he had asked: *"Are you ashamed of me?"* Quickly, I shoved the memory away and said, "Anyway, before I had a chance to bring up the subject, I got a phone call. You'll never believe who it was from."

Cassie grinned. "Let me guess. The Old Biddies."

"How did you know?"

She laughed. "Well, they haven't been involved in anything crazy for a while so I figured it was about time."

I rolled my eyes. "Crazy is an understatement. They rang me to tell me that they were stuck on a balcony at the Cotswolds Manor Hotel!"

Cassie gave a shout of laughter. "You're not serious?"

I gave her a look. "I wish I wasn't. In fact, I thought they were joking—until I arrived in the car park and looked up and saw them there!"

"What were they doing?"

"Snooping, of course, what do you think? It was the balcony to Tyler Lee's room—you know, that guy who turned up at the funeral claiming to be Rex Clifford's love child."

Cassie raised her eyebrows. "Posh place for someone to stay, isn't it?"

I frowned as I began brushing the tops of my scone rounds with an egg-and-milk wash. Now that Cassie had mentioned it, that was a good point. The Cotswolds Manor Hotel was one of the luxury hotels in the area. And even though Tyler Lee had one of the cheaper rooms, it still wouldn't have been cheap. I didn't get the impression that he was rolling in money back in China. Of course, appearances could be deceptive. Still, I wondered if somebody could have been bankrolling him...

"Earth to Gemma... Are you there?"

I jumped. "Sorry, Cass. I just thought of something..."

"So you didn't finish—how did the Old Biddies end up in Tyler Lee's room?"

"They tricked Housekeeping to open the door. They thought they'd hide on the balcony until after the maid left, except that they didn't expect her to notice the open balcony door and shut it, locking them out."

Cassie chuckled. "Gemma, you have to hand it to them—I mean, there are people half their age who wouldn't have the guts to do the things the Old Biddies do."

"You mean they wouldn't have the craziness to do the things the Old Biddies do," I said sourly. Then I gave a reluctant grin. "I suppose you're right. There is a part of me that sort of admires their spirit. I suppose, given a choice, I'd rather be like Mabel than huddled in some rocking chair, with a blanket over my knee, scared to do anything."

"So how did you rescue them?"

I told Cassie about my ploy of walking into the hotel lobby dressed only in a towel and pretending to be locked out of my room, which made her burst out laughing. By the time I got to the part where the Old Biddies and I held the poor American couple hostage in their own bedroom, she was practically crying with laughter.

"Bloody hell..." said Cassie, wiping tears from her

eyes and leaving flour marks all over her face. "It sounds like something out of a comedy farce on TV!"

"You wouldn't have been laughing if you had been there," I said darkly. "I swear, I think I lost five years off my life when we were in the corridor, trying to get into that couple's room before Pratt saw us. And that poor couple! I wouldn't be surprised if they cancelled the rest of their trip and flew straight back to Texas!"

"What's so funny?" asked Dora as she came back into the kitchen.

"Uh... nothing," I said as Cassie hastily went back to her own work.

Dora stopped short and glared at Cassie. "Miss Cassandra Jenkins! What have you done to my scone dough?" she demanded, hands on her waist.

I glanced over. Cassie had been so intent on speaking to me that she had kneaded her dough to within an inch of its life. It had been reduced to a sorry-looking mess of what looked like a giant piece of bubblegum, smeared all over the surface of the table.

Oops.

Cassie ducked her head and gave Dora a guilty look. "Maybe we can just stick it in the oven and bake it anyway? Call it a 'Pizza-Scone'?" she suggested hopefully.

Dora rolled her eyes and heaved an exasperated sigh. She shooed Cassie from her place at the table and bent over to rescue the doughy mess. "Be off with you! Go and do something useful outside!"

Cassie grinned and escaped to the sink, where she washed her sticky hands. Then she came back over to where I was putting the finishing touches to my scones and said:

"So *did* you pick up any clues in Tyler Lee's room?"

"We didn't really get enough time to search it properly," I said regretfully. Then I perked up. "Oh! There was one thing—although I don't know how relevant it might be to the murder."

"Yeah?"

"I stopped off at the lawyers' office this morning—ostensibly to see if my mother might have left her iPad there—but really to have the chance to question Gavin Sexton," I explained. "I thought he might be able to tell me a bit more about Rex Clifford's sudden decision to change his will... Anyway, while I was there, Sexton's briefcase fell open and a packet of cigarettes fell out."

"So?" Cassie looked puzzled.

"So... it was a packet of *Chinese* cigarettes. Not something you would buy down at the local newsagent. *And*—this is the big thing—I saw an identical packet in Tyler Lee's room last night!"

"So what are you saying? That Tyler Lee and Gavin Sexton are smoking buddies?"

I shrugged. "I don't know. But it's a weird coincidence, don't you think? It seems to suggest that Sexton and Lee know each other—or at least, have had contact. In fact, Gavin Sexton got really defensive and hustled me out when I started asking him about the funeral reception and why he was talking to Tyler Lee there. And it works the other way too. I met Tyler Lee in the Covered Market yesterday morning, and when I told him I saw him talking to Sexton at the funeral, he acted really spooked. He gave me some lame story about Sexton asking him where the toilets were..." I rolled my eyes at Cassie.

She snapped her fingers. "Maybe that's it! Maybe Gavin Sexton knew that Tyler Lee was coming from China—like maybe he was even bribed to give Lee details of the will—and then when Lee showed up at the funeral, and Adele got murdered, Sexton panicked. He realised that Lee probably murdered Adele to get his share of the estate—and that he, Sexton, was indirectly responsible in a way, because if he hadn't told Lee the details of the will, the murder might never have happened! So now he's worried and terrified that his connection with Lee might come out—so he's trying to cover up and pretend he didn't know him."

I frowned. It was a good theory and I had to admit that my own mind had been leaning in that direction. But still, there was something that didn't feel right, that didn't quite add up...

"Do you really think that Asian chap could be the murderer?" Dora spoke up.

I thought for a moment. "It's hard to tell, really, since I don't know him that well. From the little interaction I've had with him, I wouldn't think so... I mean, he's a smooth talker and a good actor—I wonder if a lot of that emotional sob-story stuff at the funeral was just acting—but a murderer? He seems too weak, in a way, to be able to kill someone in cold blood."

"But poisoning someone is very different to stabbing them or shooting them," Cassie pointed out. "They say poison is the coward's weapon, don't they? Because you're removed from the site of the death and don't have to deal with it. So in that case, it might fit Tyler Lee's personality perfectly."

"But where would he have got the poison?" asked Dora. "I thought arsenic was very hard to get hold of these days."

"Not in China," I said. "And Tyler Lee just flew in from there a few days ago. He could have brought some arsenic in with him in his luggage."

"You see?" said Cassie triumphantly.

"And what about Rachel Clifford? Does this let her off the hook?" asked Dora.

"It looks like it," I said thoughtfully. "She doesn't have easy access to arsenic and Tyler Lee does— and he has an equally good motive, plus he had the same opportunity to give Adele some poisoned pudding."

"Lee's your guy," said Cassie, nodding. "You just have to find a way to prove it."

CHAPTER TWENTY

I placed the tray of scones in the pre-heated oven, then washed my hands and followed Cassie out to the dining room. We started checking the tables, straightening the chairs, and pulling back the drapes, ready to open for business. Then the door to the tearoom burst open and my mother hurried in, carrying a large laundry bag.

"Darling! I was just on my way to the dry cleaners and I thought I'd pop by to see if you've got it?"

"Got what, Mother?"

"My iPad! Did you find it at Sexton, Lovell & Billingsley?"

"Oh, no... sorry, Mother. No, it wasn't there."

"Oh..." My mother looked crestfallen. "I did think it was only a slim chance. I was there last Friday, you see, and I actually think that I lost my iPad on Saturday or Sunday..."

"Have you thought of every place you visited, Mrs Rose?" Cassie asked. "Go back over your movements last weekend—where did you go? What did you do?"

My mother set the laundry bag down and leaned against the counter, her brow furrowed in thought. "Well, as I said, I'm not sure if I lost it on Saturday night or Sunday... oh, wait a minute—it must have been Sunday because when I was over at Helen's place for tea on Sunday morning, I remember showing her a Times Online article on my iPad."

"Okay, good—now we've got a starting point," I said. "So you know you still had it with you on Sunday morning. Where did you go after that?"

"I went to the sale at Debenhmans... and then I stopped off to pick up the St Frideswide's charity gala tickets... speaking of which, are you getting your hair done for the event this evening, darling?"

Oh bugger. I'd completely forgotten about the charity gala ball. My hair was the least of my problems. I hadn't even given any thought to what I was going to wear, and now I wondered idly if I'd have time when I got home to remove that horrible stain from my black cocktail dress...

"Um... no, I'm fine, Mother, thanks." I ruffled my short pixie cut. "My hair doesn't need much styling."

My mother pursed her lips as she eyed my

Audrey-Hepburn-style crop—in her book, no real lady would have short hair—but for once, she didn't comment. Instead, she resumed going through her movements on Sunday.

"...and then I stopped by the garden centre—oh, there's a wonderful sale on yuccas, darling, you really must get one for your cottage; they have fleshy roots that search for water, you know!"

"Ooh, Gemma, sounds like a perfect housemate for you," teased Cassie, stifling a laugh. "Haven't you always wanted to live with something that has fleshy roots searching for water?"

I gave my best friend a mock glare, then turned back to my mother. "Uh... thanks, Mother, but I really don't need any more indoor plants right now. So... um... after the garden centre?"

She frowned. "I think I stopped at M&S, and then Sainsbury's to pick up a few supplies that were running low—or was it the other way around? Oh, and I popped into Boots the Chemist as well, on the way back... and then I went home. I made a late lunch for your father... and it wasn't until afterwards, when I was sitting down with a cup of tea and thinking of doing a crossword, that I realised my iPad was missing."

"And you've checked all of those places?"

"Yes."

"I'm sorry, Mother. I don't really know what else to suggest. But don't worry," I added quickly, seeing her woebegone expression. "If you've really lost your iPad, we can always get you a new one to replace it."

My mother sighed. "I would just hate to spend the money and then have the old one turn up..." She looked down and gave an exclamation of annoyance. I followed her gaze and saw that the laundry bag had fallen over and half the clothes had spilled out.

"How's Muesli, by the way?" I asked as I helped her pick up the clothes and stuff them back into the bag.

"Oh, she's a little darling. Your father gave her some pieces of roast chicken this morning and then he went out with her into the garden while she did her morning ablutions."

It sounded like Muesli was getting spoilt rotten. I wondered if she would want to come home with me tonight!

"I'll pick her up on my way back from work," I said.

"Wonderful, darling. Now, I must dash!"

With a peck on my cheek and a swirl of perfume, my mother was gone. Twenty minutes later, the tearoom was open and already bustling with customers. I smiled to myself as I stood at the counter, surveying the room. There might have been a murderer on the loose—and my troubles with Devlin still hung like a grey cloud on the horizon— but at least here, in my little world, everything was going well. People were busily eating and drinking, enjoying the delicious baking and traditional English teas, and the warm hubbub of happy conversation filled the tearoom.

And then—just as I was carrying a tray with teapot, teacups, and scones to the family sitting by the fireplace—the peace was shattered by a piercing scream.

"AAAAAAAAEEEEHHH!"

I jumped, nearly losing my grip on the tray, and I heard the clatter of crockery all around me as several people nearly dropped their cups. I turned quickly to see a woman standing up, pointing beneath her table.

"A cat! I saw a cat!"

Cassie and I exchanged startled looks. I hurried towards the woman.

"Excuse me, is there a problem?"

She turned to me, clutching a hand to her chest. "Oh, I got such a fright. I felt something furry brush against my leg, you see, and I looked down and there it was!"

"I think you must have imagined it," I said soothingly. "We don't have any cats here at the tearoom."

"No, no, I didn't imagine it!"

"Maybe you saw someone's shoe or bag and mistook it for a cat?"

She shook her head vehemently. "No, I'm telling you—it was definitely a cat. A little grey tabby."

A little grey tabby?

Suddenly I had a horrible suspicion.

"Er... could you describe the cat some more?" I asked.

"It was a grey tabby, with white chest and paws—and a little pink nose. Very big green eyes. Quite cute, actually."

Oh God.

The horrible suspicion was now a very bad feeling. The description sounded too much like Muesli to be coincidence. But how could she have been here?

I bent and looked nervously under the table. To my relief, I saw nothing. There was no cat. I straightened up again.

"There's nothing there," I told the woman.

She bent to look as well, then raised a bewildered face to me. "But I saw it! I swear I saw it—a little tabby cat."

I gave her a weak smile. "Well, there's nothing there now, so you don't have to worry about it anymore. I'm sorry you got a fright. Can I get you anything? Complimentary on the house."

"Oh, no, that's all right," said the woman with a smile. "I wasn't really frightened—I like cats—I was just startled, that's all. The food is delicious, by the way. The scones are absolutely scrumptious."

"Thank you!"

I kept my smile in place as I hurried back to join Cassie at the counter, but when I got there, I let the mask slip.

"What is it?" she asked me in an undertone.

"She thought she saw a cat."

Cassie rolled her eyes. "She must have been hallucinating—"

"Uh... actually, Cass..."

She stared at me. "What? You're not telling me you believe her?"

"When she described the cat, it sounded just like Muesli."

"Muesli? How can Muesli be here? I thought she was with your parents today?"

Without answering, I turned back to scan the room. Then I crouched down so that I could look through the legs beneath the tables. A sense of déjà vu assailed me. I remembered a fateful day, not long after I opened the tearoom, when I had been here, doing exactly the same thing: looking for Muesli while she ran loose in the tearoom... and then she had run under an American tourist's table...

I blinked, coming back out of my reminiscing, and straightened again. "I don't see her anywhere. Maybe it *was* just a coincidence," I said. "After all, grey tabbies are one of the most common cat colours so it's the one most people think of, right? So if you imagined that you saw a cat, that's probably how you'd describe it."

Cassie started to reply but she was interrupted by a yell of surprise. We turned to see a German tourist standing by his chair, looking down at it in bewilderment. I dashed across.

"What's wrong?"

"*Ja, da war eine katze...* there vas a cat," he said, pointing at his chair.

I looked. The chair was empty.

"*Ja... ja...*" He scratched his head, looking confused. "A *katze* vas here." Then he shrugged and sat down again, giving me a sheepish smile. "Maybe I am vrong."

I had a sinking feeling that he *wasn't* wrong but I was grateful that he seemed happy to forget the incident. I offered him more tea, then hurried back to the counter where Cassie was waiting.

"They can't have both imagined it," I said miserably. "Muesli must be here in the tearoom."

"But how did she get here?" Cassie demanded.

"The laundry bag!" I said suddenly. "She must have stowed away in the laundry bag!"

"Huh?"

"When my mother came in, she brought a laundry bag with her. I think Muesli must have climbed into that without my mother seeing. She can be really naughty like that. The other morning, she tried to stow away in my bicycle basket so she could come to work with me." I snapped my fingers. "Remember when the laundry bag fell over and all the clothes spilled out? Well, I don't think that was an accident now—that must have been Muesli scampering out. She must have hidden somewhere and no one noticed."

I turned to scan the room once more, hoping to

see a sign of the mischievous little feline. Then Cassie made a strangled noise next to me. I glanced back to see her staring through the tearoom windows.

"Oh shi—!" she bit off a curse, her eyes bulging. She grabbed my arm and pointed frantically. "Gemma! I think... I think that's the Food & Safety inspector!"

I followed her gaze, and my heart sank to my feet.

Oh my God. This couldn't have been happening to me. All those days of preparing for this inspection... and now the food inspector was here and I had a cat running loose in the tearoom!

CHAPTER TWENTY-ONE

I watched nervously as the food inspector approached our front door. It was the same pompous little man, with wire-rimmed glasses and a wispy goatee beard, who had come to inspect the tearoom when we first opened. Like last time, he was wearing a prim brown suit with the shirt buttons done up tightly all the way to his collar, and a white laboratory-style coat over one arm. He paused outside and leaned over to peer at our menu, which was displayed next to the front door, then opened the door and stepped in.

"Er... Mr Perkins, isn't it?" I said, a bright smile pinned on my face as I sailed forwards to greet him.

"You may call me Reginald," he said stiffly. He gave me a limp handshake, then wiped his hands fastidiously with an anti-bacterial wipe. "I trust that it is convenient for me to conduct an inspection?"

"Oh... yes, of course." I gave a nervous laugh. "I assume you'll be starting with the kitchen?" I said, trying to lead him in that direction.

But he resisted, instead glancing around the dining area. "No, I think I will start outside today. While we tend to concentrate on the food preparation areas, it behoves us to scrutinise the dining area thoroughly as well."

As he spoke, he began pacing the room, his hands clasped behind his back, his small eyes darting around. The customers looked at him curiously as he walked past, but he ignored them, his eyes scanning the windowsills and checking the floors around the tables. Finally, he finished his circuit of the room and came back to the counter to join me and Cassie. Leaning against it, he drew a notepad out of his suit pocket and began making some notes.

I stood politely next to him, all the while peering over his shoulder, trying to see any sign of Muesli around the tables. I was terrified that one of the customers might yell out suddenly about seeing a cat again. If only they could keep quiet and Muesli keep out of sight for the next half an hour, just until the inspection was over...

Cassie suddenly made a choking sound. I looked down and saw to my horror that a grey stripy tail was poking out from beneath the counter! It twitched backwards and forwards, just next to the food inspector's shoes.

"Ahh... shall we go in the kitchen now?" I blurted, desperate to move him away from the counter before he saw Muesli's tail.

"Just a minute," said the food inspector. "I'd like to inspect your lavatory facilities, to ensure that they are adequate and connected to an effective drainage system, and do not open directly into rooms where you handle food."

"Oh... but you checked last time, didn't you? It's exactly the same—"

"Nevertheless, I shall make another inspection."

Reluctantly, I turned to lead him out of the dining room. As I let him pass me out of the room first, I glanced back over my shoulder and made frantic gestures at Cassie. She nodded and crouched down. Hopefully, she'd catch Muesli while we were out of the dining room and shove the little minx somewhere safe until the food inspector left.

I dragged out the visit to the toilets as long as I dared, showing Reginald the flush mechanisms and soap dispensers with the enthusiasm of a bathroom plumbing salesman. We were there for a good five minutes and I was beginning to feel sanguine, confident that Cassie would have sorted out Muesli by the time we returned. But as we were about to step back into the dining room, my best friend suddenly rushed out to meet us.

"I'll see the kitchen now—" the food inspector was saying when Cassie stepped into his path.

"Um... er... why don't you have a look outside... er... Reginald?" she said brightly. "There's a small courtyard area where we serve customers. I'm sure you'd like to inspect that."

I looked at her in surprise.

The food inspector shook his head. "No, that's fine. I'm happy with what I've seen of the service areas. Now, it's time we got to the main reason for my visit—the kitchen." He rubbed his hands in anticipation.

"Wait... er...." Cassie gave him a dazzling smile. "Um... Reginald... Reggie... can I call you Reggie? I was wondering... um... would you be free this Saturday night?"

He blinked. "I'm sorry?"

Cassie gave him a flirtatious wink. "Well, I just thought... it might be nice to have a... a drink together or something..."

I stared at Cassie in astonishment. Next to me, the food inspector turned a bright shade of red and adjusted his collar, seeming at a loss for words. And no wonder. With her dark gypsy looks and voluptuous figure, Cassie was every man's idea of a dream date—and the last person that Reginald the Stuffy Food Inspector would have expected to ask him out for a drink!

While he was stammering a reply, Cassie made frantic beckoning motions to me behind his back. I looked at her quizzically.

She leaned over and said, low, "Er, Gemma...

you know that Swiss cereal we were talking about earlier? I thought you'd like to know... it's in the kitchen."

"In the *kitchen*?" I stared at her in horror. "What's she doing—*ahem*," I coughed and hastily amended: "What's the cereal doing in the kitchen?"

Cassie shrugged helplessly. "It... uh... sort of slipped in when I was... uh... trying to put it somewhere else."

Oh help.

I glanced at the food inspector, who was still flushed and stammering: "... m-much as I am f-flattered by your... interest... er, that is to say... er... in-invitation... for s-social interaction outside the w-workplace... I-I-I feel that it would b-be a breach of my... er... p-professional..."

Leaving him still stammering to Cassie, I hurried past them and rushed into the kitchen. I burst in to find Dora peering under the big wooden table.

"Oh, Gemma—I'm glad you're here," she said fretfully. "I don't know how but your cat, Muesli, is here at the tearoom! She darted into the kitchen just now when I opened the door to have a word with Cassie—and now I don't know where she's gone!"

"It's even worse," I said. "The food inspector is on his way in here. Cassie's trying to stall him, to give us more time, but—"

Before I could finish, the kitchen door swung open behind me and the food inspector stepped in, his cheeks still red, followed by Cassie, looking slightly queasy. She raised her eyebrows at me and I gave her a faint shake of my head.

"I'll go out and look after the customers while you're busy in here," Dora offered, giving us both an encouraging smile.

We hovered uneasily behind Reginald as he began walking around the kitchen, inspecting surfaces, looking under counters, running his finger along shelves, even shining a torch into every nook and cranny. As he went, he absent-mindedly straightened the jars and boxes so that they lined up perfectly on the shelves, and adjusted the ingredients in the pantry so that all the labels were facing outwards. Cassie and I exchanged a look: talk about OCD!

Still, I was grateful that he was too absorbed to pay much attention to his surroundings—just in case a twitching grey tail should suddenly appear. But thankfully, Muesli seemed to have decided to make herself scarce and the inspection was completed at last without any sign of a paw or whisker. Cassie and I exchanged another look, this time filled with relief, and we relaxed slightly. *Almost there!*

The food inspector paused by the wooden table in the centre of the kitchen and looked down its long length. "Is this surface regularly disinfected?"

"Oh, certainly," I said.

"Hmm..." He looked at the table again, then

220

reached out to the tray of lemon meringue pies cooling next to him and fastidiously re-arranged them with a pair of tongs, so that there wouldn't be a gap in the centre. As I watched him, something clicked in my brain. In my mind's eye, I saw a similar collection of lemon meringue pies, also with a gap in the centre.... I frowned, puzzled as to why the image had come to my mind. Then I remembered: the funeral reception. It had been after the service, when I had come back to transfer the remaining food from the fridge to the buffet table; I had noticed the platter of lemon meringue pies with a gap in the middle.

Reginald looked up and gave me a nod. "I believe that completes my inspection. You shall have my report in a few days." Then—with a last wistful look at Cassie, which made her squirm—he bade us goodbye and left.

Cassie and I collapsed into chairs, weak with relief. As soon as the kitchen door had swung shut behind him, Muesli's little head popped out from behind the pantry door.

"*Meorrw?*"

"Muesli!" I glared at her. "You minx—look at the trouble you nearly got us into!"

The little tabby ignored me, trotting sedately over and hopping up on the chair next to us, to begin washing her face.

Cassie gave a great sigh. "Bloody hell, that was close! I thought he was going to catch us out for sure!" She pulled a face. "And I nearly ended up having to fend off dear Reggie's fastidious advances on Saturday night!"

I laughed. "That would have been a pretty noble sacrifice."

"Thank goodness his professional ethics saved me!" Cassie chuckled. She reached a hand towards the lemon meringue pies. "Do you think Dora will notice if I nick one? Ohhh... I really need a sugar fix after that!"

She snagged one of the pies from the tray, leaving a big gap in the centre, and bit into it blissfully. I glanced at the empty space in the middle, then shook my head and laughed at my friend.

"You're terrible, Cass—I know you love the lemon meringue pies but you're developing a bad habit." I gave her a teasing look.

"What do you mean?"

"You're always pinching one from the tray!"

"No, I'm not!" she protested.

"Yes, you are—you did it at the funeral last weekend."

She stared at me. "What on earth are you on about, Gemma? I didn't pinch any food at the funeral."

"Yeah, right," I said, grinning. I glanced at my little tabby cat, who had finished washing and was now curled up happily on the chair, dozing off. "Anyway, do you think it's safe enough to leave

Muesli here for the rest of the day?"

Cassie finished off the pie and licked the crumbs from her fingers. "Yeah, I think she'll probably sleep for a few hours now."

The kitchen door swung open and Dora poked her head in. "Is the inspection finished? I saw the man leaving."

Cassie and I sprang up guiltily. "Oh, yes—sorry, Dora. Didn't mean to leave you alone out there with the customers."

"That's all right. There aren't so many at the moment—and I've served most of them. There's just the Canadian gentleman in the far corner who hasn't had his order taken yet."

"Canadian gentleman?" Cassie said hopefully.

Dora gave her an apologetic look. "No, not him, Cassie. This is someone else. I'm sorry."

"Oh." Cassie's face fell.

"He might still come back," I consoled my friend. "Maybe he's gone to some of the other Cotswolds villages to do some sightseeing and he'll pop back in when he comes round this way again."

Cassie nodded silently but I could see her shoulders drooping and the sparkle going out of her eyes. I sighed. I wished there was some way I could help. I was half tempted to call her up anonymously and pretend to be a buyer—but I knew that she would never forgive me if she found out that I had done that just to soothe her feelings. What Cassie needed was a "real" buyer for her art—and that was something I couldn't conjure up, no matter how much I wanted to.

***

We were almost closing for the day when I had a nice surprise: the door to the tearoom opened and a red-haired girl stepped in.

"Caitlyn!" I said with delight as she came up to the counter. "How nice to see you!"

The other girl smiled shyly. "I hope you don't mind—you said I should come to see your tearoom..."

"Of course I don't mind!" I said, laughing. "I'm delighted that you took me up on my invitation. This is my best friend, Cassie Jenkins." I introduced the two girls. "This is Caitlyn—sorry, I never got your last name?"

Caitlyn smiled and held out her hand. "It's Le Fey. Caitlyn Le Fey."

"How's your ankle?" I asked.

She held her foot up and rotated it for us to see. "Almost as good as new."

"It's healed really quickly," I said.

"Actually, it was still quite sore yesterday morning," Caitlyn said, grimacing at the memory. "I think I might have torn a ligament or something. Anyway, my cousin rang from the States and told me that I should get some acupuncture... and I remembered Professor Clifford mentioning that he had regular sessions. So I called him yesterday and got the name of his therapist. She's a lovely lady from Taiwan and has been practising traditional Chinese medicine for years. She's got a clinic here in the village. That was one reason I came out to Meadowford today. I've just been to have a session with her and I have to say—although the needles look scary—my ankle feels fantastic now!"

Cassie shuddered. "Rather you than me. I think I would have just popped a bunch of painkillers."

"How did you come out to Meadowford?" I asked. "You didn't take the bus?"

"No, I wanted to, but my ankle was a bit too painful, so I got a taxi," said Caitlyn. "Is that what you do—take the bus in every day?"

"No, I cycle," I said.

"Really? All the way from Oxford?"

"It's not that far—and if you know some of the back lanes, you can avoid a lot of the main roads with traffic. Besides, cycling helps keep off the calories." I gave her a wry smile. "Occupational hazard of running a tearoom famous for delicious baking is that you end up eating your own menu all day."

She laughed. "I can imagine. Actually, it must be so much nicer to cycle and get the exercise and fresh air, rather than commuting by car. I hate long road trips—maybe because I've had to do so many of them." She saw my curious expression and added, "My mother was a singer, you see. She was often on the road, touring and giving concerts, plus she didn't like to settle anywhere for too long, so I pretty much grew up like a nomad."

"Is your mother touring in the U.K. at the moment?" asked Cassie.

"No, my mother's dead," said Caitlyn softly. "She died in a car crash a few weeks ago."

"Oh! I'm so sorry to hear that," I exclaimed.

She hesitated, then said, "Well, actually, she wasn't my real mother. I only found out after the funeral... I was adopted."

"Wow," said Cassie, giving her a sympathetic look. "That must have been a pretty big shock for you."

The red-haired girl gave an ironic smile. "Yeah, understatement of the year."

I looked at her curiously. "If you don't mind my asking—what were you doing in Professor Clifford's office the other day?"

"Well, it's a bit of a long story..." She hesitated. "The reason I came to England is because I'm trying to find my real mother—my real family—and I thought Professor Clifford might be able to help me. He's an expert on ancient stone circles, like Stonehenge, and especially on the rune symbols carved on them."

I wondered how that would help her find her family but since she didn't volunteer any more information, I didn't want to pry. Instead, I gave her a smile and said, "I haven't even asked you: would you like a cup of tea?"

Caitlyn laughed. "I just love that about England. Everyone is always offering you tea, any time of the day or night!" She nodded. "Yes, I'd love a cup."

"Have something to eat too," said Cassie, handing her a menu. "We might have run out of some items though, since it's quite late in the day."

Caitlyn scanned the menu. "Wow, everything sounds so good... Oh, and they're even marked as vegetarian and gluten-free—that's really thoughtful."

"Yes, that was Cassie's idea," I said, giving my best friend a grateful smile. "The customers really appreciate it. Although, I have to say, we were debating how far to go. I mean, with the special diets going around nowadays, you could end up adding a whole extra page to the menu. There's gluten-free, lactose-free, organic, vegetarian, vegan, Paleo, contains eggs, contains nuts..."

"I know!" Caitlyn chuckled. "You should see my cousin, Pomona. She lives in Hollywood and she's always on some fad diet or another. She's tried the Atkins Diet, the Grapefruit Diet, the Three-Hour Diet, the Lemonade Diet... Oh, and the latest one she's trying is the Blood Type Diet—you know, when you eat according to your blood type."

I looked at her with interest. "You know, that's really funny. Someone was telling me about the Blood Type Diet the other day. She was really raving about it."

"She should get together with my cousin," said Caitlyn with a laugh. "Pomona's been talking my ear off about it! I now know far more about blood groups and their appropriate diets than I'll ever want to."

"It sounded really restrictive to me, though," I said, making a face. "For instance, this girl, Rachel, was telling me that she can't digest meat properly so she has to stay away from chicken and red meat; she can't eat shellfish, she can't eat... a whole bunch of things—even oranges, because supposedly they will irritate her stomach and interfere with her absorbing minerals or something... I mean, what's there left to eat?"

"She sounds like a Type AB," said Caitlyn. "Apparently, they've got it the worst because they inherit all the problems of Type As and Type Bs combined."

Cassie snorted. "Sounds more like a load of bollocks, if you ask me."

Caitlyn laughed. "You're probably right. Anyway, I don't care what diet I'm breaking but I'm going to have a big order of scones with home-made jam and clotted cream."

"Very good choice," said Cassie with an approving grin. "Now, that's what I call a Delish-Type diet!"

CHAPTER TWENTY-TWO

"I hope we can find parking," Lincoln commented as he drove his Land Rover into the car park adjacent to St Frideswide's College.

We were arriving late to the charity gala ball, as Lincoln had had an emergency callback to the ICU just as he was leaving the hospital. When I found out that my mother and Helen Green were going too, I had suggested that it would be simpler for me to go with them first—to save Lincoln having to come and pick me up—but they insisted that we go together. *No doubt to give me and Lincoln more "alone time" in the car*, I thought, rolling my eyes.

Still, I didn't mind being a bit late. To be perfectly honest, I would have been happy to skip the evening altogether. What with the tense family dinner followed by the Old Biddies' hotel escapades the night before, and then the stressful episode with the food inspector today, I was really desperate for a quiet evening at home and an early night, just to relax and recharge. But it wouldn't have been fair to Lincoln to stand him up at the last minute, so I had reluctantly dragged out my black chiffon cocktail dress, put on some make-up, and made myself ready for the evening.

"If you can't find any spaces here, there's more parking over on that side, behind that row of trees," I said, pointing to the far end of the car park.

"You seem to be very familiar with St Frideswide's parking," Lincoln said with a chuckle.

"Not really. It's only because I was here a few days ago and I happened to notice the extra parking spots then, when I was looking out of Professor Clifford's window. Miles Clifford," I explained at his puzzled look. "He's Rex Clifford's younger brother and Adele Clifford's brother-in-law; you know, the woman who died from the arsenic poisoning."

"I didn't realise that he's an Oxford don. What's his subject?"

I frowned. "Some obscure thing I'd never heard of—archaeo-something? Astro-something? Archeo... archeoastronomy. Yes, that's it. It's the way ancient man used to understand the sky, I think." I leaned forwards suddenly and peered through the windscreen at a tall, distinguished-looking older man and a young woman getting out of a car. "Oh—talk of the devil—that's him there! And that's his niece, Rachel Clifford, Adele's stepdaughter."

"They must be coming to the charity gala as well," said Lincoln, observing their formal attire. "Probably not surprising, given that it's being held at his college."

We found a space and parked, but as I was following Lincoln towards the side entrance of the college, I glanced back and noticed that Rachel and her uncle were huddled by a lamp post at the far end of the car park. I frowned. What were they doing?

"Gemma?" Lincoln stopped a few yards ahead and looked back at me questioningly.

"Um... Listen, Lincoln, do you mind going in alone first? I've just got to do something. I'll see you in a moment."

Before he could protest, I turned and hurried back across the car park. As I got closer to Rachel and her uncle, I slowed my steps, approaching more cautiously and hunching down slightly, so that I was hidden behind the row of cars between us. I was glad now that I'd chosen to wear black and could blend easily into the shadows. I was able to get quite near them without being seen, and realised that they were not alone. There was someone talking to them. I caught a glimpse of a black trench coat.

Tyler Lee.

Cautiously, I crept closer, until I was huddled behind the car parked next to where they were standing, and strained my ears to hear what they were saying.

"...your ridiculous demand!" came Rachel's voice, sharp and angry.

Tyler Lee started to say something in reply, but Miles Clifford's deep voice cut in.

"I don't think we should waste any more time speaking with this gentleman, my dear." He put a hand under his niece's elbow, but she shook him off.

"No! I'm not letting this go. It was bad enough at the funeral—and now he has the bloody cheek to come and tell me he wants half my father's estate!"

"I have just as much right as you," said Tyler Lee, sounding like a whining teenager. "You might not like it but your father loved my mother and he would have wanted to provide for me! You can't deny me my share of the inheritance."

Rachel tossed her head. "How do I know you're not a fraud? You don't even carry his name—how do I know you are who you say you are?"

"I have a letter from Rex Clifford to my mother," Tyler Lee blustered.

"That's hardly proof! Letters can be easily forged," said Rachel scornfully. "I want something definite—like a DNA test."

Tyler Lee scowled. "No! Why should I have to take a DNA test to prove myself to you? I mean, you could be a fraud as well!"

Rachel gave a shout of laughter. "Are you

serious? You've got to be joking! I've lived with my father all his life! My mother was married to him. This is the most ridiculous conversation—"

"Well, if you don't have to provide DNA evidence to claim his estate, then I don't see why *I* should," said Tyler Lee stubbornly.

"Fine!" snarled Rachel. "I'll call your bluff. If you do the test, then I will too. And if you can prove that you're a Clifford, then I'll honour your claim. In fact, I'll go and take the test tomorrow. There! Then we'll see how you—"

"Wait, Rachel... is this wise?" asked Miles Clifford urgently. "You don't know anything about this man. You could be placing yourself in—"

"Oh, don't worry, Uncle Miles," said Rachel with a derisive laugh. "I doubt he'll be able to come through."

Her uncle made a sound of impatience. "Yes, but you shouldn't even be speaking to him without consulting a solicitor. In fact, you should really just let Sexton deal with—"

A sports car drove into the car park suddenly with a roar of engines, its headlights swinging in an arc and catching us in its glare. I ducked down quickly behind the body of the car and peeked from the side. I saw Miles Clifford take advantage of the interruption to grasp his niece's elbow and try to lead her away from Tyler Lee. Rachel seemed to resist for a moment, then allowed herself to be steered away. They hadn't gone a few steps, however, when Lee called after them. I couldn't hear what he said over the sound of the car engine throbbing in the background, but I saw Professor Clifford's mouth tighten. He turned back and said something to the young man, then grabbed his niece's elbow again and hustled her away. Lee stood watching them for a moment, then he, too, melted into the shadows beyond the car park and disappeared.

I waited until Rachel and her uncle had gone into the college's side entrance before straightening up from my cramped hiding position. Slowly, I followed them into the college, my mind going over what I had seen and overheard. It had been bold of Tyler Lee to approach Rachel like that. Could he have really been Rex Clifford's son, and able to back up his claim to the inheritance?

I entered the ballroom and found Lincoln standing with our mothers, a glass of wine in each hand. He looked up with relief as I joined them and offered me one of the glasses.

"I was just about to come and look for you," he commented.

"Sorry," I said as I accepted the glass. "I... um... had to fix something with my dress."

"Darling, why don't you have a dance with Lincoln?" said my mother from behind us. "Helen says he is the most wonderful dancer!"

"Actually, that is most definitely *not* true," said Lincoln to me in an undertone. "The most I can promise is to try my best not to step on your toes."

I laughed and let him lead me onto the dance floor. Like a typical Englishman, Lincoln had talked himself down and I discovered that, in fact, he was a pretty good dancer. The dance floor was quite crowded and yet Lincoln led me expertly through the steps without stepping on my feet or bumping into anyone else.

"You dance well," I said.

He flushed slightly. "Thank you. It's easy when one has a lovely partner," he added gallantly.

I smiled and let him twirl me around. As I stepped back into his arms, I caught sight of both our mothers sitting together, nodding their heads and beaming as they watched us dance. I felt a pang of guilt. I knew that nothing would make my mother happier than for me to be with Lincoln and—as I glanced surreptitiously up at him—I had a momentary, treacherous thought that life with this man would be so simple and uncomplicated. Maybe I was silly not to appreciate that? It would be like this evening, I thought—I hadn't wanted to come but, now that I was here, I found that I was enjoying myself. There was something to be said for the simple pleasures of good music, nice atmosphere, pleasant company... and not a sinister suspect or mysterious murder in sight...

Even as I had the thought, my eyes caught sight of someone on the other side of the ballroom and my grip on Lincoln's hands tightened inadvertently.

Surprised, Lincoln turned his head to see who I was looking at and said:

"Oh, I didn't realise Kate would be here tonight."

"Do you know her?" I asked as I watched Rachel Clifford talking earnestly to her girlfriend. I wondered where her uncle was, then I caught sight of him quite close to us, dancing with a middle-aged woman in a green velvet dress.

"Kate Markby? Yes, she's a nurse at the hospital."

"Is she nice?"

Lincoln gave a polite laugh. "Well, I don't know her socially, of course. She's... she's a good nurse, but she can be quite... er... difficult to work with."

I'll bet, I thought. From the little I'd seen of Kate Markby, I doubted she would win Personality of the Year.

"How do *you* know her?" asked Lincoln.

"Oh, I saw her at the Clifford funeral and also met her when I went to visit Rachel. She's Rachel's friend."

"Ah yes, actually, that was one of the reasons I'd seen more of Kate recently. When Rex Clifford was in Intensive Care after his operation, she used to often accompany Rachel when the latter came to see her father."

"Was he in the ICU for long?"

"Yes. He had major heart surgery and became profoundly anaemic, and needed a blood transfusion. Because he was Type O—that's the hardest one to match—the blood banks were in short supply, so he ended up having an extended stay in ICU."

"Why is Type O the hardest to match?" I asked curiously.

Lincoln shrugged. "That's just the way it is. Type O is known as the 'universal donor'—they can give blood to all the other types: A, B, and AB—but they can only receive blood from other Type Os."

"Couldn't his daughter have given him blood? I mean, she's his daughter, so they must share the same blood, right?"

"No, it's not like DNA. You can have a totally different blood type from your parents—although their type does affect your possibilities."

"What do you mean?"

"Well, for example, if you're Blood Type AB, then your parents have to be Type A or B or AB. They can't be O."

"Oh—you mean like eye colour? Like you can only have blue eyes if one of your parents has blue eyes?"

Lincoln laughed. "Eye colour is what we call polygenic inheritance, so it's more complicated than that. You *can* actually have blue eyes, even if both your parents have brown eyes."

"Well, I suppose—oops! Sorry!"

I felt myself bump into another body and step on the hem of a dress. I turned around to find an irate-looking middle-aged woman in a green velvet gown glowering at me. It was the woman I had seen dancing with Professor Clifford. He was standing next to her, his face set in its usual courteous expression, and I felt slightly embarrassed, wondering if he might have overheard us discussing his family again.

We danced away from them and when they were safely out of earshot, I said to Lincoln:

"Um... I don't suppose you've heard any rumours about Kate?"

"What sort of rumours?"

"Well... there's a lot of gossip in the village that she and Rachel are closer than usual girlfriends."

"Ah." Lincoln gave me an understanding smile. "I'm afraid you're asking the wrong person. I'm not really plugged into the hospital grapevine. And as I said, I don't know Kate that well myself, since we don't work in the same department."

"Oh? She isn't in Intensive Care? Which department is she in, then?"

"She's on the Oncology Ward," said Lincoln. "She deals with cancer patients, organises their chemotherapy."

I stared at him. "Did you say chemotherapy?"

"Yes. Why?"

"When we were talking about arsenic the other night, you told me that it's really hard to get hold of the poison these days and that one of the few sources was from chemotherapy drugs, right?"

Lincoln looked slightly surprised. "Yes, you're

right. Just one particular chemotherapy drug, actually. Arsenic trioxide, which is used to treat acute promyelocytic leukaemia. It comes in concentrated ampoules."

"And would Kate have easy access to those ampoules?"

Lincoln frowned. "Possibly. It depends on what type of cancer patients she looks after. But, wait... you're not suggesting that Kate is the murderer?"

"I don't know what I'm suggesting," I said grimly. "All I know is that, previously, Rachel was considered a lesser suspect because there seemed to be no way for her to get access to the poison. But now I'm discovering that her girlfriend can easily get her hands on some concentrated arsenic solution..."

Lincoln laughed. "You never stop, do you, Gemma? Even at a party, your thoughts are on the murder."

I gave him a sheepish smile. "Sorry. Okay, I promise—I won't mention the murder again tonight."

"Oh, don't worry on my account! I enjoy listening to you speculate. At least conversation with you is never boring."

As he spoke, Lincoln suddenly twirled me around again. The motion caught me unawares and I tripped, falling against him.

"Oops!" said Lincoln, laughing as he caught me in his arms.

"Sorry!" I said, holding onto his shoulders and

laughing as well. The spin had made me slightly dizzy and I had to lean on him for support. "Looks like I'm going to be the one stepping on *your* toes," I giggled, tossing my head back and laughing up at him.

Then I glanced over Lincoln's shoulder and looked straight into Devlin's stony blue eyes.

CHAPTER TWENTY-THREE

I gasped, the smile fading from my face, and jerked away from Lincoln, putting as much distance between us as possible. Lincoln looked at me quizzically, then turned and followed my gaze. He saw Devlin and a look of guilt crossed his face, which didn't exactly help matters. Devlin stared at us for a moment longer, then he turned and disappeared into the crowd.

I felt my heart pounding uncomfortably. *What is Devlin doing here? Did he see me trip and fall? Does he realise that I wasn't in Lincoln's arms on purpose?* I knew how compromising it must have looked with me in another man's arms, leaning against him, laughing up at him... I had a sudden urge to rush after Devlin and cry: "It's not what you think!"

Then I felt a flicker of irritation with myself. Why

should I have felt guilty? I knew I hadn't been flirting with Lincoln Green! I hadn't done anything wrong and it wasn't my fault if Devlin should jump to conclusions.

"Um... that was Devlin, wasn't it?" said Lincoln nervously. "Do you think we should... Maybe we should get off the dance floor."

I hesitated, then tossed my head. I refused to scurry off the dance floor like some guilty miscreant. "No. Let's finish the dance," I said firmly.

Lincoln gave me a dubious look. However, he obediently took my hands and we fell back into step with the music once more. But all the gaiety and enjoyment was lost. We finished the dance in silence, then Lincoln escorted me to the side of the room. As the crowd parted, I suddenly saw Devlin. He was in conversation with the Toastmaster, but his eyes flickered as he saw us. He nodded to the man, thanked him, and walked over to meet us.

"Uh... Hi Devlin," I said as casually as I could.

The two men nodded at each other, Devlin aloof whilst Lincoln looked intensely uncomfortable.

"I'm... er... just going to see if our mothers need any more refreshments," said Lincoln and hurried away.

Left alone with Devlin, I said with forced cheerfulness, "Fancy seeing you here! I... um... I was going to call you today but then things got a bit crazy at the tearoom... We had this nightmare visit from the food inspector and then... anyway, um...

so what are you doing here?"

"I'm working," he said coldly. "I'm looking for Tyler Lee."

"Tyler Lee?"

"He's done a bunk from the hotel. They found his room empty, his things gone, and his bill unpaid. They rang the police and CID got involved, since he's connected to an open murder inquiry. I managed to track him here via a taxi company that had a record of picking him up from the Cotswolds Manor Hotel."

"What about Inspector Pratt?" I asked. "I would have thought that he wouldn't want anyone stepping on his turf."

"A message has been sent to Pratt but I got the call first and I'm not waiting around for that joker to get his act together," said Devlin. "He should have put a tail on Lee. Now he's let a potential murder suspect escape. I'm not leaving the investigation in his hands any longer."

"Have you seen Tyler Lee?"

"No, I've just spoken to the Toastmaster and he hasn't seen anyone fitting Lee's description."

"I saw him outside."

Devlin looked at me sharply. "Outside?"

"Yes, in the car park. When I arrived with Lincoln—I saw Tyler Lee talking to Rachel Clifford and her uncle."

"Where?"

"On the far side, by one of the lamp posts... I... I

can show you, if you like?"

Devlin's eyes flickered across the room. "What about your date?"

I flushed. "Lincoln's not my date. I mean, he is... but more in the sense of being an escort than a... a romantic partner..." I trailed off uncomfortably.

Devlin said nothing for a moment, then he turned and waved mockingly towards the ballroom entrance. "Shall we?"

I led the way outside, trying to keep my steps casual and my expression serene, but inside, I felt like a tightly wound spring. I wished Devlin would just come out and say something—anything—about Lincoln and me, about what he had seen. I had dreaded a confrontation but this icy reserve was almost worse.

We stepped out into the now deserted car park. The music from the ballroom drifted out faintly behind us, sounding almost eerie in the still night air. I led the way past the rows of parked cars to the far side where a lamp post stood on the boundary which divided the car park from the trees and shrubbery beyond.

"It was here." I pointed to the spot underneath the lamp post. "I saw them standing there together, talking."

"Didn't they see you?"

I shook my head. "I kept hidden behind this row of cars—they couldn't see me at all. In fact, I got quite close—close enough to hear some of what they were saying."

I repeated the conversation I had overheard and Devlin listened, his brow furrowed thoughtfully.

"Hmm... DNA test..."

"There's more," I said. And I told him what Lincoln had told me about Kate Markby and her access to arsenic trioxide ampoules in the Oncology Ward. "It means that Rachel could have had an easy source of the poison, through her girlfriend."

Devlin didn't comment.

I looked at him and gave a hesitant smile. "I'm so glad you're back on the case, Devlin. At least there's a real chance of finding the murderer now, with you in charge. Pratt is useless—all he does is hound Mabel Cooke—we need you and your brains."

"I'm surprised you need me for anything," said Devlin caustically. "Why don't you just ask the eminent Dr Green? He seems to have all the answers."

I flushed. "Devlin... what you saw... it isn't what you think—"

"You don't have to explain anything to me," said Devlin tightly. "I'm well aware that everyone thinks I'm not good enough for you, Gemma, but I thought that you would at least have the decency to tell me to my face if you felt the same way. Not string me along, while playing around behind my back."

"That's unfair!" I cried. "I told you, it's not what you think—"

"I know what I saw."

"If you would just let me explain instead of jumping to conclusions!" I cried, angry now. "I never thought you'd be like this, Devlin O'Connor—behaving like a Neanderthal just because I had a dance with another man!"

"I would have thought that my reaction was perfectly reasonable considering that I found my girlfriend *in the arms of* another man!" he said through clenched teeth. "Or maybe that kind of behaviour is considered acceptable in polite society? I may not be posh but where I come from, trust and fidelity in a relationship mean something."

"Oh, that's rich, coming from you!" I said hotly. "Like you haven't been secretly running around town yourself with some mysterious blonde!"

Devlin frowned at me. "What? What are you talking about?"

"Don't pretend you don't know!" I snapped.

"I *don't* know!" said Devlin impatiently. "You sound like you're insinuating that I'm cheating on you."

"I'm not insinuating—I know! You were seen! Lincoln told me he saw you with an attractive blonde woman—"

"Oh, *Lincoln* again... How convenient that *he* should be the one to see me..." said Devlin savagely. "And how nice of him to rush off and tell you."

"It wasn't like that! Lincoln just happened to see you at the hospital the evening I had that injury from the Krav Maga class and he mentioned it to me because he thought you were coming to visit me. He wasn't trying to... to snitch on you on purpose—he's a gentleman."

"And I'm not?"

I flushed. "That's not what I meant!" Taking a deep breath, I added, "Anyway, you haven't answered my question. I asked you about her—the blonde woman—when you took me on that picnic to the Botanic Gardens, and you acted all weird and evasive. So..." I swallowed. "So if you're not having an affair... then who is she?"

Devlin was silent for a long moment. Then he said quietly, "She's my mother."

I stared at him. *"Your mother?"*

"My mother came down to Oxford for a visit. She needed some treatment at the hospital and I was escorting her."

"B-but..." I stammered, confused. "But if it was your mother... why didn't you just say so? Why didn't you tell me?"

He hesitated. "It's complicated."

"What's that supposed to mean?" I asked, annoyed. "What could be complicated about telling your girlfriend about your mother?"

Devlin gave an impatient sigh. "It's hard to explain, okay? I wasn't sure I could trust you to understand—"

I drew back, stung. "You couldn't trust me?"

"Yes, I didn't think I could trust you, Gemma," said Devlin, giving me a bitter look. "And to be honest, the way you behaved at dinner with your parents made me think that I was right!"

"I just wanted you to make a good impression," I said defensively.

"No, you wanted me to be something I'm not— something I'll never be—just to please your parents and their stuck-up friends!"

I glared at him. "You know what your problem is, Devlin? You always want everything on your terms! You're never willing to bend a little, to try and meet people halfway! It wouldn't have killed you to play along a bit, to show a different side and impress everyone—but no, you wouldn't do it, just because of your stubborn pride!"

"And you know what *your* problem is, Gemma? You care way too much what other people think! I thought you'd changed after all these years, grown a bit of a backbone at last—but no, you're still Mummy's Little Girl, desperate for her approval!" He took a step towards me, his voice coldly furious. "You threw away our chance of happiness eight years ago because you were scared that people would disapprove of me. Well, guess what? We're back here again."

I stared at him, trembling. Angry tears smarted in my eyes and I fought them back, determined not to cry in front of Devlin. I felt so hurt and furious and confused and... a million other things.

With a strangled sob, I turned and ran back into the ballroom.

CHAPTER TWENTY-FOUR

If getting up the morning before was hard, this morning was even worse. I really didn't feel like facing the world. All I wanted to do was curl up with a blanket over my head and try to forget last night ever happened—except now that I was awake, that terrible fight with Devlin kept playing like a loop in my head, with every horrible thing we'd said to each other echoing over and over. Pushing the memory away, I got dressed and, still trying not to think about it, went down to my usual routine of checking emails over breakfast.

Muesli wolfed down her own breakfast, then sauntered over to the garden door and looked back at me expectantly. *"Meorrw?"*

Argh. Not this again.

I got up and went to open the door. Muesli

hesitated on the threshold, but this time I didn't let her play her little game. I put a foot behind her furry bum and gently nudged her through, then shut the door firmly behind her and went back to my chair at the dining table, feeling smug.

There. That's how to deal with cats. Show them you're the boss—

A faint but persistent sound came from the garden door.

"Meorrw! Meorrw! Meorrw! Meorrw…"

I looked over. Muesli had her little face pressed up to the glass, demanding impatiently to be let back in.

Aaaaarrggghh! I groaned and dropped my head on the table.

No, I decided. *I said I'm the boss. I'm not going to let myself be dictated to by an eight-pound ball of fur.* She wanted to go out in the garden—well, now she could stay out. Resolutely I turned back to my computer screen. But after a moment, I couldn't help flicking my eyes back towards the garden door. Muesli was still there, staring intently at me through the glass.

I gritted my teeth and looked back at the screen. But it was as if Muesli's eyes were a laser beam, trained on me, making me feel more and more uncomfortable. Finally, I sighed and gave up. I got up, stomped across the room, and opened the door.

"Meorrw!" Muesli flicked her tail, sounding like she was saying: "About time!"

Then she sauntered slowly back into the room. I shut the door, making sure it was locked, then glared at my little cat.

"That's it! No more visits outside. You've got your litter tray, you've got your toys—I'm leaving now."

I stomped upstairs, checked that Pricklebum had clean bedding, food, and water for the day, then collected my bike and left the cottage. I arrived at the tearoom, still in a foul mood, and walked into the kitchen to find Cassie and Dora talking excitedly.

"Why the long face?" said Cassie when she saw me. "It's not because of the news, is it?"

"What news?" I asked.

"Haven't you heard? Tyler Lee has been found dead."

"What?" I stared at her disbelievingly.

Cassie nodded. "His body was found this morning, in the bushes next to the St Frideswide's College car park."

"Bloody hell..." I sank slowly into a chair.

Cassie cocked her head at me. "You're not really upset, are you?

I looked up at her. "What? Oh, no. I mean, it's terrible to have another murder, of course—I didn't particularly care for Tyler Lee but I wouldn't have wished him harm."

"Then why did you look so glum when you came in?"

I darted a glance at Dora, then said, "Shall we go

out and check the tables?"

Cassie obediently followed me out to the dining room, where we could have some privacy. "Well?" she said. "Is it something to do with the charity gala last night?"

I sighed. "It was a nightmare."

Cassie grinned. "Don't tell me: Lincoln tried to make a pass at you."

I winced. She couldn't have known how close that joke cut to the bone. "Devlin came to the ball and saw me with Lincoln."

Cassie gave me a sideways look. "You guys weren't—"

"No, of course not!" I cried. "How could you think that?"

Cassie shrugged. "Well, I know things have been a bit rocky between you and Devlin recently... and I knew you always sort of liked Lincoln—"

"Even if I did, I would never do anything behind Devlin's back! What do you take me for?"

Cassie put out a placating hand. "All right, all right—sorry! I know you wouldn't do it on purpose but sometimes when things get a bit messed up and you're unhappy... well, people make mistakes, have a lapse of judgement. It's only human."

"There was nothing between me and Lincoln," I said firmly. "We were just dancing and then I tripped and fell against him. He caught me in his arms and we were both laughing about it—and then Devlin walked in at that moment and saw us."

"Ouch." Cassie gave me a sympathetic look. "Did you explain?"

"I tried! He wouldn't listen! He was being an absolute pig, jumping to conclusions and making sarcastic comments about Lincoln... and accusing *me* of betraying the trust in our relationship! Can you believe it? When *he's* the one who's been running around with some strange woman and hiding things from me!"

"Did you ask him about the blonde?" asked Cassie.

"Yes." I calmed down slightly and gave my friend an exasperated look. "She's his mother."

"His *mother*?" Cassie gaped at me. "But... if it was his mother, why didn't he just tell you about her from the beginning?"

"That's exactly what I said! He told me it's 'complicated'." I rolled my eyes. "What on earth does *that* mean? I don't understand why it's such a big deal—why couldn't he just introduce us!"

"Do you know anything about his mother?" asked Cassie. "I've never heard Devlin mention her and I've known him a long time."

I gave a helpless shrug. "No, he would never talk about his family much, even back in college. All I knew was that his father left them when he was young and things were quite tough. Whenever I've tried to ask him more about his mother, he'd look uncomfortable and change the subject."

"People can be funny about their mothers

sometimes," said Cassie.

"Yeah, but he didn't even *try* to share things with me! In fact, he said he didn't trust me to understand. That's ridiculous! Why can't he trust me?" I cried, still hurt and angry. "He made some stupid comment about the way I acted at dinner with my parents—"

"Well..." Cassie gave me a sombre look. "I can sort of understand where he's coming from."

I looked at her indignantly. "What do you mean?"

"I can see why Devlin would feel a bit defensive and wary about opening up to you. I mean, that evening at your parents' place sounded like a disaster, with you and everyone else making him feel pretty sensitive about his working-class roots. I can just imagine it: him sitting at this table, surrounded by all these upper-middle-class snobs, and even *you* were putting pressure on him to fit into this perfect world..."

"Cassie! I thought you'd be on my side!"

"I *am* on your side," she said quickly. "But, Gemma, you've got to see it from his point of view."

"Well, *Devlin*'s not making any effort to see it from *my* point of view," I said, jutting my bottom lip out. "Why should I always be the one who is expected to change, when he won't at all? He was being so bloody pig-headed last night—and then he said I care too much about what other people think and that I was still desperate for my mother's approval... Don't you dare say he's right!" I said fiercely to Cassie.

She raised both hands in a gesture of surrender. "I'm not saying anything."

I glared at her, then crossed my arms and stalked to the tearoom windows. I stood there, looking out and fuming. For once, the view of the rolling Cotswolds hills in the distance didn't bring me a sense of peace and contentment.

Cassie came up to me and patted my arm gently. "Gemma, look... I know you're angry... but I think you need to go and speak to Devlin. Maybe even apologise."

I raised my chin. "Why should *I* be the one to apologise? He's just as much at fault as me!"

"Pride won't keep you warm at night," said Cassie.

I gave her a sour look. "Is that some cheesy line you picked up from a Hollywood movie?"

She laughed. "Probably. It doesn't make it less right, though. Look, Gemma, do you want to be with Devlin or not? If you do, then swallow your pride and go and speak to him. You're not—"

She was interrupted by the door bursting open and Glenda, Florence, and Ethel hurrying into the tearoom.

"Oh Gemma!" they cried. "You have to come quickly! Inspector Pratt's at Mabel's house. He says he's come to arrest her for Tyler Lee's murder!"

"What? Is the man a complete moron?" I said in disgust. "Why on earth would he think that Mabel has anything to do with Tyler Lee's death?"

The Old Biddies looked slightly guilty.

"Well, they found Tyler Lee's things near his body—his travel bag and such—and Mabel's fingerprints were on several of the items," explained Glenda.

I covered my face and groaned. I remembered now: the night we were in Tyler Lee's room at the Cotswolds Manor Hotel, Mabel had rummaged carelessly through the young man's things, dropping several on the floor and picking them back up again. Yes, her prints would be all over his stuff.

"Inspector Pratt asked Mabel why her prints were there, and of course she couldn't tell him the truth, otherwise he'd know that we'd sneaked into the hotel room when we shouldn't have—"

"And her caginess makes her look even more suspicious," I said with another groan. I glanced at Cassie. "Can you manage if I—"

"Go," said Cassie. "Don't worry about the tearoom. Dora and I will hold the fort."

I followed the Old Biddies back to the Cooke residence and found Pratt facing Mabel in the front hall, waving a piece of paper aggressively under her nose.

"...you're not going to get away with it anymore, Mrs Cooke! You think you're so smart, eh? Well, I'm smarter. And you know what this is? A search warrant for your house. I'm going to come in and I'm going to turn the place upside down—and I won't stop until I find proof that you are the murderer!"

Signalling to the two uniformed constables with him, Pratt pushed past Mabel and marched into the house. She pressed her lips together angrily but could do nothing to stop him. I hurried up to her and put a concerned hand on her arm.

"Mabel... are you all right?"

She drew herself up to her full height. "I'm fine, dear. Just a silly bit of nonsense!"

Nevertheless, I sensed that underneath the bravado, Mabel was slightly shaken. There was a horrible sense of violation when your house was invaded and all your possessions searched against your will. I stood together with the Old Biddies in a corner of the sitting room and watched helplessly as Pratt and the constables went through the house.

"Ah... what have we here?" said Pratt, eagerly opening a cardboard box that had been sitting on the coffee table. He began emptying the contents onto the table, then paused and snatched up a tiny bottle. He held this up to the light, reading the label on the bottle.

"What's this? It says '*Arsenicum album*'!" he cried triumphantly. He came over to Mabel and brandished the bottle in her face. "What do you have to say for yourself, Mrs Cooke?"

"What do you mean? That is a homeopathic remedy," said Mabel.

"Don't play the innocent with me! Do you think I

can't read the label here?" He jabbed a finger at the bottle. "It says *'Arsenicum album'*... this is an arsenic solution!"

My heart sank, but I spoke up: "Inspector, those are just herbal and alternative remedies to help digestion. I remember Mabel showing me that box the other day. Her daughter sent it from Australia—"

"Quiet!" he snapped. "I'm not asking you. I'm asking the suspect." He turned to Mabel. "Do you deny that this bottle of arsenic solution was found in your house?"

"I never denied it," said Mabel with great dignity. "But if you'll let me explain, you'll see that it doesn't—"

"I think you'd better do your explaining down at the station, Mrs Cooke," said Inspector Pratt. He raised his voice. "I'm hereby arresting you on suspicion of the murder of Adele Clifford and Tyler Lee. You do not have to say anything, but it may harm your defence if you do not mention, when questioned, something which you later rely on in court. Anything you do say may—"

"This is ridiculous!" I cried. "You can't arrest Mabel!"

"Madam, I can and I have," said Pratt smugly. He caught Mabel's arm and began leading her out of the house.

It was almost like a déjà vu of what had happened in the tearoom a few days ago, except that this time, Pratt looked triumphant and Mabel looked slightly stunned.

"Don't fret, dear," she murmured. "I'm sure it will all be sorted."

But for once, her voice lacked its usual conviction and the words felt empty. In fact, she seemed almost to have shrunk slightly, as she was led by Pratt out of the room. I followed them out of the house and watched, troubled, as Mabel was put into the police car and driven away. Next to me, the other Old Biddies huddled together, seeming suddenly older and a lot more vulnerable. It hurt me to see them like that.

"Mabel will be all right, won't she?" asked Ethel in a small voice.

"It's just a misunderstanding," said Florence weakly. "I'm sure they'll see that."

Glenda nodded hopefully. "Nobody could think that Mabel could really be a murderer."

I didn't say anything. But I didn't share their optimism. I knew that Mabel was innocent—but people had been wrongly convicted before on the flimsiest of circumstantial evidence. Pratt was too obsessed now with proving that Mabel was guilty to listen to reason. Even if he couldn't pin the murder on Mabel in the end, he could make life very unpleasant for her until the case was solved. And at the rate that he was proceeding, it could take weeks, even months.

No, I couldn't just sit here and watch Mabel

being harassed. But there was no point trying to reason with Pratt.

"Listen, where's Mabel's husband, Henry?" I asked.

"He's gone on a bird-watching trip with some friends. He's a very keen twitcher."

"Okay, do you know the Cooke's lawyer? Get in touch and make sure Mabel has a solicitor down at the station with her as soon as possible."

The three old ladies nodded soberly. Then they looked at me. "Where are you going, Gemma?"

I gave them a grim smile. "To find Devlin."

CHAPTER TWENTY-FIVE

I hesitated outside the courthouse, wondering if I should go inside. The duty sergeant had told me that Devlin would be here this morning, waiting to give evidence in a trial, and I had hoped to catch him in the waiting area outside the court. But now I felt torn. After our fight last night, I squirmed slightly at the thought of running back to Devlin for help. It seemed almost like a sign of weakness. But I also knew that I had important information which could be key to solving the case: I'd never told Devlin about my meeting with Tyler Lee in the Covered Market, nor my conversation with Gavin Sexton and my suspicions that the two men knew each other. With Lee now dead, that information could be crucial to finding his killer.

This was not personal, I told myself firmly. No,

no, this had nothing to do with our fight and I was *certainly* not here to apologise! I was just doing my civic duty—and helping Mabel—that's all.

The waiting area was disappointingly empty when I finally went into the building. I could hear the sounds of a court in session and wondered if Devlin was inside. For a moment, I debated sitting down and waiting, then changed my mind. I had no idea how long the trial was going to last and I didn't want to sit here twiddling my thumbs. I might as well go back to the tearoom first.

As I came out of the courthouse, however, I spied a black Jaguar XK parked on a side street and recognised Devlin's car. I walked over and hovered uncertainly beside the gleaming vehicle. *Should I leave him a note?* I could always just call him, of course, and leave him a voicemail, but for some reason I recoiled from doing that.

Then I heard a step behind me and a familiar deep male voice said:

"Gemma?"

I turned swiftly to see Devlin, looking as handsome and debonair as ever in a smartly tailored navy suit, his dark hair slightly ruffled by the breeze. He was holding a cup of takeaway coffee in one hand. I licked suddenly dry lips and wondered what to say. All my cool poise and carefully prepared speeches deserted me.

Devlin's blue eyes softened and he said gently, "You wanted to see me?"

He leaned against the car and looked at me expectantly. His manner was polite and formal, and in a strange way, it helped me relax a bit. It was easier to match his manner and pretend that this was just a "business" meeting, with no connection to the emotional scene the night before.

"Inspector Pratt has arrested Mabel!" I blurted.

Devlin cursed beneath his breath. "The stupid sod. What's he playing at?"

"You know Tyler Lee's body was found this morning?"

He nodded. "Yeah, I heard. He was strangled sometime last night, just before midnight. I've been tied up in the courts all morning on another case so I haven't been able to do much, but I was planning to get up to speed as soon as I got back to the station." He looked at me sharply. "But even Pratt can't arrest Mabel for no reason. There must have been something—"

"He... he found her fingerprints on Tyler Lee's things," I said, then rushed on before Devlin could ask why her prints were there. "And then he got a search warrant for her house and he found a bottle of arsenic solution."

"Arsenic solution?" Devlin looked startled.

"It was one of her stupid digestion remedies—you know how Mabel is always obsessed with her bowels—and her daughter had sent her a box of goodies from overseas. She was showing them to me the other day and I didn't even pay attention when she mentioned it. It's something called 'tincture of *arsenicum album*' and—"

"*Arsenicum album*?" Devlin repeated. He furrowed his brow. "That sounds familiar. I was doing some research on arsenic compounds the other day and I'm sure I came across that term..."

"It looks bad, though, doesn't it?" I asked. "I mean, it's *arsenic!*"

"It might not be as bad as you think," said Devlin, his voice reassuring. "I have a feeling this tincture of *arsenicum album* might be a red herring—something that Pratt would have known if he had done his research properly... But I need to get back to the station to check my sources..." He straightened from the car.

"Wait, Devlin... there's something else. It's about Tyler Lee. I... I don't know if it's important but I thought I'd better let you know, just in case... I should have mentioned it last night but..." I trailed off awkwardly.

"It's all right, just tell me now," said Devlin.

I took a deep breath and recounted my encounter with Tyler Lee in the Covered Market, followed by my conversation with Gavin Sexton at the lawyer's offices.

"Oh, and there was another thing," I added. "Gavin Sexton had some cigarettes—Chinese cigarettes—which are exactly the same as the ones found in Tyler Lee's room."

"How can you know that?" Devlin asked,

frowning at me. "The SOCO team only searched Lee's hotel room this morning and I haven't even seen the forensics report yet."

"Um... well, the Old Biddies and I sort of had a preview..."

Devlin gave an exasperated sigh. "What have you and those meddling old coots been doing now? Don't you realise that entering someone's hotel room without permission is illegal?"

"Of course I realise that! But you try telling that to Mabel and the others. They were already in the room when they called me. That was the night we were having dinner at my parents' place—you know, when I got that phone call—"

"Yes, I remember," said Devlin, his cheeks reddening slightly. "I didn't realise it really was the Old Biddies. You looked so guilty and were so keen for me to be gone after that, I thought it might have been... well, I thought it might have been Lincoln Green."

"What?" I stared at him. "Why on earth would you think that?"

Devlin gave a sheepish shrug. "I don't know... You're very friendly with him... His family is close to yours... He lives around the corner from your parents' house... I thought maybe he was calling you to invite you over for a nightcap or something."

"And you think that's why I rushed off?"

Devlin shrugged again, looking uncharacteristically unlike his usual confident self.

I felt my previous anger and indignation melt away. For the first time, I really saw things from his point of view: suffering through that dinner with his girlfriend sniping at him, seeing his "rival" being welcomed by my family, and then, the very next night, finding me in Lincoln's arms—it wasn't surprising that Devlin had lost his famous cool at the charity gala ball.

"Devlin, I promise you, there's nothing between Lincoln and me," I said gently. "We were dancing and I tripped and he caught me—that was all. And..." I hesitated, looking down, shamefaced. "And you were right... I... I behaved really badly at that dinner. I got so caught up in trying to impress my parents... I didn't think about how you would feel..."

Devlin stared at me for a moment, then he cleared his throat and looked away. "Yes. Well. To get back to the case... So you went to the Cotswolds Manor Hotel?"

"Yes, I found the Old Biddies stuck on a balcony—"

"Stuck on a what?"

"A balcony. *The* balcony to Tyler Lee's room, actually."

"How the hell did they get on his balcon—" Devlin broke off and shook his head. "Never mind. I don't think I want to know. In fact, the less I know about the Old Biddies' shenanigans, the better—otherwise I might be forced to arrest Mabel myself! I take it this is the reason her fingerprints were on Tyler Lee's things?"

I grinned. "Well, anyway, I... er... found a way to get into Tyler Lee's room—you don't want to know about that either," I added hastily, as I saw Devlin open his mouth to ask. "And while I was in there, I happened to see a packet of cigarettes on the desk. A Chinese brand. The same as the ones I saw the next morning in Gavin Sexton's briefcase. When I asked Sexton about it, he made up some lame story—just like he did when I asked him about speaking to Tyler Lee at the funeral. I saw them talking to each other, you see. Sexton claims that he was just checking to make sure Tyler Lee wasn't a gate-crasher, whereas Lee says Sexton asked him where the toilets were!" I rolled my eyes. "But I *saw* them—they were arguing about something. They definitely didn't look like two men who had only just met."

"Mmm..." Devlin narrowed his eyes thoughtfully. "Yes, it certainly sounds like Gavin Sexton and Tyler Lee knew each other—*and* were taking great pains to hide the fact. The question is why. By the way, there's something interesting you should know—it looks like your instincts were right, Gemma," he said with a ghost of a smile. "Interpol got back to me this morning. Tyler Lee's real name is Tai Lung Lee. He's a small-time actor model from Hong Kong."

I leaned forwards excitedly. "So you mean... he's

not Rex Clifford's love child?"

"Well, I suppose he could still be—and just happens to be an actor too—but my money's on him being hired to play the part."

"By Gavin Sexton!" I said.

Devlin inclined his head. "Yes, I think it's time I had a chat with Mr Sexton."

"Won't Pratt mind you muscling in on his case?" I asked uneasily.

"It isn't 'his' case any longer. I think even the DCC is rapidly losing patience with Pratt and rethinking his 'favour' to Pratt's uncle. He called me last night and told me that I was officially back on the case."

"What about Mabel?"

Devlin hesitated, then said, "I'm sorry, Gemma, I think it's actually best to let Pratt have his chance to question her—if I try to intervene and prevent it, that would really be stepping on his turf. And it would only make him more defensive and dig his heels in. But don't worry about Mabel. She'll be treated well at the station. And unless he has substantial proof and is able to charge her with the murder, Pratt will have to release her by tomorrow. In any case, it won't come to that—when I get back to the station, I'll make sure that Pratt releases her."

"But what about this arsenic solution that he found?" I said worriedly. "Isn't that 'substantial proof'?"

"The *arsenicum album*? No, I'm pretty sure that's a false alarm. I need to double check with Toxicology when I get back to the station—I want to make sure before I confront Pratt—but from what I remember, it's a very dilute solution of aqueous arsenic trioxide. So dilute that there is practically no arsenic in the solution."

"Huh? But if there's no arsenic in it, how can it have any effect?"

"Well, I think, like many homeopathic remedies, there is no scientific evidence of any real effect, and if there are any changes, it's probably more of a placebo effect. You know, people believe it works... so it does. The mind is a powerful thing."

"Oh." I felt a wave of relief sweep over me and looked at Devlin gratefully. It was wonderful to have him back in charge.

"In the meantime, while Pratt is busy questioning Mabel, we can do something more useful—we can work on finding the real murderer." Devlin hesitated a moment, then added casually, "It might be helpful if Sexton is confronted with a witness who saw him with Tyler Lee... Would you like to come along?"

I stared at him. "M-me? I'd... I'd love to!" I gave him a tremulous smile. "Thank you."

Devlin gave me a brief smile in return and I caught a faint twinkle in his blue eyes. I realised suddenly that he was offering me an olive branch. He was also probably breaking CID rules by inviting me along, but he was doing it anyway because he knew how much I wanted to be involved. Somehow, that meant more to me than words of endearment because it showed that he really understood me and cared.

He opened the passenger door for me and I got into the car. As we pulled away, I felt my spirits lifting. It wasn't quite a reconciliation—not yet—but it was a first step.

***

We arrived at Sexton, Lovell & Billingsley and marched into Gavin Sexton's office to find the lawyer talking to a balding, middle-aged man. Sexton sprang up in indignation as we entered and said, "Do you mind? I'm with a client—"

"I'm afraid I'm going to have to ask you to postpone your meeting, Mr Sexton," said Devlin, flashing his CID badge. "I need to ask you some questions."

"Can't it wait?" asked Sexton irritably. "As you can see, I'm the middle of something here—"

"I'm in the middle of something too," said Devlin coolly. "A murder investigation, in fact. And unless you'd like your client to listen while I question you as a possible suspect, I would suggest that you re-arrange your meeting to another time."

The lawyer stiffened. He darted a look at his client, who was listening avidly, eyes agog, and said hastily, "Er... perhaps we'd better postpone our meeting, Mr Nelson. If you'll step outside and see my secretary, she'll arrange a new time for you..."

As soon as the man had left, Gavin Sexton turned around and said peevishly, "There's no need to start making accusations like that in front of my clients. I could sue you for slander!"

"You could," said Devlin. "But perhaps you'd be better employed using that time to prove your innocence."

"I don't know what you're talking about," blustered Sexton. "I am the Clifford family solicitor, yes, but I had nothing to do with Adele's murder. You have no right to hound me like this."

"Who said I'm here about Adele's murder?" said Devlin pleasantly.

"Then what's this about?" asked Sexton, his voice thick with annoyance.

Devlin didn't answer. Instead, he said, "Do you smoke, Mr Sexton?"

"Yes, sometimes. Why—is that a crime?" asked Gavin defensively.

"Which brand of cigarettes do you smoke? Benson & Hedges? Regal?"

Sexton gave a lofty smile, relaxing a bit. "Well, to tell you the truth, I prefer foreign brands."

"You mean like a Chinese brand, perhaps?"

Sexton's smile slowly disappeared. "Yes, actually, I do like Chinese cigarettes... How did you know?" he asked warily.

"Because Miss Rose here noticed a packet in your briefcase the other day. The same brand that was found in Tyler Lee's hotel room. How do you explain that?"

"H-how should I know? Why don't you ask this Lee chap—whoever he is!" snapped Sexton.

"I would... except that he's dead."

Sexton went pale. He swallowed. "Dead?" he said hoarsely.

Devlin nodded. "His body was found this morning. He had been strangled."

Sexton sat down suddenly in his leather chair.

"Mr Sexton, can I ask what you were doing between the times of ten o'clock and midnight last night?"

"What?" Gavin Sexton sprang back to his feet. "Wait, wait... are you suggesting that you think I killed Tyler Lee?"

"It's a suggestion that's going to become an assumption, unless you can prove me otherwise."

"That's crazy! I didn't even know the man!"

Devlin's voice hardened. "That's a blatant lie and you know it. Now, I'm going to give you a choice, Mr Sexton. You can either start telling me the truth—or I can arrest you and take you down to the station for questioning."

CHAPTER TWENTY-SIX

Gavin Sexton stared at Devlin, his lips quivering, then all of a sudden, he crumpled. Sitting back down in his chair with a weary sigh, he said, "All right, all right... I'll tell you everything."

I let out the breath I didn't realise I had been holding and shot Devlin a look of admiration. There was something thrilling watching him in action, like watching a panther skilfully stalk and bring down prey. He hadn't raised his voice once, or made any kind of overt physical threat—and yet there was no doubting the commanding force of his presence.

Sexton took a deep breath and began talking. "We have a branch of the office in Hong Kong and I've been out to visit a few times in the past year, to get to know the ropes, as I've been taking over my uncle's responsibilities. I met Tyler Lee on one of those trips. He was an actor and a model, and I decided to hire him to… well… to play a particular role."

"You mean, to help you perpetrate a scam to embezzle the Clifford estate," said Devlin. "You asked him to impersonate Rex Clifford's love child."

Sexton winced at the word "scam" but he didn't contradict it. "It seemed like a good idea at the time. I knew the terms of Rex Clifford's original will and I thought that the vague way it was expressed—with his 'next of kin' inheriting the estate—would enable me to slip in a 'second child' who could also have a claim on the inheritance. I was to be the executor for the estate, so all the transactions would be under my supervision anyway. I could direct the money into my own off-shore account, using the name of Rex Clifford's fictitious love child. Of course, this was all in theory—I'd primed Lee with all the details of the plan but I'd warned him that Rex might not die for a while. In fact, after his operation, the old man seemed to improve greatly and looked set to live for several more years."

"But then Rex Clifford changed his will," I spoke up.

Sexton looked at me, his expression bitter. "Yes, then Rex Clifford changed his will out of the blue. In fact, it was a shock that night when he called me out to Clifford House and insisted on making a new will, with everything left to Adele instead."

"So that's when you decided to murder Adele to

get her out of the way—"

"What? No, no, you've got it wrong!" cried Sexton. "I immediately tried to get hold of Tyler Lee, explaining what had happened and telling him that the whole scheme was off—for good. With Adele in the equation, it just became too complicated. But Lee started getting all paranoid, accusing me of trying to cut him out of the deal and saying I had hired someone else to play Rex Clifford's love child... I tried to reason with him but he wouldn't listen. To tell you the truth, I didn't realise what a nutter he was until then. Kept saying that I was 'denying him the role of a lifetime'. I told him it wasn't some bloody part in a movie! Anyway, the next thing I knew, Lee said he was coming to England." Sexton ran a harassed hand through his hair. "I thought that he was just bluffing... but when he showed up at the funeral, I nearly had a heart attack!"

"That's when I saw you talking to him," I said.

Sexton nodded. "I asked him what the bloody hell he was doing there and the blighter had the cheek to tell me he was there to get his inheritance!"

I thought back to the day of the funeral and the sense I had got that the handsome Eurasian enjoyed the attention, milking his moment in the limelight for all it was worth like any needy actor...

"And then Adele got ill and the ambulance came and it was chaos everywhere... and Lee disappeared before I could speak to him again," continued

Sexton. "When it came out that Adele had been murdered, I started panicking. The last thing I needed was for Lee to be wandering around, like some kind of loose cannon, while a murder investigation was going on! I found out that he was staying at the Cotswolds Manor Hotel—he was planning to send the room bill to me, the tosser!—and I contacted him, trying to reason with him again and convince him to return to Hong Kong. But can you believe it? Lee told me that he didn't need me anymore! He'd obviously got overconfident about his own acting abilities and decided that he could run the scam on his own. And he told me that if I dared report him or get in his way, he would expose the whole scam and my part in it."

"It seems to me, Mr Sexton, that you've simply provided even more reason for you to kill Tyler Lee," observed Devlin. "After all, the man was threatening your career, your reputation—*and* your share of the money."

Gavin Sexton shook his head vehemently. "But I didn't kill him—you have to believe me!" he pleaded. "I just wanted him to go back to Hong Kong and disappear. The whole thing had blown up under my feet and turned into some kind of nightmare. I mean, do you think I wanted Adele murdered and the police suddenly breathing down my neck? All I wanted was for Rex Clifford to die peacefully so I could quietly dispose of his estate." He stopped suddenly and turned to Devlin. "When did you say

Tyler Lee was murdered?"

"I haven't seen the full report yet but I believe the preliminary estimate is between the hours of ten and midnight last night."

"Well, I have an alibi for then!" said Sexton triumphantly. "I was out at a law society dinner until eleven and then I went with some friends to a bar on George Street. You can check with them if you like. There were several people with me."

"I'd like the names, please," said Devlin. "I will verify your alibi with them. But in the meantime, Mr Sexton, you are not to leave Oxford without advising the police."

Gavin Sexton nodded and scrambled to comply. We left the lawyer's offices a few minutes later with a sheet of paper in our hands.

I looked at Devlin in disappointment. "I thought he was going to confess."

Devlin gave me a weary smile. "This is pretty normal in an investigation. One step forwards, two steps back. But don't worry, Gemma. We'll get there—in fact, I have a feeling that we're just about to crack this case."

"How can you say that? It seems to me that we're back to square one! Maybe... maybe Gavin Sexton didn't murder Tyler Lee, but he *did* murder Adele?"

Devlin shook his head. "Anything is possible but it's very unlikely. The two murders are linked and most likely committed by the same person. Therefore, if Gavin Sexton did not kill Tyler Lee, chances are he didn't kill Adele either." He paused as his phone rang and he answered it. "O'Connor." He listened for a moment, then he said, "All right. I'll be right there."

Putting the phone back in his pocket, he gave me an apologetic glance. "Sorry, Gemma, I've got to go. Something's come up on another case. Can I drop you off anywhere?"

I felt a stab of disappointment. In spite of the aftermath of last night's fight still hanging over us—not to mention the gruesome spectre of the murders—a part of me had been enjoying the morning. There was something wonderful about being with Devlin, working a case together.

"That's okay. I can find my own way back. Um... maybe we can catch up later?" I didn't say it, but the words "...and talk about the other stuff..." hung in the air between us.

Devlin looked at me for a moment, then a smile touched the corner of his lips. "Why don't we catch up over dinner?"

My heart leapt with happiness. "You're on! Just call me when you're done."

***

When I arrived back at the tearoom, I found it to be fairly quiet for once. In fact, Cassie was hunched behind the counter, happily working on a sketch, when I walked in.

"What happened?" she asked. "The village has been all abuzz with Mabel being arrested!"

I pulled a face. "Yeah, Pratt found a bottle of arsenic solution in her house—"

"A *what*?"

"Don't worry, Devlin says it's some kind of homeopathic remedy which is so dilute that it doesn't really have any arsenic in it," I said.

"Hah!" said Cassie gleefully. "I'd like to see Pratt's face when someone tells him that!"

"Yes, so Devlin says Pratt won't really be able to keep Mabel in custody. He's gone back to the station now and he'll make sure that she's released as soon as possible."

"So you saw Devlin?"

I tried to look nonchalant. "I went to find him... just to tell him about my encounters with Tyler Lee and Gavin Sexton, of course. And then... he... um... invited me to accompany him to question Sexton."

Cassie raised her eyebrows but didn't comment. I felt my cheeks growing warm and said quickly, "Anyway, it turns out that Lee was an imposter—an actor hired by Sexton to impersonate Rex Clifford's love child. It was all part of a scam to embezzle money from the Clifford estate."

Cassie whistled. "That's pretty brazen."

Before I could answer, the tearoom door opened and a blonde woman with short cropped hair and a slightly scowling expression stepped in. I did a double take as I recognised Rachel's friend, Kate

Markby.

"Gemma, isn't it?" she said briskly as she approached the counter.

"Hi," I said tentatively. "Uh... Kate... what can I do for you?" Somehow, I doubted that she was here to sample my scones.

"I'm the Volunteer Coordinator for the Happy Hedgehog Friends Society," she said.

I had to struggle to hide my surprise. Of all the people in the world, the surly nurse was the last person I would have expected to be an animal rescue volunteer! I guess it just showed how deceptive appearances could be. Although maybe it was ironically fitting that Kate should be championing a creature covered in prickles, I thought with a smile to myself.

"Oh... er... right," I said. "I didn't realise you were interested in the charity."

"It's crucial that some of us take an interest!" she growled. "The British hedgehog population is in a terrible decline. We've lost fifty percent of these wonderful creatures since the start of the century, and if things go on like this, they could soon become extinct!"

"Uh... right... yes, of course," I said, slightly taken aback by her vehemence. I saw Cassie eyeing her askance as well.

Kate gave me a grudging look of approval. "I didn't realise you're helping out with the hedgehogs until Mabel Cooke told me that you were fostering

Pricklebum. That's very good of you."

"Oh, I haven't done much," I said, embarrassed.

"Every little bit of support helps!" said Kate. "All it takes is a bit of thoughtfulness—like checking bonfires and compost heaps for hibernating hedgehogs or providing gaps in your boundary walls and fences, so they can move through gardens easily. Do you know how many hedgehogs die needlessly every year, from being poisoned by slug pellets or injured by grass trimmers? It's sad how little respect there is for nature and—"

She caught herself and stopped, then gave me and Cassie a sheepish smile. "Sorry. I feel very passionate about this and tend to get carried away."

No kidding. Still, I was seeing Kate Markby with slightly new eyes. Surely anyone who cared so passionately about the welfare of hedgehogs couldn't be that bad? Could you really be a murderer and love animals too?

Kate leaned across the counter. "Anyway, I'm actually here because one of our new volunteers has the ideal foster home for Pricklebum. She lives out in Marston and her garden backs onto the meadows there. It will be the perfect place for Pricklebum to stay until his leg heals fully and he can be released back into the wild."

"That sounds great," I said, surprised to find that I felt slightly wistful. To be honest, my prickly guest had grown on me in the last few days and I was sorry to see him go. But still, I knew that no matter how fancy a cage I bought for Pricklebum, it would be much nicer for him to convalesce in a home with a nice garden where he could hopefully return to his natural habitat and continue his life in the wild. I couldn't offer him that living in central Oxford.

"Is there any chance you could take him over today?" asked Kate. "Only because Marie, the volunteer, is also a nurse at the hospital. She has the day off and is home today, so it would be the perfect time to receive Pricklebum and settle him in."

"I'm afraid I don't live in Meadowford, so I'd have to go back to Oxford to get Pricklebum," I explained. "I'd have to wait until the tearoom closed for the day."

"Why don't you pop back now?" suggested Cassie. "Things are really quiet here anyway. I'm sure I can manage on my own."

I hesitated. "Well, if you're sure..."

"It's fine." Cassie waved a hand. "Then you won't have to worry about running around after work."

I remembered Devlin's suggestion of dinner. Not having to worry about delivering Pricklebum to his new home would mean that I would be free as soon as the tearoom closed this evening.

"Okay, thanks, Cass!"

"Thank you, that would be great," said Kate, breaking into a rare smile. "I'll ring Marie now and tell her you're coming. By the way..." She glanced at the table next to us, where a couple was enjoying some freshly baked scones with jam and clotted cream. "Uh... I don't suppose I could get some of your scones to go? I had some at the funeral reception and they were really fabulous," she said to me with sincere appreciation.

I blinked. *Bloody hell. Next thing, Kate Markby will be giving me a hug!*

"Sure, we can put some in a paper bag for you. But..." I gave her a teasing look. "Are you sure you're allowed to have them? Would Rachel approve of them as the right food for your blood type?"

Kate rolled her eyes. "Between you and me, I think the Blood Type Diet is a load of nonsense. But Rachel believes in it passionately, so I humour her. Although sometimes I wish she didn't have such a difficult blood group! You should see us in restaurants, with her trying to decide what she can eat from the menu... Not that all the blood groups don't have restrictions, but Type AB seems to be the worst!"

"Rachel is Type AB?" I asked.

"Yes. Why?"

"Oh... nothing." I frowned, my mind suddenly whirring. Something was niggling at me, although I couldn't put a finger on what it was. "Um... by the way, I heard that you're an Oncology Ward nurse?"

"Yes, I am. Why?" Kate gave me a curious look.

"Um... I just wondered what kind of cancers you work with."

She looked at me a bit oddly, but answered

readily enough. "A whole mixture, really. A lot of breast cancer... and some bowel and prostate."

"What about blood cancers?" I asked casually. "Like... um... leukaemia?"

She shook her head. "No, those are treated in Haematology."

"Oh, right." I didn't dare probe any further.

Kate gave me the foster volunteer's address, collected her scones, and left the tearoom. As I cycled back to Oxford a few minutes later, I found my thoughts returning to her visit. I couldn't quite shake off the feeling that I was missing something important—some vital piece of the puzzle. It was only as I was gently lifting Pricklebum out of his cage that it came to me.

The blood types. At the charity gala ball, Lincoln had told me that Rex Clifford was Type O. He had also said that Type AB could only have parents with A, B, or AB.

Never O.

But according to Kate, Rachel was definitely Type AB.

Which meant that Rachel couldn't be Rex Clifford's daughter!

CHAPTER TWENTY-SEVEN

I drew a sharp breath as the realisation hit me. Was this what Adele had found out and revealed to Rex Clifford on Tuesday last week? It would have certainly explained why the businessman got so upset. Not because his daughter might be lesbian, but because she might not be his daughter at all!

I suddenly recalled Gavin Sexton's remarks: *"He kept muttering to himself as we were going over the papers—something about everything being a lie and how he had been fooled all his life."*

Yes, it was all beginning to make sense now. And it was no wonder that Rex Clifford felt shocked and betrayed enough to suddenly change his will completely.

But what about Rachel herself? Did she know? Had she been furious with her stepmother for revealing the truth and depriving her of her inheritance? Was that why she had murdered Adele? And had Kate helped her by stealing ampoules of arsenic trioxide from the hospital?

Now that I had seen Kate's nicer side, I was loath to think of her as an accomplice to murder. But I had to admit that people weren't black and white; Kate Markby could be kind to animals on the one hand but still help her girlfriend murder someone on the other. And after all, it wasn't as if Adele was a saint either. The widow had been a horrible woman in her own right and the two girls might even have felt justified in killing her. Even the Old Biddies and other senior residents of the village had thought that it would be a "community service" to murder Adele...

So did that mean that Rachel had murdered Tyler Lee as well? But why? I thought back to the conversation I had overheard in the St Frideswide's College car park on the night of the charity gala ball. With his talk of DNA tests, Tyler Lee had been forcing Rachel to prove her identity as Clifford's daughter and her claim to the estate. It was no surprise, perhaps, that Rachel would feel the need to silence him. And it would have been easy for her to slip out from the ballroom at the gala event, meet up with Tyler Lee again, and kill the unsuspecting young man...

I came out of my thoughts to realise that I was still holding Pricklebum. The hedgehog had relaxed and uncurled in my hands and was now waving his tiny snout around, sniffing the air curiously. His bright black eyes peered myopically up at me and he made a sort of cute purring noise.

I smiled at him. "Well, whatever happens, I'll take you to your new home first," I told the hedgehog. *And I'll call Devlin after that and tell him my discovery regarding Rachel's identity*, I decided.

I started to put Pricklebum back in the cage, then paused. I'd been planning to let the hedgehog ride in his cage, which I would put in my bicycle basket, but now I wondered if that might be quite uncomfortable for the little creature. If he was loose in the cage and the bicycle swerved or had to brake sharply, he would get thrown around and have a pretty scary, bumpy ride. It would probably be safe—and nicer for him—if he could travel more snugly.

So I found an old towel and wrapped the hedgehog carefully in its folds, leaving a little gap for his face—then tucked it into the bottom of my tote bag. I then placed the cage in my basket, tilted at an angle so that it would fit, with my tote bag wedged into the corner, on top. As long as I cycled very slowly, Pricklebum should have a fairly smooth ride.

I was about to wheel the bicycle—with my prickly passenger—out of the house when my mobile phone rang. A faintly familiar male voice spoke into my ear when I answered.

"Is this Miss Rose?"

"Yes?"

"This is Professor Clifford. Miles Clifford."

"Oh, yes... hi," I said, surprised.

"I rang your tearoom and your friend gave me your number." He hesitated, then said, "Er, Miss Rose... I have been thinking about things since you visited me at St Frideswide's the other day. If you will recall, you... er... asked some questions about my family."

"That's right," I said cautiously.

"Well, I have been doing a lot of thinking and..." He hesitated again, sounding slightly embarrassed. "I am sorry I was so brusque with you last time. Er... in view of what has happened in the last few days, I... er... I feel that perhaps it's time some things were brought out into the open. I have always believed in maintaining a dignified silence but... perhaps I am wrong. I think... there are some things you ought to know. So I was wondering if I might speak to you again?"

"Of course," I said.

"Is there any chance you could come and see me in my college rooms sometime this morning? I don't have any tutorials today."

"Actually..." I glanced down at the hedgehog cage in my wicker basket and thought quickly. St Frideswide's College was very close to my cottage— in fact, I would have to cycle past it to get onto the road for Marston—so it was an easy detour to stop off on the way. "Sure, I could come now, in fact. I'm actually at home—I live down by Folly Bridge—so it'll only take me ten minutes at most to get there."

"That would be marvellous," he said warmly. "Well, I'll see you shortly."

It was a short ride to St Frideswide's and I looked around as I entered the car park beside the college, marvelling at how different everything seemed in the daytime. On the far side of the car park, an area of shrubbery beyond the gravel had been sectioned off by crime-scene tape: a grisly reminder that a murder had taken place here only last night. I remembered that the last time I had been here, Tyler Lee had still been alive, and felt an uneasy twinge.

I parked my bike against one of the bicycle racks, then slung my tote bag carefully over my shoulder. I was glad now that I had opted to carry Pricklebum in my bag—otherwise I would have had to worry again about leaving him unattended outside in his cage. Instead, he was snugly wrapped in a towel and riding comfortably in my bag as I carried him with me across the main college quadrangle, through the arched entrance into the Library Quad, and then across the open space to Staircase 5.

Ugly scaffolding still covered one side of the quad and, as far as I could see, no progress had been made since I last visited: other than several paving stones having been prised up from the pathway next to Staircase 5 and a deep hole dug below them, everything else looked the same. A cement mixer and a pile of sand stood next to the hole but there were no workmen in sight. *Looks like British builders haven't got any better since I've been away Down Under*, I thought sardonically.

I hurried up the staircase and knocked on the heavy oak door, then noticed that it was slightly ajar. I stepped inside and saw Professor Clifford at his desk, a pair of half-moon spectacles perched on his nose. He looked up as I entered, took off his spectacles, and came forwards warmly to greet me.

"Miss Rose! Thank you for coming," he said. He gestured to a tray on a shelf nearby. "Would you like a sherry?"

I laughed. "Isn't it a bit early in the day for sherry—even by Oxford don standards?"

He chuckled. "I won't tell if you don't."

"No, I'm fine, thank you."

"Please, have a seat."

I walked over to his cluttered desk, placed my tote bag carefully on the surface, then sank into the bergère chair next to it.

"You said you wanted to talk to me about... the family?" I said tentatively.

"Yes..." Miles Clifford was still by the door, fiddling with the latch. He gave an irritable sigh. "Excuse me a moment... these old doors..."

I glanced idly at a framed photo on his desk: it showed a much younger Rachel, her head tilted back and her mouth stretched into a wide smile. The photograph had obviously been taken just before some kind of formal event—her university ball, perhaps—as she was wearing a satin dress and smoky eye make-up, as well as bright red lipstick which clashed slightly with the pink of the dress.

I blinked suddenly as I stared at the photo—and in particular at the bright red lipstick on Rachel's lips. Lipstick... *red lipstick*... Something flashed in my mind, like a camera flashbulb going off. I was back at the funeral again, standing at a discreet distance from the coffin, watching the mourners crowded around the graveside... Rachel and Kate taking their places... everyone fidgeting impatiently... the vicar looking back towards the parish hall... and still no Adele... and then, finally, the widow sauntering out, escorted by Miles Clifford, making a great show of dabbing her eyes with a tissue and hastily reapplying her lipstick...

Hastily re-applying her lipstick.

Why had Adele been re-applying her lipstick? I remembered her wanting to taste one of the mini lemon meringue pies when I was stowing them in the fridge. She had restrained herself, making some comment about having just applied her lipstick and not wanting to mess up her lips. So if her lipstick had already been perfectly applied, why had she been putting it on again?

Because it had come off. Because she had been

eating something in the parish hall.

And suddenly, something else which had been niggling at me became clear. The day the food inspector had come to the tearoom, he had adjusted a tray of lemon meringue pies because they had been arranged unevenly. After he'd left, Cassie had pinched one of the pies, leaving a large gap in the centre of the tray. I'd teased her then about doing the same thing at the funeral reception, but she had insisted that she hadn't.

Now I realised that Cassie had been telling the truth. Which meant that someone else had pinched one of those pies while they were still in the kitchen. And that someone must have been Adele. Which also meant that it wasn't just the three puddings she ate at the reception—the treacle tart from Mabel, the sticky toffee pudding from Rachel, and the Victoria sponge cake from Tyler Lee—that could have been poisoned. No, the poison could also have been in a *fourth* pudding—a lemon meringue pie—that Adele had eaten *before* the reception.

And I realised suddenly who could have placed poison in that fourth pudding. The only person who had been left in the parish hall with Adele. The same person who had escorted her outside: her brother-in-law, *Miles Clifford.*

I felt my heart lurch and begin thumping uncomfortably in my chest as the truth dawned on me. Why hadn't I seen it all along? I remembered telling the Old Biddies that murderers were most often known to the victim, someone "closer to home"—I had fixated on Rachel without ever once considering her uncle.

Slowly, I turned my head back towards the door where Professor Clifford was still fiddling with the lock.

He turned the knob and I heard the deadbolt slide in with a loud *CLICK*.

Then he swung around to look at me, his eyes smiling.

"Now, my dear, shall we have a little talk?"

CHAPTER TWENTY-EIGHT

I sprang up from my chair, trembling. "Er… actually, I've just realised that there's something I need to do. I have to go…"

I took a step forwards, then faltered to a stop. Miles Clifford stood between me and the door, and I didn't like the manic gleam in his eyes.

"Oh, don't rush off, my dear," said Professor Clifford. "We still have a little business to take care of. And don't worry—it won't take long. Death by strangulation can take as little as fourteen seconds. It will be slightly uncomfortable at first, but you'll soon be unconscious and won't feel a thing."

He's completely barking, I thought, panic surging through me as I backed away. My hips bumped against something. The edge of the desk. I was hemmed in, with the desk behind me, my chair on my right, a bookshelf on my left, and Miles Clifford in front of me.

"You... you'll never get away with it," I said hoarsely. "We're in the middle of an Oxford college! How are you going to get rid of my body without anybody noticing?"

"Ah, well, I've given that matter considerable thought," said Professor Clifford. "It's very fortunate, you see, that the college is doing renovations to this side of the quad. And, in particular, that the workmen have helpfully unearthed a hole in the pathway outside. I know that they are planning to pave over it with new stone tiles tomorrow. So all I need to do is wait until tonight when I will have the cover of darkness. This is the Library Quad and most of the student rooms are on the other side of the college, so there is very little activity here late at night. I will carry your body down—suitably wrapped in canvas, of course—and drop it in the hole. There is a convenient pile of sand nearby and a few shovels into the hole should cover up the sight of your body. Then tomorrow the builders will fill up the hole and seal it with the new paving slabs. Your body will disappear and no one will be any wiser!"

He beamed at me, like someone discussing a successful DIY project. Then he took a step towards me, saying, "But first, of course, we need a body..."

I swallowed. *Keep him talking*, I thought frantically. Isn't that what heroines always did in novels when faced with a murderous villain? Keep him talking, keep him distracted, and think of a way to escape.

Not that I have any ideas for the last one, I thought despairingly. Even if I managed to dodge around him and get to the door, it was firmly locked with what looked like an old complicated deadbolt and double latch, which would take me a few minutes to unlock—by which time, Miles Clifford would be on top of me, his hands around my throat...

I shuddered and thrust the image away. Quickly, I asked, "Aren't you going to tell me why? Why did you kill Adele?"

But Miles Clifford didn't respond. Instead, he was advancing slowly towards me, eyeing my throat with a sort of speculative anticipation which made me feel sick. I realised with a sinking heart that he wasn't some cardboard villain in a cartoon, just waiting to deliver the final monologue explaining his motives—*bwahaha!* No, Miles Clifford didn't have the kind of criminal ego that needed to show off or justify things.

"Wh-what about Tyler Lee?" I stammered. "Why d-did you kill him? Was it because he was trying to muscle in on Rachel's inheritance?" A light bulb went on in my head. "Oh my God—*you're* Rachel's father, aren't you?"

Miles Clifford's eyes flickered and he paused. "I wondered when you would figure that out. When I overheard you talking with your dance partner about blood types at the charity gala last night, I knew that it wouldn't be long. You are a bright young lady—I've seen students like you and I know how your minds work—so I knew it was only a matter of time before you arrived at the truth." He smiled at me benignly. "That was why I had to work fast today to get you here, to silence you quickly."

"But... but what does Rachel's parentage have to do with Adele's murder? Or Tyler Lee? Why did you kill them?"

He didn't answer.

"Does Rachel know you're her father? Who else knows?" I pleaded.

Still no response. He came closer... He was only a few steps from me now... I recoiled, grasping the edge of the desk behind me for support.

Then, in a last desperate attempt, I raised my head, looked him straight in the eye, and said, "Professor Clifford, do you think your actions were the product of an internal repressed desire or an external environmental stimulus?"

Without consciously thinking of it, I had adopted the tone and expression I used to use, back when I was attending tutorials myself as a student. And it worked. Miles Clifford might have been a psycho murderer but he was also an Oxford don, conditioned from years of habit to respond to an enquiring mind and a challenging intellectual debate.

He stopped advancing towards me, his expression becoming thoughtful. "Hmm... that is a very good question, my dear. Of course, I may have subconsciously nurtured the desire to kill Adele from the time I first met her—it is hard to analyse one's reactions in an objective manner, you understand—but I believe the real intention germinated and grew after she contacted me early last week to inform me that she had found out about my affair with my sister-in-law."

"Y-your affair?" I asked faintly.

He nodded. "Oh, only a brief one, mind you. Many years ago—twenty-five years, to be precise. Rex was frequently travelling to the Far East, often leaving Susan alone, and—as we were closer in age—we shared the same interests and enjoyed doing many things together, such as going to the cinema and the theatre, visiting art galleries, sampling foreign cuisines... I suppose it was inevitable that friendship should turn into something deeper, and we began an affair. It was over almost as soon as it began and I regretted it bitterly afterwards. I looked up to my big brother, as I told you, and I never wanted to do anything to betray him. Susan agreed with me. She loved Rex too and didn't want to break up a happy marriage for the sake of a brief fling. It had been a moment of madness, a lapse of judgement on both our parts. So we decided to pretend it never happened." He dropped his head and lapsed into silence, obviously regressing into the past.

I hesitated. I didn't want to break the spell—but I also had to keep him talking. "It didn't end as simply as that, though, did it?" I asked softly. "I mean, Rachel was born…"

"Yes," said Miles Clifford with a sigh. "Shortly afterwards, Susan came to me and told me that she was pregnant. And the timing was such that it had to have been my baby. We decided to hush it up— Rex would never suspect that it wasn't his—and they had long wanted a baby. I didn't mind that Rachel would never know the truth about her parentage—I was content to watch her grow up from afar." He gave me a whimsical smile. "I'm a solitary man, Miss Rose. A confirmed bachelor. I like my academic life, the long field trips out to Central America, the focus on my work and my research. I am not suited to family life. So this seemed to be the best of both worlds. Rachel grew up in a loving family unit, with the kind of father that she needed—and I enjoyed being her doting uncle, taking pride in her accomplishments and able to remain a part of her life, without committing to it."

"It sounds like the perfect arrangement," I murmured.

Miles Clifford's mouth twisted. "It was. Until Adele arrived on the scene."

"How did she find out about your affair?"

"She was going through some old boxes in the

attic and found a diary that Susan had hidden away. It was foolish of Susan, really, but I suppose the burden of secrecy became too much for her to bear. So it was all there, written in black and white—our affair, Rachel's parentage, the life-long deception we had played on Rex together." His eyes darkened with anger. "Adele was a spiteful woman. And a greedy one. She had long been trying to find a way to convince Rex to change his will in her favour—and now she had the perfect excuse. She went to him with the diary and told him everything. As you can imagine, Rex was devastated. He sent for me immediately to ask if it was true—and, of course, I couldn't lie to his face. I will never forget his expression that day..." The Oxford don passed a hand over his own face. "I think learning the truth killed my brother—in fact, I know it did. The heart attack he had later that night was the direct result of the shock of this discovery."

He looked up at me, his eyes calm again. "So I actually think my murder of Adele is quite justified. She killed my brother, so I returned the favour. In any case, there was a more practical reason." He raised his eyebrows at me, as if expecting me to impress him with the right answer.

"She was standing in the way of the inheritance," I said, like a dutiful student. "With Adele dead, the estate would go to Rachel."

Professor Clifford nodded approvingly. "Yes, but not just that. When Adele learned that Rachel might contest the new will, she called me and threatened to tell Rachel everything too if I let the appeal go ahead. I couldn't allow that! She had already destroyed my brother's faith in me and indirectly killed him—I wasn't going to let her hurt any more of my loved ones. Rachel had been happy in her ignorance—and she can remain happily ignorant for the rest of her life. I will make sure of that."

He flexed his hands as he spoke, and I gulped. Quickly, I said, "Where did you get the poison, though? Arsenic isn't easy to source."

He gave a modest laugh. "Oh, in actual fact, it was not too difficult. You see, my acupuncturist is a TCM practitioner as well and it was merely a case of fabricating a few ailments, pretending a few symptoms, and some clever exaggeration of weight... and I received the necessary sachets of powder containing arsenolite—or what you and I know as arsenic trioxide. Highly soluble in water, of course, and very toxic."

"And... and what about Tyler Lee? Um... was his death a matter of causation or correlation?"

"Oh, causation, definitely causation," said Professor Clifford, sinking into his tutor role once more. "Lee was threatening to reveal the truth to Rachel as well. All that talk of DNA tests! I knew then that he had to go. The only problem was how. I managed to arrange with him to come back and meet me at the same place three hours later. I promised I would make it worth his while. He was completely unsuspecting."

I remembered how I had seen Miles Clifford—while hustling Rachel away—suddenly stop and go back to the young actor and say something to him. I hadn't been able to hear what was said because of the loud engine of the sportscar in the background, and I had assumed that the Oxford don had simply been protecting his niece, warning Tyler Lee away from her.

Well, he *had* been protecting his niece/daughter. Just not in the way I had imagined.

"Having the element of surprise is always a benefit," said Miles Clifford thoughtfully. "But of course, one is able to work without it—if necessary!"

And he lunged at me, his hands reaching for my throat.

I screamed and flung myself backwards, flattening myself against the desk behind me. Papers flew everywhere as my hands flailed around, groping for something to use as a weapon. But there was no time. He was on me almost immediately and I felt his fingers on my throat, pressing down hard, squeezing—

I spluttered and choked, trying to scream again but producing nothing more than a faint, gasping squeak. I clawed uselessly at his hands, trying in vain to peel his fingers away from my neck.

Miles Clifford loomed above me, his eyes wide and bulging, a vein throbbing in his temple.

I choked and gurgled, still trying to break his

grip with one hand while groping desperately on the desk next to me for a pen, a paperweight, a stapler—anything that I could use as a weapon. But my fingers felt only the slippery smoothness of paper... and then the folds of something soft...

Dimly, I realised that it was my tote bag. But my strength was already fading... I couldn't breathe... couldn't think... I gasped and wheezed... Everything was going dark...

My hand fluttered weakly, sliding into the bag... and then something sharp pricked my fingers, the sudden pain piercing through the red haze...

Pricklebum.

I grabbed the hedgehog, ignoring the sharp pinch of pain as his quills dug into my hands, pulled the spiky creature out of the bag, and, with the last ounce of my strength, shoved him into Miles Clifford's face.

"AAAAAGGGHHH!"

Clifford reeled back, clawing at his eyes and releasing me from his choking grip. I gasped and wheezed as I leaned against the desk, my throat burning with pain. The hedgehog fell from my hands and rolled across the desk.

"UUUNNGGH!" Miles Clifford staggered sideways, still scrabbling at his eyes, which were red and weeping. Several of the hedgehog quills must have gone into his eyes. He turned blindly, tripped, and fell over, hitting his head against the side of the bookshelf as he went down.

Thunk.

His body slumped to the floor and he lay still.

I held my breath and peered slowly over the edge of the chair between us. Miles Clifford was out cold on the other side, lying face down on the floor.

I sagged against the desk, trembling all over. My throat felt like it was on fire and each breath was agony, but at least I could breathe. I wheezed and choked and gasped, feeling like crying and laughing at the same time.

Then I remembered Pricklebum. I gasped and turned to the desk, staring at the ball of prickles. The hedgehog seemed to be ominously still.

"Oh no... Pricklebum...No, you've got to be all right..." I whispered, choking back a sob.

There was a faint snuffling sound, then—very slowly—the prickly ball uncurled slightly and the hedgehog peeked out, his nose quivering.

"Oh Pricklebum!" I croaked, scooping him up as tears jumped to my eyes. I had to fight the urge to hug the spiky little creature—I think neither of us would have enjoyed the experience—and instead cradled him in my hands and raised him to my face.

He gave a little huff, as if grumbling at me, and his bright black eyes regarded me reproachfully.

I sniffed and gave a watery laugh. "Sorry. You're quite right. Next time, I'll provide a better hedgehog taxi service!"

CHAPTER TWENTY-NINE

The only bad thing that came out of a hedgehog saving my life was that Devlin and I had to cancel our dinner date once again, since I was too busy having my bruised throat examined at the hospital and he was too busy arresting Miles Clifford for double murder.

Still, the upside was that business at the tearoom boomed the next morning as every nosy old biddy in Oxfordshire (and her sister), rushed to the Little Stables to get a first-hand account of my escape from death and compare it with the six other versions which were already doing the rounds in the county.

By the time lunchtime rolled around, I was exhausted. My throat was still raw and the doctors had told me sternly not to speak too much for a day or two, but that was practically impossible with the number of people begging to hear my story. I was relieved when Mabel Cooke stepped in and decided to start telling my story for me. Okay, I did wince slightly when I heard some of her embellishments—such as when she declared that Professor Clifford's homicidal tendencies were probably due to his severe constipation—but overall, it was a great arrangement. Mabel loved holding court in the tearoom, surrounded by a crowd of avid listeners, and I got the chance for a bit of peace and quiet at last.

I'd barely sat down behind the counter, though, when the tearoom phone rang. Cassie picked it up, then handed it to me, saying, "It's someone from Food & Safety."

Yikes.

In all the excitement since, I'd completely forgotten about the food inspector's visit. I wondered uneasily now what his report said. What if he had found a problem which could threaten my licence?

"Hello?" I said hesitantly.

"Hello, Miss Rose," came a pleasant female voice. "I was just calling regarding a recent inspection conducted at your premises."

"Yes?" I said nervously.

"I have the report here and all seems to be in order. However, there was one point which was raised. The food inspector noted that there seemed to be evidence of a cat about the premises?"

"A-a cat?" I said weakly.

"Yes, apparently he observed a tail beneath the counter in the main dining room. He also chatted to a few patrons outside, after they left your tearoom, and several of them swore that they had seen a cat around the tables."

I swallowed. "Ah... yes, well, you see, that... that was a special... uh... occasion. I can assure you, it's certainly not the norm. I know animals aren't allowed in cafés and restaurants so—"

"Oh, that's not strictly true."

"I'm... I'm sorry?" I said, confused.

"Well, animals are not allowed in the food preparation areas, that is true. So definitely not in the kitchen. But there is no official rule that says they may not be in the other areas of the establishment, providing that standards of hygiene are maintained. It's really down to the owner's discretion. This is why many pubs allow dogs to accompany their patrons. And of course, service dogs should always be made to feel welcome."

"Wait... are you telling me that I'd be allowed to have my cat at my tearoom, as long as she doesn't go in the kitchen?"

"Well, she shouldn't be on any surfaces where food is served either—such as on the customers' tables—but yes, in theory, there is no reason why you may not have a cat at your tearoom, as long as she stays away from the food and drink."

I gave a whoop. "Thank you! Thank you so much!"

"I must warn you, though, that should you have an animal on the premises, you will be subject to much more stringent and frequent inspections as we will have to make sure that hygiene standards are being met."

"Yes, thank you. That's fine. I'm more than happy to have the inspections and I'll make sure that I meet all the requirements necessary."

I hung up, a big smile on my face.

"What was that all about?" asked Cassie.

"Oh Cass, it's great! They said I can have Muesli here at the tearoom!"

"Really?"

"Yes, as long as she stays out of the kitchen and off the surfaces where food is served."

"Do you think she will?" asked Cassie sceptically.

I nodded. "She's actually very good at home. I've trained her to stay off the kitchen counter and the dining table and it's one thing she's very obedient about. I think I could do the same here. It's worth a try! I've been feeling so bad about leaving her alone at home all day—this would be the perfect solution! She'll be delighted to be back in the tearoom again." I made a face. "And maybe she'll be so tired when we get home that she'll stop her new game."

"What new game?"

"Oh, Muesli's started this thing where she keeps getting me to open and close the garden door for her. It's driving me batty."

"Why don't you install a cat flap?" suggested Cassie. "Then she can come and go as she pleases and you don't have to worry about opening the door."

"Hmm... that's not a bad idea," I said. "I'd have to contact the rental agents and get the landlord's permission first... but it might be worth it."

"And you could also—" Cassie broke off suddenly as the door to the tearoom swung open and a tall man dressed in a denim shirt and jeans stepped in.

"Hi Cassie!" He gave her a wave and came over to the counter.

"H-h-hi Scott," stammered Cassie, all her usual poise deserting her. "I... I thought you'd left. England, I mean. I... I hadn't seen you in d-days."

Scott gave her a rueful smile. "Sorry—I meant to come in again before I left for London but I never got the chance. I went down to visit some friends for a few days. But I'm back now—and look who I've brought with me!"

He turned and gestured to a slim, fashionably dressed young man who had entered the tearoom with him and who was now admiring the paintings displayed on the walls. "This is my friend, Brett. He owns an art gallery in London. I've been telling him all about your paintings."

Cassie's eyes bulged and she became even more tongue-tied. Hastily, I stepped into the breach and offered both men refreshments.

"Thanks, maybe we could have some of your famous scones—and a pot of tea—and then Brett can discuss with Cassie which paintings he'd like to host at his gallery," said Scott with a grin. "Except not that one," he added, pointing to the largest canvas on the far wall. "That one's got my name on it. I'm taking that back to Montreal with me."

"You... you still want it?" Cassie said, looking dazed.

He beamed at her. "Sure do! And I might take that little one next to it too."

"Hey, don't be greedy, Scott," Brett spoke up with a chuckle. "Leave some for me. I'd like that one at my gallery. In fact, I think it would look perfect in my window display."

Cassie looked as if she might faint. I smiled to myself and quickly led the two men over to a free table, then served them a big plate of freshly baked scones, still warm from the oven, accompanied by home-made jam and clotted cream. I loaded a tray with a teapot and three teacups, and handed it to my best friend.

"Go on, Cassie, this is your moment," I said softly, smiling at her.

She looked at me, her eyes shining, then she squeezed my hand gratefully, took the tray, and walked over to join the men. I watched her, my heart brimming with happiness for her. Then I glanced across the room as I heard the bells attached to the tearoom door tinkle, and new customers stepped in. There were two girls: a familiar-looking shy red-head and a curvy blonde with big hair and an even bigger smile.

"Hi Gemma," said Caitlyn, giving me a wave. "This is my cousin, Pomona, who's come over from the States. I've been telling her all about your tearoom and the delicious baking here, so she told me I had to bring her! She can't wait to try your scones."

I flushed with pleasure. "Thanks! Have a seat and I'll bring some menus over." I waved a hand. "Choose any table you like."

As the two girls went to choose their table, I grabbed two menus from the stack on the counter, then paused for a moment as I looked around the dining room. I gave a happy sigh as I surveyed my little kingdom: the Old Biddies gossiping excitedly with their friends in the corner, the big group of tourists enjoying their finger sandwiches and toasted teacakes at the long table, the family with the toddler smearing whipped cream on her face, the backpackers poring over a map of the Cotswolds while enjoying their treacle tarts... and Cassie laughing with her new fans at the table nearby. I gave another contented sigh. I couldn't imagine anything that could make things better.

Well, okay, maybe one little thing, I thought with a smile. A little feline addition named Muesli...

CHAPTER THIRTY

"Darling, are you *sure* you don't want a yucca plant?" my mother asked brightly as she walked into the living room carrying a full Royal Doulton tea service on a tray. "The man at the garden centre told me they're wonderfully easy to grow, and you can even cut them in half when they get too tall and plant the severed parts in new pots!"

Ugh. Between the fleshy roots searching for water and the severed parts looking for new homes, yuccas sounded like something from a horror movie and definitely not a plant I wanted as a housemate.

"No, thanks, Mother," I said. "I told you—I really don't have the space for another houseplant."

"Well, then, what about some nice little bonsai trees? They don't take up a lot of room," suggested my mother as she set the tray down on the coffee table and began pouring out the tea. She handed a cup to my father—who was sitting in his customary armchair, with spectacles perched at the end of his nose and a history book on his knee—and then offered him a plate of home-made shortbread biscuits.

I heaved a sigh. I was beginning to regret accepting the invitation to stop off at my parents' for tea on my way back home from work. "No, Mother, I really don't—"

The doorbell rang, surprising all of us.

"Whoever can that be?" said my mother. "We're not expecting anyone..."

"I'll get it," I offered, rising and going into the foyer. I opened the front door and my eyes widened as I saw Devlin O'Connor standing on the threshold.

"Devlin!" I cried, smiling in delight. "How did you know I was here? Did Cassie tell you?"

He looked amused. "No, actually, I came to speak to your mother."

I stared at him, dumbfounded. "M-my mother?"

"Darling, who is it?" My mother wandered into the front hallway and stopped short when she saw Devlin. She came forwards hesitantly. "Er... hello, Devlin. How nice to see you again."

Devlin inclined his dark head. "Mrs Rose... may I have your car keys?"

"My car keys?" My mother stared at him.

I looked at Devlin in puzzlement. "Why do you

want her car keys...?"

He gave me a smile. "Just trust me."

Looking very bemused, my mother got her car keys and handed them to Devlin. We followed him outside to where my mother's car was parked in its usual position, on the street in front of the house. Devlin unlocked the car, then opened the front passenger door and leaned in. I could see him rummaging around in the glove compartment. A moment later, he straightened and held something up for us to see: a flat, rectangular-shaped screen with a bright red cover.

"My iPad!" my mother squealed, rushing across to him and pouncing on her long-lost tablet. "You found it!"

"How did you know—?" I looked at Devlin in amazement.

He grinned. "With a bit of help from a service called Find My iPhone. It's provided by Apple and uses the inbuilt GPS in the devices to track their location. I did a bit of cyber-detective work, logged in on Apple iCloud, and then used the service to track the iPad... to here." He gestured to the car.

"Oh, how silly of me," exclaimed my mother. "I remember now—I decided to place the iPad temporarily in the glove compartment when I popped into St Frideswide's College to pick up the charity gala tickets. It was too big for the handbag I had that day, you see, and it was too cumbersome to carry around. I meant to take it out again when I got back to the car, but with all the hectic running around I was doing that day, I must have completely forgot!"

She gave a trill of laughter and looked up at Devlin in admiration. "But that was so clever of you, Devlin, to find it!"

I stared incredulously at my mother. *Did she just compliment Devlin?*

"Now, would you like to come in for some tea?" My mother beamed at him. "You must come in! I'm sure Philip would like to hear about your prowess in locating the iPad."

"Thank you, I would love to, Mrs Rose," said Devlin.

My mother linked her arm through his and began leading him into the house. "Do you like shortbread biscuits? I have just baked some. If not, you must tell me what your favourite tea-time treat is, Devlin, so I can bake it for you the next time you come!"

I stood open-mouthed as they walked past me, my mother still chattering about how clever my boyfriend was. Devlin glanced back and gave me a smirk. I stared at their retreating backs. *Unbelievable.* Here I was, worrying myself to death about how to get my mother to approve of Devlin... if only I'd known that the way to her heart was through her iPad!

Following them into the house, I sat back down in the living room and had the surreal experience of watching my mother fuss over Devlin as her new blue-eyed boy. My father, meanwhile, discovered that while Devlin might not have shared his love of cricket, my boyfriend did share his passion for a good bacon sandwich, and the two men spent the rest of tea discussing whether the best "bacon butty" was made with smoked or unsmoked bacon, tomato or brown sauce.

As I watched Devlin and my father passionately debate whether adding an egg to a bacon sandwich could be considered sacrilege, and my mother eagerly poured everyone another cup of tea, I felt a warm glow steal over me. *Maybe Cassie was right—maybe my parents will learn to love Devlin... just as he is.*

"Now, Devlin... there was one thing I've been wondering," my mother said. "You are such a clever boy with numbers and I remember Gemma saying you graduated with First Class Honours... Don't you think it's a shame that you haven't gone into a career in Finance? Why, Dorothy Clarke was telling me that her cousin's daughter has married a London stockbroker and he's made *millions* in the City!" She looked at him reprovingly. "A policeman's salary is so modest—it seems hardly worthy of you."

Devlin opened his mouth, but before he could answer, I spoke up.

"I think it's wonderful that Devlin's a detective."

Everyone turned to look at me, Devlin with surprise in his eyes. I smiled at him and reached out to clasp his hand.

"Devlin is brilliant at his job; Oxfordshire CID are lucky to have his talents… I wouldn't want him to do anything different." I looked at my mother. "I think you should be proud of him, Mother—I know I am."

Devlin looked slightly stunned. Then he smiled and squeezed my hand. Later that evening, when we finally left my parents' place together, he said quietly to me: "Thank you for what you said, Gemma. It meant a lot to me."

I stopped and looked up at him. "It's the truth, Devlin, and I'm only ashamed of how long it's taken me to realise that." Then, to lighten the mood, I added with a grin, "By the way, what was really brilliant was the way you found my mother's iPad. You couldn't have made her happier if you'd told her that she'd won the lottery."

He chuckled. "Well, for my part, I have to say it's easier than slaying a dragon to prove that I'm worthy."

I flushed. "Devlin, I wanted to say I'm sorry again… for that night at the charity gala ball. I… I know I said some things—"

"No, it's all right, Gemma. I think we both said a lot of hurtful things to each other that night… I'm sorry too." Devlin reached out and gently tipped my chin up, so that I was looking into his eyes. "I know things won't always be easy for us. You and I come from different worlds, in a way, and there will always be challenges..." A ghost of a smile touched his lips. "But you're worth fighting for."

I felt my heart swell with emotion. "So are you," I whispered, and I threw my arms around his neck and pressed my lips to his.

We broke apart at last and Devlin gave a laugh. "Hmm... kissing me on your parents' doorstep, Gemma Rose? You *are* getting bold." Then he hesitated and said, "My mother will be coming down to Oxford again in a few weeks. I was thinking... perhaps you'd like to have dinner with us and meet her?"

I smiled at him. "I would love to."

EPILOGUE

It was the first day of June and the end of a perfect English summer's day, with a warm orange sun low on the horizon and a soft breeze bringing the scent of freshly cut grass and wildflowers to the rambling garden where I stood. The Old Biddies were standing with me, and together we were waiting for the guest of honour at this special farewell party.

A sound behind us made me turn around, to see Kate, Rachel, and another girl coming out of the French doors which led from the kitchen into the garden. Kate was carrying a small bundle in her hands and, as she approached us, I saw a familiar pointed snout and two bright black eyes peek out from the folds of the cloth. I smiled as Pricklebum the hedgehog sniffed the air around him curiously.

"Will he stay, do you think?" I asked Kate.

She smiled. "I hope so. Marie has set up a little hedgehog home for him as well." She pointed to a wooden box placed around the side of the shed.

Marie the foster volunteer spoke up. "There's a

hole in my hedge so he can easily get out and back in again. Hedgehogs have quite a large territory and Pricklebum will probably visit several gardens each night, as he hunts for food."

"It's why it's so important to have holes in fences and hedges, so they can get about freely," said Mabel, nodding emphatically.

"Yes," Kate agreed. "And that's one of the things that Happy Hedgehog Friends is going to highlight in their new campaign—which Rachel has just supported by a large donation from the Clifford estate," she added, smiling gratefully at her friend. "Hopefully, if we can just educate people, we won't lose this wonderful little British native."

We all watched as Kate walked to the back of the garden, which had been left wild and overgrown, and carefully placed the bundle down beside a row of bramble bushes. A pile of logs, surrounded by leaf litter, had been set up nearby, as well as a shallow ceramic bowl filled with cat food and some dried mealworms. We all watched with bated breath as Pricklebum slowly uncurled and took a look around him, his nose quivering.

Then he turned and ambled through the long grass, making snuffling sounds as he went. My last sight of him was of his prickly little bum waddling away as he disappeared into the undergrowth.

FINIS

THE OXFORD TEAROOM MYSTERIES

A Scone To Die For (Book 1)

Tea with Milk and Murder (Book 2)

Two Down, Bun To Go (Book 3)

Till Death Do Us Tart (Book 4)

Muffins and Mourning Tea (Book 5)

Four Puddings and a Funeral (Book 6)

Another One Bites the Crust (Book 7)

Apple Strudel Alibi (Book 8)

The Dough Must Go On (Book 9)

The Mousse Wonderful Time of Year (Book 10)

All-Butter ShortDead (Prequel)

For other books by H.Y. Hanna,
please visit her website:
www.hyhanna.com

GLOSSARY OF BRITISH TERMS

* **"in / to hospital"** – in British English, this phrase is used without the article, for example, "take him to hospital" or "my sister is in hospital"

a dog's dinner – a complete mess or muddle, also sometimes expressed as "a dog's breakfast" (*may come originally from an expression referring to a cooking mishap which is only fit for a dog's consumption.*)

Bacon butty – slang term for bacon sandwich

Barking (mad) – crazy (eg. "He's absolutely barking")

Biscuit – small, hard, baked product, either savoury or sweet (*American: cookies. What is called a "biscuit" in the U.S. is more similar to the English scone)*

Blighter - a contemptible, worthless person, especially a man; a scoundrel

Blimey – an expression of astonishment

Bloke – man *(American: guy)*

Bloody – very common adjective used as an intensifier for both positive and negative qualities (e.g. "bloody awful" and "bloody wonderful"), often used to express shock or disbelief ("Bloody Hell!")

Bollocks! – rubbish, nonsense, an exclamation expressing contempt

Boot – rear compartment of the car, used for storage (*American: trunk*)

Bugger! – an exclamation of annoyance or dismay

Bum – the behind *(American: butt)*

Car park – a place to park vehicles *(American: parking lot)*

(to) Catch someone out – to detect that someone has done something wrong or made a mistake

Canteen - a restaurant provided by an organization such as a military camp, college, factory, or company for its soldiers, students, staff, etc

Clotted cream - a thick cream made by heating full-cream milk using steam or a water bath and then leaving it in shallow pans to cool slowly. Typically eaten with scones and jam for "afternoon tea"

Cripes – an exclamation of surprise or dismay

(to) Do a bunk – to make a hurried or furtive departure or escape

Finickity – very fastidious and meticulous, derived from "finicky" but more often used in British English.

Foolscap - a standardized paper size (about 13 × 8)

Football – known as "soccer" in the United States

Gormless – lacking sense, very foolish

Half-arsed – half-hearted, not done with proper effort or thought *(American: half-assed)*

Hooligan – a young man who does noisy and violent things as part of a group or gang

In a jiffy – in a moment, very quickly

Lift – a compartment in a shaft which is used to raise and lower people to different levels (American: elevator)

Lippie - slang term for lipstick

(to) Nick - to steal

O.A.P. – Old Age Pensioner

On to a loser - be involved in a course of action that's bound to fail

Nosh – food (usually of the slang variety)

Nutter – a crazy person, a madman (*but often used in an affectionate way, e.g. "You nutter!" as you laugh at a friends's joke*)

Pants! – rubbish! (an exclamation of contempt) – can also be used to express dismay

(to) Pinch - to steal

Plod – a slang term / nickname for a policeman

Porter – usually a person hired to help carry

luggage, however at Oxford, they have a special meaning (see *Special terms used in Oxford University* below)

Posh – high class, fancy

Post shop – post office combined with a shop selling a variety of everyday items and groceries, often found in small towns and villages

Prat – idiot, often a superior, condescending one

Quid – slang term for one pound

(to) Ring – to call (someone on the phone)

Row – an argument

(to) Scarper – to escape, run away

(to) Send someone off/away with a flea in their ear – to reprimand someone sharply, to deliver as stinging reproof or rebuff which makes someone go away, feeling discomfited.

Semi – short for "semi-detached", a type of house which shares ones wall with another, i.e. is joined to another house on one side.

Shag – (v) to have sexual intercourse with or (n) the act

Sod – a term used to describe someone foolish, idiotic or unfortunate. Can be used in both a contemptuous manner ("He's a lazy old sod!") or in an affectionate or pitying way ("Poor sod—he never saw it coming.")

Stuff (something)! – an expression of frustration, showing contempt and apathy towards something (another way to say "I don't care! Or "Who cares about...!")

Takeaway – food that's taken away from the restaurant to be eaten elsewhere *(American: takeout)*

Telly – television

Tosser – a despicable person

Twitcher – a particular type of birdwatcher whose main aim is to collect sightings of rare birds

Yob – rude, uncouth, thuggish person, often used by snobs to describe the lower classes (It was coined in 18th century England as part of the fad amongst upperclasses to speak backwards. Formed by spelling 'boy' backwards)

SPECIAL TERMS USED IN OXFORD UNIVERSITY:

College - one of thirty or so institutions that make up the University; all students and academic staff have to be affiliated with a college and most of your life revolves around your own college: studying, dining, socialising. You are, in effect, a member of a

College much more than a member of the University. College loyalties can be fierce and there is often friendly rivalry between nearby colleges. The colleges also compete with each other in various University sporting events.

Don / Fellow – a member of the academic staff / governing body of a college *(equivalent to "faculty member" in the U.S.)* – basically refers to a college's tutors. "Don" comes from the Latin, *dominus*—meaning lord, master.

Porter(s) – a team of college staff who provide a variety of services, including controlling entry to the college, providing security to students and other members of college, sorting mail, and maintenance and repairs to college property.

Porter's Lodge – a room next to the college gates which holds the porters' offices and also the "pigeonholes"—cubby holes where the internal University mail is placed and notes for students can be left by their friends.

Quad – short for quadrangle: a square or rectangular courtyard inside a college; walking on the grass is usually not allowed.

STICKY TOFFEE PUDDING RECIPE

(courtesy of Kim McMahan Davis - *Cinnamon and Sugar... and a Little Bit of Murder* Blog)

INGREDIENTS:

Cake:
- 1 cup (180g) dates, pitted and chopped
- 1 teaspoon baking soda
- 1 cup (236ml) boiling water
- 2 tablespoons butter, room temperature
- 1 cup (200g) dark brown sugar
- 2 eggs, room temperature
- 1 teaspoon vanilla extract
- 1-1/2 cups (230g) self-rising flour*

Toffee Sauce:
- 1 cup (200g) dark brown sugar
- 3/4 cup (177ml) whipping cream
- 1 teaspoon vanilla extract
- 2 tablespoons butter

INSTRUCTIONS:

Preheat oven to 350 degrees (F) / 180 degrees (C).

Cake:

1. Place dates in a heat-proof dish and add baking

soda.

2. Pour the boiling water over the dates and stir. Allow to cool to lukewarm temperature while you collect the remaining ingredients.

3. Grease an 8-inch round or 8-inch square cake tin and set aside.

4. Beat the butter and brown sugar together for about 2 minutes until the sugar is coated with the butter.

5. Add the eggs, one at a time, beating well after each addition.

6. Mix in the vanilla extract.

7. Slowly stir in the flour, beating on low until just incorporated.

8. Using a hand-held stick immersion blender, pulse the date mixture until only small pieces of dates remain. (If you don't have a stick blender, you can, instead, finely chop the dates prior to adding the baking soda and boiling water, then proceed with the recipe as follows.)

9. Add the cooled date mixture to the cake batter and mix to combine.

10. Pour the batter into the prepared cake tin and bake for 30 - 40 minutes. A wooden skewer inserted into the center should come out mostly clean, with a few moist crumbs clinging to it.

11. Allow the cake to cool in the pan for 10 minutes then invert onto a serving platter.

Toffee Sauce:

1. Combine the brown sugar, whipping cream, vanilla extract, and butter in a small saucepan.
2. Bring just to a boil over medium heat, then reduce heat and simmer for 5 minutes, stirring frequently.
3. Cut the cake and serve on warmed plates. Pour a generous amount of the hot toffee sauce over the cake and garnish with fresh whipped cream or vanilla ice cream.

Tips:

- If you don't have self-rising flour, substitute 1-1/2 cups all-purpose flour and add 2-1/4 teaspoons baking powder and 3/4 teaspoon salt.
- The toffee sauce can be made ahead of time. Refrigerate until needed then gently rewarm over low heat just before serving.

Enjoy!

ABOUT THE AUTHOR

USA Today bestselling author H.Y. Hanna writes British cosy mysteries filled with humour, quirky characters, intriguing whodunits—and cats with big personalities! Set in Oxford and the beautiful English Cotswolds, her books include the Oxford Tearoom Mysteries, the 'Bewitched by Chocolate' Mysteries and the English Cottage Garden Mysteries. After graduating from Oxford University, Hsin-Yi tried her hand at a variety of jobs: advertising exec, model, English teacher, dog trainer, marketing manager, educational book rep... before returning to her first love: writing. She worked as a freelance writer for several years and has won awards for her novels, poetry, short stories and journalism.

A globe-trotter all her life, Hsin-Yi has lived in a variety of cultures, from Dubai to Auckland, London to New Jersey, but is now happily settled in Perth, Western Australia, with her husband and a rescue kitty named Muesli. You can learn more about her and her books at: **www.hyhanna.com**

Sign up to her newsletter to be notified of new releases, exclusive giveaways and other book news! Go to: **www.hyhanna.com/newsletter**

ACKNOWLEDGMENTS

My grateful thanks as always to my wonderful beta readers: Basma Alwesh and Charles Winthrop for always finding time to squeeze me into their busy lives and for their helpful feedback. Special thanks also to Connie Leap, for lending her eagle eyes to the manuscript (as well as my official editor and proofreader).

I am especially grateful to the talented Kim McMahan Davis of *Cinnamon and Sugar... and a Little Bit of Murder* blog, for acting as my "baking consulant" and in this case, providing and testing the wonderful Sticky Toffee Pudding recipe, (as well as providing U.S. measurement equivalents!)

And last but not least, to my wonderful husband for his patient encouragement, tireless support, and for always believing in me—I couldn't do it without him.

Made in the USA
Monee, IL
11 July 2020